THE
LONG WAY
AROUND

QUINN
ANDERSON

RIPTIDE
PUBLISHING

Riptide Publishing
PO Box 1537
Burnsville, NC 28714
www.riptidepublishing.com

The Long Way Around

Cover art: L.C. Chase, lcchase.com/design.htm
Editors: Stella Li, Carole-ann Galloway, Rachel Haimowitz, May Peterson
Layout: L.C. Chase, lcchase.com/design.htm

ISBN: 978-1-62649-837-2

First edition
August, 2018

Also available in ebook:
ISBN: 978-1-62649-836-5

THE LONG WAY AROUND

QUINN
ANDERSON

To Lou, the antique car that I drove all throughout my formative years. We went on many amazing road trips together, until he couldn't anymore. Now, every time I drive with the windows down, I swear I can smell his old leather seats.

TABLE OF CONTENTS

CHAPTER ONE

Williamsport, Pennsylvania, was a city in a loose sense of the word. Nestled between low mountains and the Susquehanna river, it looked like the sort of Colonial-era, red-brick town that most people only saw on postcards. The streets were clean and lined with neat houses, their pointed roofs begging for a layer of snow no matter the season. "Downtown" consisted of a cluster of old buildings—none tall enough to tickle the sky, let alone scrape it—whose stone edifices were elaborate without ostentation.

It wasn't an exciting city. It wasn't the sort of place a kid would dream of living someday. But as Sam Cooper looked out over it from the window of his third-floor apartment, he thought, *This place feels more like home to me than Montana ever did.*

"You there, Sam? Did the signal cut out?"

Filmy curtains swished back into place as he turned away and glanced at his laptop. "I'm here. Sorry, I was lost in thought."

A grainy version of his sister's face smiled at him from a Skype window. "What else is new?" Jessica laughed, and her black curls trembled. "Something on your mind?"

"I should be asking you that. You're the one who's getting married in—" he walked over to the glass coffee table and peered at his laptop's task bar "—seventeen days. Wow. Is it June already?"

"Sure is. Speaking of the wedding..."

Sam groaned, slumping onto the cushiony couch. "Please, not this again."

"Yes, this again! What kind of little brother misses his favorite sister's wedding?"

"You're my only sister, Jess, and I told you. I have to work." His tongue was thick as he delivered the lie, despite how accustomed he'd become to it.

He checked his reflection in the little side window that showed his camera feed. His blond hair—the polar opposite of his sister's inky locks—had fallen across his big brown eyes. They looked black in the low resolution. He was normally meticulous about shaving, but after his last job had unceremoniously dumped him, he'd allowed stubble to creep over his jaw, emphasizing its squareness. His expression had a hint of discomfort. A stranger wouldn't notice, but Jessica would.

Sure enough, she squinted at him. "Your internship ended a week ago. There's nothing stopping you from hopping on a plane to Helena. You would have told me if they'd offered you that tech job at the end of your contract." Her expression softened. "I'm sorry you didn't get it. I know you had your fingers crossed."

Sam shrugged and shifted into a sitting position across from the computer. "It happens. Lots of people are going into coding these days, so the competition was fierce. They probably found someone who wasn't fresh out of college to fill the position. You know, someone who has that mythical 'experience' I've heard so much about."

"I thought the point of an internship was to get experience?"

"That was the idea, yeah, but I guess the company had other ones."

There was no way to know for sure, but Sam had suspicions as to why he hadn't gotten a job offer after a year with the same small tech company. On all of Sam's quarterly evaluations, one phrase had come up over and over again: *Not a team player.* Sam didn't spend his time gossiping by the watercooler or sucking up to his superiors. He kept to himself and finished his work quietly and expeditiously. As a result, a year later, some of his superiors still didn't know his name.

I bet Wesley would have gotten the job if he'd been in my place. He would have charmed them all.

His gaze fell to his lap. He rubbed his thumbnail with the pad of his index finger. He'd chewed it down to a stub.

"Are you sure nothing's bothering you, Sam?" The camera feed showed Jessica studying him with concern. "You look pensive."

His mouth twitched. "I'm making dinner plans in my head. Boxed mac and cheese is serious business."

Jessica snorted. "Uh-huh. And when you were staring broodily out the window earlier, you were thinking about new curtains, right?"

"I was watching the sunset. It's so beautiful here. I'd stay forever if I could." He chewed on his lower lip. *If I can get a job.*

Jessica's concern warped to sympathy. "You'll find a way, little bro. You work so hard, and it's only been a week since your internship ended. There's a reason you landed it right out of college. You may not be the most . . . gregarious. But employers are going to see how valuable you are."

"I appreciate your faith in me." Sam wiped his mouth with the back of his hand. "Can we change the subject?"

"Fine by me. Let's talk about the wedding."

Damn, I walked right into that.

"I'm so sorry, Jess, but I mean it when I say I can't make it."

Jessica's serious face snapped into place. "Samuel Patrick Cooper." Her tone crackled like a live wire. "If you're not at my wedding, what are people going to say?"

"If by 'people' you mean our parents, then probably 'Thank God.'"

She rolled her eyes. "They love you, Sam. They'd love to *see* you. It's been over a year. You can't avoid them forever."

We'll see about that.

"Even if I weren't too busy to go—and I still maintain that I am—I wouldn't want anything to distract from your special day. If I show up, it'll be returning to the scene of the crime."

"There was no crime, Sam. You called off a wedding. Big deal."

He gave her a pointed look.

"Okay, so you called it off the night before, and that was kind of a big deal. But at least you didn't marry someone you don't love."

I did love Michael. But I couldn't marry him.

Out loud, Sam said, "If the family Runaway Bride shows up at your wedding, it's going to get our relatives talking. I don't want to take the focus off you on your special day. Or expose myself to all that gossip and scrutiny, for that matter. I'll spend the whole night dodging cousins asking me why I did it."

Jessica pressed her lips together, eagerness written all over her face. She wanted to ask him herself. He'd only ever given perfunctory explanations, and they'd had to be pried out of him.

Mercifully, she restrained herself. "Sam, I would take all the gossip in the world if it meant I got you too. It hurts my heart when I think that you won't be there. What if I got Mom and Dad to call you, and—"

"No!" Sam exhaled and forced himself to speak at a normal volume. "Please don't. I can't handle any more terse conversations with them."

"It's your choice: either talk to them on the phone, or talk in person at my wedding."

Sam opened his mouth, hesitated, and shut it again. His eyes wandered around his apartment, taking in the cream walls, tidy kitchen, and the bedroom sectioned off by bookcases. His bed was made with two perfectly fluffed pillows resting against the headboard.

Looking at his pristine apartment would make most people think Sam had his shit together, but he knew better. It was *too* clean. When he started washing baseboards and bleaching grout, it was a sure sign that he was spending too much time at home. He needed to get a life in a big way.

It wouldn't be a bad idea to take off for a long weekend. Break out of my routine. I know what happens when I spend too much time alone in this little apartment. Now that I don't have the internship to make me leave the house, I'm going feral.

He swished words around in his mouth. "I'll think about it. I can't promise anything more than that, but I swear to consider it seriously. You know how much you mean to me. I'd be there in a second if things weren't so complicated. Okay?"

"Okay." Jessica eyed him. "Regardless of what you say, I'm not giving up hope. There's going to be a seat for you at the reception. Right up front. If you leave an empty spot at one of my tables, you'll be pissing off a bride on her wedding day. That's a minimum of one gajillion years of bad luck."

Despite the anxiety twisting his insides, Sam laughed. "Noted. I love you, Jess."

"I love you too, little bro. Talk to you soon."

Sam ended the video call, stomach still churning. He stared at his computer's wallpaper: a photo of him and Wesley Reed—his best friend—when they'd left Penn State a little over a year ago.

Back then, it'd seemed like nothing could stand in Sam's way. He'd graduated with honors, was about to start a promising internship, and was set to marry his wonderful fiancé only a week later.

Even after they'd broken up, Sam still thought Michael was wonderful. Smart, handsome, funny. The whole package. Sam's parents had been very vocal about wanting Michael to join the family. Then Sam had gone and ruined everything. He'd wasted tens of thousands of dollars—most of which was his parents'—and Michael had never spoken to him again.

Sam couldn't blame him. Hell, he was half-convinced his family was only still speaking to him because Jessica had loudly proclaimed her support. Thank God for her. And the fact that he'd chosen to go to school all the way across the country.

His phone buzzed on the sofa next to him. Grateful for the distraction, he plucked it up and glanced at the screen. He had a text from Wesley.

Meet me at Corner Bar? After the day I had, I need booze and Sam-time.

Corner Bar was a pub located, shockingly, on the corner of Fifth and West, three blocks from Sam's place. Sam composed a quick reply. *That's what you always say.*

True, but I really mean it this time. Please? I haven't seen you all week.

Drinking sounded like exactly what Sam wanted to do right now. Drinking meant not thinking, and he would desperately love to not think. Plus, Wesley had a talent for uncomplicating things. Everything seemed clear and simple when he talked about it.

Wandering over to his dresser, Sam pulled out some clothes that would be suitable for both a bar and the unseasonably cool summer they were having. He changed, grabbed his things, and was out the door a few minutes later. Knowing Wesley was waiting for him was apparently all the motivation he needed.

Night had settled like soot over the city. The streets were still slick from the warm afternoon rain that had fallen earlier. Despite what the calendar said, the air had a hint of bite to it. If today was any indication, they were in for a gorgeous summer.

Corner Bar was busy for a Wednesday. Through the clear windows, Sam saw people spilling over barstools and huddling together at pub tables. Wesley wasn't in sight. Sam's anxiety ratcheted up a few degrees, but he pressed forward.

He bypassed the people smoking outside, ducked beneath the low green awning surrounding the brick building, and let himself in through the painted double doors. Inside was much warmer than outside, probably thanks to all the bodies. He'd picked a hell of a day to wear long sleeves.

The bar smelled like fried food and beer, in a good way. Sam could almost feel the carbonation tickling his nose already. Three steps in, he heard a familiar voice.

"Sam!"

He turned toward the sound and spotted a dark head tucked away at the bar behind a big party. Wesley.

"There you are." Sam hurried over, a smile sliding onto his face.

Wesley had his long, trouser-clad legs propped up on the stool next to him. He moved them when Sam approached. "Perfect timing, Sammy. I just got here."

"You know how I feel about that nickname." The familiar argument was equivalent to a greeting at this stage in their friendship.

Wesley's blue eyes glinted with mischief. "You pretend to hate it and argue that nicknames shouldn't be longer than the name itself, but deep down, you find it endearing."

Sam rolled his eyes. This was the problem with best friends. They knew too much. "I stand by my argument."

"And I counter by saying your name isn't Sam. It's Samuel, which has more syllables than Sammy. So, there." He drained the beer in front of him and signaled to the bartender. "If I can still hold my own in an argument, then I'm not drunk enough. You want?"

"Yeah, I'll take a beer."

While Wesley ordered for them, Sam gave him a once-over out of the corner of his eye. Wesley looked good, as per usual. He'd dressed up in a navy suit that didn't look expensive but fit him perfectly. A blue button-down brought out his eyes, clear as the summer sky. He'd run some product through his dark hair, smoothing its usual messiness.

"You had an interview today?" Sam asked needlessly.

The bartender appeared with two pint glasses. Wesley stood to grab them, set one in front of Sam, and then took a healthy gulp from his own. "Yup. Hence the alcohol."

"It didn't go well?"

"When I walked in, I went to shake hands with my left instead of my right, which caused my interviewer to switch sides just as I put out my right hand. Then I switched again the second he switched. It was like a Russian kick dance. What are those called?"

"A prisiadka."

"Yeah, that. Anyway, I'm not kidding when I say it went on for a solid minute while we both stared at each other with growing horror."

Sam snorted into his beer. "But you're not left-handed."

"I'm sure not."

"Then why did you—"

"Hell if I know." Wesley took another long glug. "The rest of the interview went about as well. I totally choked."

"Damn. You normally make such a good first impression."

"Says who?"

"Says the three jobs you've landed since graduation."

"Yeah, but I'm pretty sure you're not supposed to job-hop like that. Doesn't look good on a résumé." Wesley rubbed his eyes. "I'd take your year of gainful employment over going on all these interviews. They're torture."

"I'll make that trade if I can have your confidence and social skills. At least you know when you go in that you're going to charm the pants off them. Russian kick-dancing notwithstanding."

Wesley laughed, the sound deep and pleasant. "Thanks. On to the next, I guess. If I exhaust all the job opportunities in Williamsport, I suppose I can look at some neighboring cities."

Sam punched his arm. "Yeah, right. Like you'd leave now after spending your whole life here. Sometimes I think half the reason you went to Penn is so you could stay local."

"Ah, good ol' Penn State. All this talk of college makes me want to do shots."

"Wow, you're really upset about this interview, huh?"

"What gave me away?" He got the bartender's attention again, shouted an order, and then swiveled on his stool to face Sam. "What about you? Now that your internship is over, you're looking for jobs, right? If you can't find anything, are you going to move back home?"

"To *Montana*?" Sam clutched his throat and made exaggerated choking noises. "No way. Someone could offer me my dream job, and I wouldn't go back. Not because there's anything wrong with living peacefully in the mountains, or whatever, but it's not for me. Besides, I can't leave you." He fluttered his eyelashes.

Wesley chuckled. "Shit like that is why people assume we're a couple, you know."

"Nah, it's because they stereotype us. Haven't you heard? It's impossible for two gay men to be friends without hooking up. To us, there is only *fresh meat*."

That got a solid laugh out of Wesley. He made Sam crack up so often, it was nice to return the favor.

The bartender returned with two shots, and to Sam's horror, she plunked one of them down in front of him. "Wesley, no."

"Wesley, yes." He held his glass up and grinned. "Remember when I got you to do shots in our dorm freshman year? You said it was one of the best nights of your life."

"Yeah, right before I threw up everywhere. Why do I let you talk me into things?" Despite his protests, he picked up his own glass. He actually wouldn't mind some hard liquor after his conversation with Jessica.

"Come on, it'll be fine." Wesley clinked their glasses together. "What should we toast to?"

"The future? Finding our dream jobs?"

"That's too generic. We can do better than that." He rubbed his chin. "Hey, isn't your sister's wedding around the corner? Let's toast to the bride-to-be."

Sam flinched and looked away to hide it, but he was too slow.

Wesley's eyes narrowed. "What happened?"

"Nothing."

Wesley set his shot down next to his half-drunk beer, propped an elbow on the bar, and planted his chin in his palm, eyes fixed on Sam.

"All right, fine." Sam sighed. "Jessica asked me to come to her wedding again today."

"And you caved and said yes, right?"

"Uh . . ."

"What?" Wesley made a rude sound. "Dude, you have to go. You know you do. Hell, I'm planning on attending."

Sam's brow furrowed. "Jessica invited you?"

"No, but only because I told her I was your plus-one."

"Oh my God." Sam rubbed his eyes. "You can't do shit like that."

"Why not? You don't have a boyfriend, and I know you'd never work up the nerve to go alone. Enter Wesley."

Sam couldn't help but laugh. "If we're going to discuss this, I need more alcohol." He downed his shot and came up sputtering.

"Fine by me." Wesley followed suit much more smoothly and chased it with beer. Then he signaled the bartender for another round. "Why don't you want to go? Weddings are fun."

"You know why. I haven't seen my family since I called things off with Michael. I can't face them in the same setting where I disappointed them."

"Sure you can. It's been a year. No way they're still mad."

Sam laughed again, but this time it was humorless. "You've met my parents. Think about it."

"Hm." Wesley tapped his chin. "I suppose they're not the most forgiving people. If it's any consolation, I think you did the right thing. You guys were way too young to get married, and you rushed into it. You met, what, junior year?"

"Sophomore."

"And you were engaged by senior! I always thought one of these days we were going to find out Michael had some deal breaker, like a gambling problem, or a husband in another city, or he listens to Nickelback."

"Well, you were right, considering it all fell apart."

"So, what's the plan? Avoid your parents until someone dies? You can't do that. It's not fair to you, them, or Jessica, for that matter."

"I know I can't, but I don't know what else *to* do."

"I'll tell you. You can suck it up, be a good little brother, and go to your sister's wedding. You'll break her heart if you don't, and instead of remembering who was there for years to come, she'll remember who wasn't."

There was no arguing with that. Sam sighed. "You're right. I'm not convinced I won't die of embarrassment, but you're right."

More shots arrived. Wesley perked up like a dog who'd spotted a squirrel. "You know what you need? Booze."

"Right. That'll help me make responsible decisions."

"We're past the decision-making portion of the program and on to drowning our sorrows."

They clinked glasses, and this time, Sam knew what to toast. "To us. Five beautiful years of friendship. Who would have thought the loud, obnoxious guy who barged into my dorm that fateful day would end up becoming my best friend?"

Wesley met his gaze, eyes bright. "And who would have thought I'd saddle myself with a total square and somehow love every minute of it? To many more years to come."

The rest of the evening was a bit of a blur.

They ordered more shots—a *lot* more shots. An inadvisable number of shots. Sam remembered to order water at some point, but it was like putting a bandage on a hull breach. There was lots of laughing and arguing with Wesley about which of them loved the other one more. Then cold air, like they'd walked outside.

Next thing he knew, he was waking up to sunlight battering his closed eyelids.

He started to lift his head and groaned when pain lanced into his skull. "Oh God."

"Are you finally awake, Sammy?"

At the sound of a muffled voice, Sam managed to convince one eye to crack open. His surroundings weren't those of his apartment, but they weren't unfamiliar either. He was lying on olive-green sheets, which smelled like laundry detergent and mild cologne. His clothes from last night were still on and looking much worse for the wear. There were framed vintage Archie posters on the wall, and the headboard had a bookshelf above it that was stuffed with paperbacks, DVDs, and comics in plastic sleeves.

Wesley's bedroom. Not where Sam had expected to end the night, but not totally unheard of either.

"Damn," he said to the ceiling. "How drunk was I that I couldn't make it three blocks to my place?"

"It was more the stairs that you couldn't handle." Wesley poked his head into the bedroom. He was wearing a rumpled version of his suit. "Morning."

"Wes, please." Sam groaned again. "Kill me."

"I would, but it's an awful mess, and I'd rather cure you." He had two steaming mugs in his hands. He set one on his nightstand before offering the other carefully to Sam.

Sam sat up and took it, taking a gulp without a care for the heat he could feel through the ceramic. Brown sugar, no cream, precisely how he liked it. "Thanks for letting me crash."

"No worries. It was my fault for pouring all those shots down your throat. I forget you're a lightweight."

"The hell I am." Sam went for a glare, but it probably looked like he was squinting. "No one can drink like you and expect to survive the night. You should pay your liver time and a half."

"Fair." Wesley gripped his own cup and blew on it before taking a ginger sip. "It's been a while since we ended up passed out in the same bed."

Sam nodded. "Not since senior year, although that time *you* crawled into *my* bed after that frat luau. I remember because you were wearing an itchy grass skirt. You mumbled something about 'murderous coconuts' and then started snoring."

Wesley crinkled his nose. "I only vaguely remember that, which means I did it right. Anyway, I know last night got a little out of hand, but I had a blast. Felt like old times. I've missed living with you since we became boring adults."

"Me too." Sam smiled. "Too bad we couldn't keep that up. I rented my little studio back when I thought it was going to be Michael and me living there. If you'd moved in, people would *really* talk."

"True. We'd probably end up bunking together every night too, instead of once in a while when we're both obliterated."

Sam laughed and then winced when it made his head throb. He was about to make a joke about how he wouldn't mind that, but he stopped himself. Close as they were, there were still lines neither of them ever crossed.

A handful of times, Sam had drunkenly admitted Wesley was gorgeous, which had earned him a round of good-natured ribbing.

Although, Wesley had returned the favor, so Sam could tease him back if he wanted. That was as far as it'd ever gone. Their friendship was worth way more than some passing attraction. Sam couldn't imagine a force powerful enough to get him to jeopardize it.

"So—" Wesley sipped his coffee, face carefully neutral "—are we going to talk about what you decided last night? About the wedding?"

Sam flinched, and this time it wasn't from the hangover. "Do we have to?"

"I'm afraid we do, my friend. You'll thank me later, when your sister's heart isn't broken and you're not kicking yourself for the rest of your life."

"Can I at least raid your pain relievers first?"

From the breast pocket of his suit, Wesley produced a small bottle of aspirin. "Have at it."

Sam popped three into his mouth, downed them with a swig of coffee, and grimaced. "Okay. Now, give me thirty minutes for it to kick in, and then we can talk."

"Oh, no, you don't. Once it kicks in, you'll say you have to get going, and then you'll be out of here as fast as you can limp. Right now, while you're weak and helpless, we're going to talk." Wesley sat cross-legged on his side of the bed, facing Sam. "Let's hear it."

"There's really nothing left to say. I'm terrified of going, but I don't see how I have a choice. I love Jessica more than I hate the idea of facing my parents, and that's really all that matters."

Wesley smiled, big and bright as the sun. "You sentimental bastard. I'm so proud of you. I guess all that's left to do is pack."

"Pack and spend the next two weeks in a state of constant anxiety."

"I've been thinking about that, actually." Wesley pulled out his phone. "Today's June sixth, and her wedding is the twenty-second. Minus today, that gives us fifteen days to get there."

"'Us'?" Sam sat up straighter. "You really want to come with?"

Wesley rolled his eyes like that was the most ludicrous question he'd ever heard. "I'm not going to send you off to face the wolves alone. Of course I'm coming with you."

The relief Sam felt was so profound, his eyes stung. "Thank you, Wesley. Really."

"You can thank me by paying for gas."

Sam frowned. "Gas?"

"Yeah. We could book some boring old plane tickets, *or* . . ." He waggled his eyebrows. "We could take the long way around."

"What'd you have in mind?"

"A road trip, baby! TJ and Amal–style."

Sam blinked. "Who?"

"Never mind. I forget you don't read comics. The point is, we haven't been on a trip together since that spring break where we drove to Jersey and spent a week drinking on the beach. Since we're apparently rehashing our college days, we should hit the road. See the country. Boldly go! It'll be more expensive to drive—hotels, gas, et cetera—but think of the fun we could have. It'd be such an adventure."

Sam frowned. "I don't know. A road trip? Being stuck in a cramped car together for all that time?"

"What, you think we'll get sick of each other? Two best buds like us?" Wesley slapped him playfully. "Come on, when are we going to get a chance like this again? I'm between jobs, and your internship is over. We don't have boyfriends or mortgages or kids we have to look after. You need to get across the country, and I need a break from all this job hunting. In two weeks, I bet we could do the whole East Coast and then zip over to California with time to spare. What's stopping us?"

This was leagues outside of Sam's comfort zone, but Wesley had made some damn good points. There really was nothing stopping them from going, and years from now, when they had nine-to-fives and responsibilities, they could look back on a more carefree time.

Wesley's lips twitched. "I can tell you're thinking about it. I like the gleam in those pretty brown eyes of yours."

"I won't deny it. Especially if it guarantees I'll have you by my side."

"Hey, if you decide you don't want to do a road trip, that's fine. I'll get on a plane and be with you through this regardless. But I think it'd be way more memorable to drive there. We've lived in America our whole lives, but how much of it have we seen?"

Sam frowned. "Um, Jersey, like you said, and, uh . . . when I was a kid, my parents took us to the Grand Canyon. But I don't actually remember it."

"Exactly. Let's make some memories that'll last a lifetime. Shit we'll look back on in fifty years from now and think 'That was one of the best times of my life.' Are you in?" Wes gave him the sweet, big-eyed look of his that could convince the Pope to go clubbing. "Please?"

Sam bit the inside of his cheek. There were plenty of cons. He couldn't job hunt while he was on the road. He had savings, but not working for two weeks while he had rent to pay wasn't something he could just *do*. Neither could Wesley.

A trip like this would be expensive, even if they ate gas-station food and stayed in shitty motels. Plus, he loved Wesley—dearly, completely, deeply—but spending fifteen days in another person's constant company made the introvert in him palpitate.

There were pros too, though. He'd have someone to hold him accountable and make sure he made it to Jessica's wedding. Wesley would give him strength when he faced his bloodthirsty relatives. Plus, Sam so seldom did anything daring. He didn't want to look back on life and see nothing but paying bills and going to bed at a reasonable hour. He wanted to *live*, for once.

If his family was going to go nuclear on him, he might as well see the world before he died. He'd managed to run out on his wedding because it was important. Somehow, this felt important too. As he debated with himself, he had the strangest feeling, low and wriggly in his gut, that whatever he decided was going to change everything.

"Okay." He nodded. "I'm in."

CHAPTER TWO

W esley almost couldn't believe how easily Sam had caved. Sam was a fun guy, in his own mellow, down-to-earth way, but his comfort zone had a five-block radius. His idea of a wild night out was Wesley's typical Thursday afternoon.

A week into knowing him, Wesley had joked that he was a balloon, and Sam was a kid holding on to him. Wesley brought fun into Sam's life, while Sam kept him from floating up into the sky. Sam had laughed and told Wesley that he watched too many John Hughes movies.

As luck would have it, it seemed Sam needed a getaway as badly as Wesley did. Another cup of coffee and some gentle cajoling later, he left Wesley's apartment with the intention of going home to pack.

After he'd gone, Wesley wandered into the living room and flopped on his futon. Excitement washed through him. This was going to be *epic*. A road trip across the country with his best friend. Two whole weeks of freedom and going wherever the wind took them. What could be better?

Not keeping a secret from Sam.

Wesley shook that thought off like a wet dog. He wasn't keeping a *secret*. He was omitting part of the reason why he wanted to go on the trip. That wasn't the same as lying. Really. And Wesley had told Sam ninety percent of the truth, so that had to count for something.

Besides, he had every intention of telling Sam the whole story, eventually. Sam was his best friend, after all. Wesley wouldn't be able to keep it from him for long. Hell, Wesley was surprised he hadn't confessed the whole sordid tale after his fourth or so shot. Alcohol wasn't truth serum for him the way it was for some people—like Sam—but it lowered his inhibitions down to "nonexistent."

Speaking of which.

Wesley heaved himself off his futon—which he'd refused to get rid of after graduating on the basis that it was the only comfortable futon in existence—and strolled into the bedroom. Sam's face imprint was still in the left pillow. Wesley fluffed it and caught the faint smell of Sam's fancy cucumber shampoo. The urge to press the pillow to his face was sudden and overwhelming.

You could have passed out on the couch, an inner voice quietly pointed out. *You were way less drunk than Sam. You chose to sleep in the bed with him. Why?*

Wesley's brain was quick to make excuses, as it always did when awkward questions about Sam came up. This time around, however, the explanation wasn't contrived. Sam was handsome in a wholesome, fields-of-wheat sort of way, but Wesley wouldn't act inappropriately toward his best friend, especially when alcohol was involved. No, he'd slept in the bed last night for a simple reason: he was lonely.

His last "relationship" had been a three-week affair with a guy from work. It'd fizzled out when Wesley quit, since sneaking sex in the copy room wasn't possible anymore. Sadly, that had been one of his more successful romances.

He couldn't fathom how Sam had gotten engaged before they were out of college. Wesley had never felt that sort of connection with someone else. Well, besides Sam, of course, but that hardly counted.

When they were kids—and by kids, Wesley meant reckless undergrads who had no business being recognized as legal adults—they'd been surrounded by peers. Making friends had never been easier. Even for Sam, who'd once introduced himself as a strange hissing sound followed by a head-to-toe blush.

Now that they'd graduated, however, it was getting harder to meet people. And they were expected to do odd things like pay taxes and have plans for the future. Adult shit. Technically, Wesley was an adult, and he knew that, but he was low on experience. He still read comics, for Christ's sake. His solution to a sink full of dishes was to order takeout. When his last boss had asked him about his 401(k), Wesley had blinked and asked, *"Is that a band?"*

Increasingly, it was Sam and him against the world, which was precisely why he wanted to go on this trip and re-create their college days. Man, he'd give anything to have that time back. But until Apple produced an iTimeTravel, he'd have to settle for the next best thing: getting some serious face time with his bestie.

Sam had been joking earlier when he'd mentioned Wesley moving into his tiny apartment, but honestly, Wesley would live with Sam forever if he could.

But if you lived with him, he'd know your secret. In fact, considering the close quarters you two are going to be in on this road trip, he might figure it out before you can tell him. Sam's sharp, and he knows you better than anyone.

Wesley frowned to himself and let the pillow drop back onto his sheets. He'd have to be extra careful. This road trip had to be epic. He wouldn't let anything jeopardize that.

Resolved, he flung his closet doors open and wrestled a battered suitcase out from the back corner. He hadn't used it since the summer after sophomore year. He'd been the most original college kid ever and had gone backpacking through Europe. As he opened it on his bed, he swore he could still smell Amsterdam on it. So, weed and questionable judgment.

It took him less than fifteen minutes to pack, mostly because his definition of *packing* involved sniff-testing his laundry and tossing everything that didn't make him wince into the suitcase. He also grabbed the Sam-pillow off his bed and tucked it under his arm. Just in case they had to sleep in the car or something.

Though he was careful to pack toiletries like deodorant and mouthwash—for Sam's sake. No one wanted to be trapped in a small space with a dude who forgot to bring deodorant. He also packed his tablet, charging cords, and converters. If there was nothing good on the radio (possible), or they ran out of things to talk about (improbable), they could listen to books and watch movies.

Finally, he wandered out to his living room, where a well-stocked bar boasted a number of opened bottles. One, however, was sealed: the fifteen-year-old, single-malt whiskey his father had given him as a graduation present. Dad probably thought it was long gone by now, but Wesley had been saving it for a special occasion.

A cross-country road trip with Sam totally qualifies. Plus, you never know when you might need to make a Molotov cocktail.

Wrapping up the bottle carefully in a shirt, he tucked it into the suitcase, did a quick check to make sure he had everything he needed, and zipped it up.

There was only one thing left to do: secure their ride. Sam would probably want to take his car—with its up-to-date safety features and terrific gas mileage and blah, blah, blah—but Wesley had another idea.

They were going to travel in style.

"You have *got* to be kidding me."

Wesley's arms—which he'd been holding out toward his car like it was a prize on a gameshow—wilted. "What's wrong?"

"We are not taking *that* to Montana." Sam set a large brown Boston bag on the stoop and shook his head so hard, his corn-field hair fell over his eyes. "No way. I'm shocked it's still running."

Wesley glanced between Sam and the aqua-blue '69 Rambler that was parked by the curb, disappointment threatening to wash over him. "I take offense to that. My dad and I restored this car ourselves."

It was Wesley's baby. On top of the striking paint color, it had a white stripe down the middle, round side mirrors, and a classic black grill set between two headlights like bright eyes. It was a "beaut," as his dad would say.

"Yeah, which is what worries me." Sam eyed the car as if it were a wild animal. "Man, when I got your text saying to come outside, I thought you were too lazy to drag your suitcase up the stairs."

"Nope, I wanted to surprise you." Wesley leaned back against the Rambler, which already had his luggage loaded into the trunk. "You're not seriously refusing, are you?"

"Damn straight I am." Despite his words, Sam picked up his suitcase again—looking at it made Wesley's biceps ache—and hauled it over, setting it down on the curb next to Wesley. He leaned on the car as well as if the effort had fatigued him. "How many miles to the gallon does this boat get? Twelve?"

"Twenty." Wesley sniffed. "On the highway, at least, which is where we're going to be most of the time. So, we should be fine."

"This trip is already going to be way more expensive than plane tickets. Can you really afford to pump money into this thing?"

"Don't you worry about me. I may not be as responsible as you, but I've had three jobs in the past year, and I saved money from all of them. My finances are sorted, for once in my life."

Sam frowned. "I'm not sold. How did you even get your dad to agree to lend you this?"

"He didn't *lend* it to me. It's mine. He signed it over to me on my sixteenth birthday. It lives at my parents' house because they have a garage, and Dad likes to tinker with it, but I can claim it whenever I want."

There was actually a lot more to that story. When Wesley had gone over to his parents' house to pick it up, the encounter hadn't been pleasant. Dad had made arguments similar to the ones Sam was making right now, only more centered on Wesley and his personal faults. But the car was legally Wesley's, so in the end, Dad couldn't keep him from taking it.

He didn't want to start this trip off on a negative note, however, so he kept that part of the story to himself.

"That's another thing," Sam said. "Neither you nor Mr. Reed are mechanics. What if your dad . . . I dunno, left a wrench in the engine core, or something? What if we break down in the middle of nowhere?"

"'Engine core'? That's not a thing." Wesley patted the chrome trim. "I know this car inside and out. I may not be a professional, but I have a lifetime of field experience. If we break down, and it's something I can't handle, we'll take it to a shop. But I promise, this baby's running every bit as well as the day it came off the assembly line. And hey, it's been on this Earth longer than either of us have, so if anything, the car should be worried about being handled by two neophytes like us."

Sam's expression wavered. "I don't know . . ."

"We gotta, Sammy. Think about it: a classic car for a classic road trip. It's perfect. Plus, it's got bench seats. If we can't find a hotel, we can sleep in it. During long treks, you can stretch your legs out in the back seat with a book while I drive. Picture yourself all cozy with a pillow behind your back. The windows cracked. Wind ruffling your hair. Oldies on the radio. Sunlight warming the leather seats. Can't you see it? Hell, I can smell it."

Sam tilted his head back, thinking. "That *is* an attractive image, and I have to admit, it'd be fitting to take a car like this out on the open road. It feels sort of magical somehow."

"*Exactly.*" Wesley clapped his hands together like an eager child. "Now you're getting the idea! So, can we take it? Pleeease?"

Sam sighed. "It's so hard being the single dad of a twenty-three-year-old. Are you certain you want to spend the extra money?"

"Money doesn't worry me. For all I know, I got that job I interviewed for after all. It could be waiting for me when we get back. Besides, I'm not too good to microwave cup noodles at a gas station. I did it all throughout college, after all."

Sam smiled. "I'd kill for your optimism."

"Please don't. I'm going to be the only person around for the foreseeable future." Wesley pulled out his keys and dangled them by his head. "Shall we?"

Sam could never resist when Wesley got excited about something. After only another second of hesitation, he nodded. "Okay. Let's get going."

Wesley whooped. "The adventure begins!"

When Wesley picked up Sam's bag, he realized why Sam had seemed drained from lifting it. "Holy shit, did you pack your entire apartment?"

"I wanted us to be prepared. I brought a first aid kit, my laptop, some books, magazines, spare clothes and shoes—"

"Jesus. I feel better about my haphazard packing now. You brought enough for both of us."

Sam ruffled his hair. "I have to take care of my bestest best friend."

Wesley made a face, but inside, his heart warmed. He stowed Sam's bag—thank God the trunk had plenty of room—and tossed the keys into the air. He caught them neatly a moment later. "All right. Where should we go first?"

Sam pulled his phone out of his pocket and checked it. "It's a little after ten now. You said this trip was about seeing the country, so

I suppose we should pick a city that's a few hours from here? We'll drive there, spend the day, crash, and then do the whole thing over again tomorrow. We can head down the coast, cut across to California, and then loop around to Montana. Two weeks is enough time for at least ten cities."

"Sounds perfect. Hop in, and I'll head for the interstate. Pull up a map on your phone and pick anywhere you'd like."

He slid into the driver's seat and took a deep breath. A familiar smell filled his nose: leather and what he swore was cigars, though neither he nor his father smoked.

Wesley had heard the story of how Dad had found this car in a junkyard so many times it was like a memory. Dad had towed it home to his pregnant wife, who'd been none-too-impressed. Dad had sworn he'd fix it up and that their baby would inherit it when they were old enough to drive. Mom had predicted Dad would give up on the car after a week, but he'd persisted, trial-and-erroring his way through a steep learning curve.

Wesley was grateful he had. Working on cars was soothing, like solving a metal puzzle. Oil and gasoline smelled like childhood to him, and although he hadn't taken the Rambler to college—everything was walking distance, and after all these years, Dad was too attached to let it go—the car was Wesley's baby.

Sam climbed into the seat next to him and whistled. "After hearing you talk about this thing for years, it's an honor to finally be in it."

Wesley patted the steering wheel. "Play your cards right, and I might let you drive."

"Yeah, right. More like beg me to drive the days you're too hungover to look at the road. How are you feeling, by the way?"

Wesley opened a console on the dashboard and pulled out a pair of sunglasses. After placing them on his nose, he grabbed a bottle of water from the driver's side pocket. "With these items, I am healed enough to begin our quest."

Sam laughed. "All right. I bet there's a road trip app we can use to plan the whole thing. I'll search for one."

If it were up to Wesley, they'd head in a random direction and probably never stop. It was a good thing he had Sam around to put a plan together.

Wesley fastened his seat belt. "Ladies and gentlemen, keep your hands and feet inside the vehicle at all times. We're ready for takeoff."

Sam followed suit and then buried his nose in his phone. Wesley turned the key in the ignition, and the engine roared to life before settling into a soothing growl. He eased the car away from the curb, excitement tingling from his toes to the tips of his fingers.

He caught a glimpse of himself in the rearview mirror. With his hair still tousled from Sam's fingers and stubble on his jaw, he looked like the star of one of those old buddy-cop films. He was the loose cannon who broke all the rules, and Sam was the by-the-book lieutenant who remained faithfully by his side.

"Here we go," Sam said, interrupting his daydreaming. "I found an app that will not only plan our route, but it'll also tell us how long it takes to get to the cities within a certain radius. Oh, and I found another one that ranks nearby gas stations by price."

"God, I love technology." Wesley clicked on the radio and was delighted when classic rock played over the speakers. "How does four hours sound for our first day? Assuming we grab lunch to-go and don't need too many pee breaks, we can be in a totally new city by three o'clock."

Sam let out a breath. "Wow, we're really doing this. It didn't hit me until you said that."

"How do you feel?" Wesley held his breath.

"Excited as *fuck*." Sam looked at him, grinning so hard his cheeks were twin red apples in his face. "No one but you could have convinced me to do this."

Wesley's heart soared. This was the shit he lived for. When people met Wesley, they assumed his friendship with Sam was one-sided. They were right, but it was Wesley who was always chasing after Sam. Sam wasn't the sort to have a ton of friends, preferring quality over quantity. The fact that Wesley was his best friend was the world's biggest compliment.

Sam consulted his new app. "There's Baltimore. Or Philadelphia. How do cheesesteaks sound for lunch?"

"Mighty tempting. That's a solid maybe. What else ya got?"

"We could go to Cape May Point in Jersey and re-create our beach week there."

Wesley made a sound like a buzzer on a gameshow. "Negative. I'd rather go somewhere new."

"All right." Sam hit some buttons. "Hey, New York City is about four hours away. Ever been to the Big Apple?"

Wesley perked up. "No. Have you?"

"Nope."

"Well, hot damn, Sam. I think we have our first destination!"

Sam laughed. "How long have you been waiting for an opportunity to say 'hot damn, Sam'?"

"Since literally the moment we met. I'm convinced: this trip is going to be *epic.*"

Up ahead an overpass appeared, bearing signs that indicated where to turn to get on the interstate. Wesley selected the one leading east and merged onto the highway, accelerating as he went. The purring engine joined the sundry sounds of traffic as they slid into the lanes of cars speeding down the gray ribbon of asphalt.

The road sloped upward, affording them a beautiful view of the silvery Susquehanna River on the right and verdant green hills to the left. The sky was the shade of baby blue that Wesley liked best. It evoked lazy Sunday afternoons and iced tea with a bite of lemon.

Most people loved the deep azure of autumn, but Wesley loved a good summer sky, especially when it paled the closer it got to the horizon. He knew the reason it did that, of course, but when he was a kid, he'd thought the sky got lighter with excitement as it stretched down, like it was couldn't wait dig its fingers into the warm dirt and smell the grass.

Mesmerized as he was by the view, Wesley still noticed the silence that had draped itself over them. Keeping one eye on the road, he turned his head toward Sam. "You all right?"

Sam jerked in his seat, like he'd crashed back to reality. "Yeah."

"Liar."

"Am I that transparent?"

"To me, you're Casper. What's up?"

Sam chuckled. "I was thinking about how funny life can be. If I'd married Michael, I'd be going to this wedding with him right now. My parents wouldn't be mad at me, and I wouldn't be ashamed to face them. I wouldn't have considered breaking my sister's heart."

Wesley's lungs compacted with sympathy. "Don't think like that. You and Michael weren't meant to be together. Jess knew it too. Did you tell her you're coming, by the way?"

"Not yet. I don't want to delay RSVPing—having planned a wedding, I know how important having an accurate head count is—but I also don't want to tell her I'm coming only to chicken out. If we get close to Montana, and I haven't given myself an ulcer, I'll call her."

"All right. Let's face some of your fears right here and now. Worst-case scenario, what do you think is going to happen when you see your folks again?"

"Mom bursts into tears, Dad hands me a bill for ten thousand dollars, and Jessica's wedding is ruined. Then Dad trots Michael out and says they want him to be their son instead. Also, Michael is now an international underwear model and married to Nick Bateman."

"Okay. That was . . . detailed. Let me posit some more-likely scenarios. Your parents, who are rational people, put on polite faces and treat you civilly because it's their daughter's day. Jessica is thrilled to see you. Some relatives say awkward things because that's what relatives do, but we don't care because we're busy telling everyone about our awesome trip. Michael is not there because your sister would *never, ever* invite your ex to her wedding. Seriously. And if he inexplicably traveled all the way to Montana to crash the party, she'd kick him out before you ever saw a hair on his blond head."

Sam shrugged. "Yeah, I guess. If you want to be rational about it."

"I do. Also, for all you know, if you'd married Michael, you'd be divorced already and going with me anyway."

Sam raised an eyebrow. "You don't think Michael and I would have made it a year?"

"Buddy, you didn't make it to your wedding day."

A bark of laughter burst from Sam. "I can't argue with that. I had no idea you thought so little of Michael."

"*Au contraire.* I think very highly of him. He's a great guy, and he could mix up a hell of an appletini, which is a fantastic quality in a husband. But I admit I never saw you two making it in the long run."

"Why'd you agree to be my best man, then?"

Wesley shrugged. "I wanted to be, for one thing. I was honored when you asked me. And I thought you were happy. If Michael was who you wanted to be with, I wasn't about to cast doubt. Much as I love to be right, I was praying I was wrong about you two."

Sam cooed. "Wes, you're giving me a toothache."

Wesley sniffed. "Well, it's true."

"I appreciate it. But you know, if you'd told me you had misgivings, you might have convinced me to call the whole thing off before the night before."

"I did! Not about Michael, but I said a hundred times that getting married right out of college was a mistake. You were both way too young."

"Yeah, but lots of people get married young. That wasn't the problem."

Wesley's tongue tingled with a question he'd been dying to ask. *Then what was?* He forced the words back down his gullet.

Sam seemed to sense them, because he quickly shifted away from the topic. "Well, what's done is done. I can't take it back."

"Would you if you could?"

"No." Sam exhaled sharply. "But there are a lot of things I'd do differently. Namely, I would have found a gentler way to break up with Michael. He still won't speak to me."

"How many times have you contacted him?"

"I called him a few times, and about six months ago, I wrote him a letter. I thought if I gave him some time, he'd write back, but he never did. I texted him the other day to see if he got my letter, but he didn't respond. That sends a pretty clear message, don't you think?"

"Yeah." Wesley furrowed his brow. "I wonder why he doesn't want to talk. If I were him, I'd need the closure."

"Isn't it obvious? He hates me."

Before he could answer, the road split, and Wesley had to read signs to see which lane to be in. So far, their path had been clear, but as they got farther from home, they were going to need to use a navigation app.

"For the record, I thought you handled the breakup as well as could be expected. You told Michael to his face, and you broke the news to both your families yourself instead of making him do it.

It's not like you disappeared in the night, or faked your death and moved to Belize. Considering how nonconfrontational you are, what you did took guts."

"Yeah, but you weren't there when I told him. You don't know." Sam's voice sounded tight.

Wesley glanced over at him. "Don't know what?"

"Let's change the subject." Sam fiddled with the radio. "We're on an adventure. We need music to get us pumped."

That was a misdirection, but Wesley let it slide. He was going to give Sam the trip of his life, no matter what it took.

New York City was *amazing*.

Wesley had seen his fair share of movies set in New York. He was familiar, in general, with what to expect. Tall buildings. Short tempers. Museums and sketchy street food. He'd heard enough songs about the city to know it was big and dirty and diverse and that the people who lived there were inexplicably loyal to it.

But it wasn't until they exited the New Jersey Turnpike, and the metal sprawl spanned out before them, that he got a real scope of the thing. It blotted out the horizon. It made his home town look like a toy village. It was an *entity*.

Next to him, Sam practically pressed his nose to his window. "Christ. I knew it was big, but *wow*."

"Yeah. I guess nothing anyone says can really prepare you for it. It's going to be hard to go home after this, and this is only the first stop."

Sam pulled out his phone and started snapping photos. "I'm putting these on Facebook. Our friends are going to be so jealous when we tell them what we're doing."

"Won't your family see?"

"My parents aren't online, thank God, and I'll block Jessica from viewing my statuses for the next two weeks." He paused. "Actually, it might be worth it to make an Instagram account for this trip. I bet people would love a photo blog about two guys traveling the country." He turned his camera to Wesley. "Smile!"

Wesley pushed his sunglasses onto his head and winked. "New York City, here we come."

They drove aimlessly for a while, looking at absolutely everything and blessing the grid system for keeping them from getting lost. Wesley's blood curdled a number of times as he avoided all the cabs that seemed to have no regard for things like lanes, traffic lights, or other cars. The pedestrians were similar, and Wesley got a handful of one-finger salutes for crimes such as turning right and driving through intersections while the light was green.

Sam used his phone to find them a hotel with parking, which was no small feat. The one he selected was in lower Manhattan and at a shockingly reasonable price.

"Be honest," Wesley said, "did someone get murdered in our room? Is that why it's such a steal?"

"If they did, would that stop you?"

"Hell no. If we're lucky, we'll see a ghost. Then it'll get attached to us, and it'll follow us from city to city, hitchhiking in the back seat. We'll never have to turn on the AC, and if anyone tries to carjack us, the joke will be on them."

Sam chuckled. "What's it like in your head?"

"Confusing, and for some reason, everything is mauve."

After they got to the hotel, they breezed through check-in—Sam put this one on his card after Wesley promised to get the next room—and hurried up the stairs, eager to drop off their shit and see the city. The second they got their door unlocked, it was obvious why it'd been so cheap.

"Holy shit, this place is a closet," Wesley said.

The door, which only opened halfway before it hit a dingy mattress, creaked worrisomely as Wesley fought his way inside. Sam had to Tetris his bag through the doorway. Wesley tried to step back to make room for him, but there wasn't anywhere to go.

The room couldn't have been more than eight feet by eight feet. The two beds they'd requested consisted of twin mattresses, sans sheets, pushed together in the corner. One of them blocked most of a tiny window, which was fine, because the view consisted of the building next door. The only other furniture was a single nightstand, on which rested a Bible, an empty coffee cup with lipstick on the lid, and a phone so old it dialed by rotary.

Wesley spent a moment soaking it in before he grinned at Sam. "We are *so* stealing the Bible."

"No way." Sam hefted his bag onto the nearest mattress and sent a cloud of what Wesley prayed was dust into the air. "I'm scared to touch anything."

"What are we going to do for sheets?"

Sam inspected a questionable green stain on the wall. "I brought a spare set." At Wesley's look, he shrugged. "What? I knew we were going to be staying in cheap places. I wanted to be prepared."

"Dude, I *love* you. You would have made a hell of a Boy Scout."

They did rock-paper-scissors for who got the dirtier mattress, stowed their things under their beds, and left to explore the city. Sam wanted to go to the Met, of course, but with only one day and so much to see, Wesley insisted they spend their time outdoors.

They took the subway to Central Park—an experience in and of itself—and practically ran through it in their effort to get to all the good parts. They took selfies with the *Alice in Wonderland* statue, and Wesley somehow earned the ire of an aggressive and persistent swan.

Lunch consisted of the questionable street food Wesley had heard so much about, and it was *delicious*. Then they hit all the big-name spots one by one: the Empire State Building, Times Square, and Wall Street. At sunset, they took a ferry past the Statue of Liberty. Wesley wanted to go in it, but Sam and a serious case of motion sickness vetoed that.

It was a blast, but all day, Wesley sensed growing tension in Sam. It was as if a spring had wound itself around his spine and was slowly tightening. Wesley made a mental note to find them some drinks somewhere. That would loosen Sam up, and Wesley could use one after a long day in the sun.

For dinner, they went with the obvious choice and found an authentic pizza joint. They got slices the size of their heads and split a pitcher of beer, chasing off the last of their hangovers. Unfortunately, it seemed to do little to ease Sam's tension.

Wesley wanted to hit up a club, but considering they were both guys, they figured no bouncer in their right mind would let them in and risk ruining the club's ratio. They headed back to their room/closet, freshened up in the communal bathroom down the hall, and then used Sam's laptop to watch movies while the city buzzed outside their window: traffic, sirens, and humming lights. It was oddly soothing.

After, Sam put his laptop away, and got up to hit the light switch. It plunged them into unexpected darkness. There was some shuffling, the rustle of sheets, and then a little sigh. Wesley could almost hear the spring inside Sam winding tighter.

He fought sleep and propped himself up on his elbows. "Sam?"

There was no sound from Sam's bed. Then, "Yeah?"

"There's something I want to ask you."

Sam stirred, but his form didn't sit up. "Hmm?"

"Why'd you call off the wedding?"

Sam fell into eerie, breathless silence. Wesley thought about saying something else—to forget he'd asked, or conversely, that Sam could tell Wesley anything—but then Sam relaxed.

"Because Michael wasn't the one."

Wesley hesitated, chewing on several possible reactions to that.

Before he could settle on one, Sam spoke again. "I know that's cliché, but it's true. Michael was *a* one, but he wasn't *the* one. I knew I could have been happy with him, but some part of me was certain there was someone else out there. Someone I could be more than just happy with. Someone who'd make me glad every day I woke up on the same planet as them. So, I called it off."

"Weren't you scared you were losing a good thing with no guarantee you'd find someone better?"

"Terrified, but some part of me knew it wasn't right all along. Michael was safe." His voice was soft, but it filled their tiny room. "All my life, I've taken the safe route. Kept my head down, my nose clean, and my feet on the ground. Going to college out of state was the wildest thing I'd ever done. Then I met Michael. He was sweet and handsome, and he loved me. But somehow, marrying him felt like giving up."

Wesley was wide-awake now. "What do you mean?"

"If I'd married Michael, I'd never have to date again. I hated dating. Working up the nerve to say hi and bumbling my way through first dates. I wanted it to be over. When Michael proposed, I figured, why not? I was all set to make yet another safe choice, but the night before the wedding, I realized what I was doing and how unfair it was to both of us."

"So you called the whole thing off." Wesley didn't phrase it as a question.

"I left Michael for the same reason I agreed to this trip. I didn't want to pick *safe* my whole life only to look back and realize I'd never had *great*. I understand why people take the easy route at times, but someone else's happiness was at stake. I couldn't do that to Michael."

Wesley nodded. "It's like I said before, you made the right call."

"I think so too, but that didn't make it any easier. There's something I've been avoiding talking about, and I don't just mean earlier in the car. I've been putting it off, because saying it out loud isn't easy."

"What is it?" Wesley tensed with anticipation.

Sam took a breath. "When I broke things off with Michael, he asked me why. I could have lied. I could have said I wasn't ready or that this had all happened too fast. But if I'd done that, he might have forgiven me. He might have still wanted to be with me, and I couldn't waste any more of his time. So, I told him the truth. I told him he didn't make me happy to wake up every morning."

"How'd he take that?"

Sam laughed humorlessly. "His *face*. If you'd seen it, you'd know why I refused to talk about it for so long. I wish he'd contact me, but the truth is, I'm glad he'll never forgive me. I don't deserve to be."

Wesley rolled onto his side, fierce emotion sweeping through him. "Don't say that, Sammy. Never say that."

"Why not? It's true."

"No, it isn't. You shouldn't feel guilty for being honest about things that are important. You gave Michael the best thing you could have possibly given him that night: closure. That's why he's never tried to talk to you. He doesn't need to. You set him free."

Sam was quiet for a minute. "Maybe."

"Definitely. If you want to be eaten up by guilt, that's your business. But you'll never convince me you did anything wrong."

Wesley's eyes had adjusted enough that he could almost see Sam's face in the darkness. He spotted a hint of a smile.

Before Wesley could say anything else, Sam rolled over. "Good night, Wesley."

"Night, Sam." He shifted onto his back and closed his eyes.

Several minutes passed, long enough that Wesley had nearly fallen asleep.

"Wesley?" Sam's voice was no louder than a whisper.

"Yeah?"

"Thank you."

They fell silent, and not long after, the sound of Sam's steady breathing joined the noise of the city. It lulled Wesley to sleep.

CHAPTER THREE

T he next day, Sam woke early. Wesley had gravitated over to his bed sometime in the night, which afforded Sam the opportunity to wake him by pushing his eyelids up and making funny faces. Wesley jerked awake with a shriek, and Sam laughed so hard, his sides hurt.

After eating breakfast in a little café and taking one final stroll through Central Park, they bid goodbye to New York City. This time, Sam got behind the wheel. He'd expected Wesley to put up a fight, but instead Wesley handed the keys right over.

"Dad and you," he'd said. "The only people I trust with my baby."

Once they were all packed up and headed for the highway, Sam gave his phone to Wesley. "I suggested our first destination, so you pick the next one."

"Sounds fair. There are a lot of cool cities to choose from. I've always wanted to go to New Orleans and eat some beignets. We could get there today if we drove nonstop."

Sam squirmed in the driver's seat. "Maybe pick somewhere closer? We have plenty of time, and I don't want to drive all day if we don't have to. Short bursts of four to five hours would work. I think it'd be easier on Grandpa here too." He patted the steering wheel.

"Don't you worry about the car. It's solid." Wesley slapped the dashboard, and it made a worrisome creaking noise. "Oops."

Sam snorted. "Hurry up and pick a destination before it falls apart."

Grumbling, Wesley consulted the road trip app. "How about Washington, DC? It's around four hours away. Seems appropriate to hit up the capital on our tour of America. I've always wanted to see that reflecting-pool thingy. What's that called?"

"The Reflecting Pool." Sam switched into the correct lane. "And that sounds good to me."

They found their way to I-95 and got on, this time heading south. According to the app, it would take them within spitting distance of Philadelphia, then past Baltimore, before depositing them in the political heart of the country.

Wesley pulled a pillow out of the back seat and put it between his side and the window, stretching out as much as he could. His knee ended up near Sam's. "We should stop in Philly and get those sandwiches we talked about."

"That's a great idea. Then we'll have had actual New York pizza and real Philly cheesesteaks. Does DC have a famous food?"

Wesley screwed his mouth to the side. "Apples? Cherries? Nothing I'm particularly excited to eat. I suppose not every city can be known for its food."

"Maybe that could be a factor in our decision-making process in the future."

"Yeah! We'll let our stomachs guide us across the country. I'm making New Orleans my one place I definitely want to hit. What's yours?"

Sam considered it for a moment. "If we make it all the way to California, I'd really like to see the Pacific Ocean."

"You never saw it when you lived on the West Coast?"

Sam shook his head. "I stayed in Montana, except when I scouted Penn State in my last year of high school. I went straight from there to here."

"I see. Well, we've got two whole weeks and nothing but open road ahead of us. We'll get you to that ocean." Wesley leaned forward and tuned the radio. "Let's get some road music going. Listening to the actual radio feels more authentic than using our phones."

Wesley managed to find an adult alternative station that played all the angsty indie rock they'd listened to in their formative years. They sang along at the top of their lungs. Sam sincerely thought he might lose his voice, and for once, he didn't care.

When commercials played, Wesley would click it off and suggest they play games instead. They ran through the classics—License Plate Alphabet, Twenty Questions, and I Spy—but Wesley also started up a truly heinous round of Would You Rather. He made Sam pick between being eternally sticky or itchy, and just thinking about it made Sam twitch.

Around lunchtime, they stopped in Philadelphia as planned. Sandwiches were easy to locate, which meant they didn't have a good excuse to explore. Time-wise, Sam knew that was best, but it seemed like a shame to skip over a beautiful new city. It was right on the water too. Also, after one bite of a real cheesesteak, Sam would have stayed for those alone. They almost missed an exit, thanks to him shoveling food into his mouth.

Don't start stalling, said a voice in his head. *You're only delaying the inevitable. No matter how much you avoid thinking about it, you know where this trip is headed. Montana. Home. Your family. You're going to have to face reality sooner or later. Right now, it's looking like sooner.*

Lost in thought as he was, Sam hadn't realized he'd left Wesley to sing solo through a few songs until Wesley noticed it as well.

"Hey." Wesley touched his arm. "Something troubling you? You got quiet."

"I'm fine," Sam lied. "Focused on the road, is all. I'll give you my undivided attention when we get where we're going."

Once they reached DC, he actually did perk up. It was overcast, but all the historical white monuments and buildings brightened it anyway. There were parks everywhere, making it seem much greener than the past two cities they'd visited.

They did the same thing as in New York and used their phones to find accommodations—a motel this time. They checked in to their blessedly normal-sized room, dropped off their bags, and hit the town.

The Lincoln Memorial was their first stop, along with the much-anticipated Reflecting Pool. There was too much wind for them to get a clear reflection of the Washington Monument, but the clouds made the water look like mercury. It was beautiful, in a somber way, as clouds tended to be.

Thanks to the weather, Sam finally got his way: Wesley agreed to go to a museum. The Smithsonian Air and Space Museum had the honor of being their inaugural choice. They toured model airplanes and rocket ships while Wesley asked Sam ridiculous questions. If they moved to Mars, would they be explorers or would they do something more practical, like start a laser farm? When the inevitable uprising occurred, would they join the resistance or submit to the authority of their new alien overlords? Sam shushed him between chuckles.

A coin toss decided their next stop was American Art. It was a farther walk than some of the other museums, but it was conveniently located by the International Spy Museum, which Wesley wouldn't shut up about.

"I don't get it," Sam said hours later, as they walked down a tree-lined street in search of dinner. The sun had finished setting a few minutes prior, and the darkening sky was still tinged with orange at the horizon. "We just saw some of the most famous paintings in the world. Work by Thomas Moran and Roy Lichtenstein. But all you can talk about is Operation Spy."

"It was *interactive*, Sam." Streetlights flickered on around them. Wesley's cheeks were flushed with excitement. "We *were* the spies. Does this mean we have a license to kill now?"

Sam couldn't help but mirror his infectious smile. "I'm sure the police would say no."

"Bunch of spoilsports."

They found a diner, ate fast, and then meandered in the direction of their motel.

"It's too early to go home," Wesley said. "Let's go clubbing or something. Get some local color."

"I don't know." Sam hesitated. "Clubbing in a strange city sounds like one of those scenarios that leads to getting mugged. Or waking up in a tub of ice."

"Oh, come on. DC is perfectly safe, and we'd never let anything bad happen to each other. Besides, we're two young, hot, virile men, and it's a Friday night. I thought you wanted to make some memories on this trip. Or would you rather sit in the motel watching movies you could just as easily watch at home?"

Damn. Wesley always knew the right argument to make. One of these days, Sam was going to find himself in a jail cell, and there Wesley would be, sitting next to him and saying, *It seemed like a good idea at the time.*

Sam relented. "All right. I don't think I brought any clubbing clothes, though."

"I doubt there's a dress code. Although, we could hit a bar instead. Oh!" Wesley stopped in the middle of the sidewalk. "Are there any gay bars around here?"

"It's a big city. I'm sure there are a few."

"Awesome. I feel like dancing." Wesley held his arms out and spun around, careful not to hit any of the people passing by them on the sidewalk. "We're in a new place, on an exciting adventure, and we should be celebrating. When was the last time you went out dancing?"

"Um." Sam thought back. "Is 'never' a viable answer? If you didn't make me do the thing, assume I haven't done it."

"That settles it. And don't think you can get out of dancing with me. We'll never see these people again, so you have no reason to be self-conscious."

That got a laugh from Sam. "How do you always know what I'm thinking before I've thought it?"

"It's a gift. Also, at this point in our relationship, we're practically an old married couple." Wesley linked their free arms at the elbow and pulled his phone out of his pocket. "You want to change clothes, or are you good to go?"

"I'm good."

Wesley googled gay bars in the area. There were, in fact, plenty of them in the city. After some debate, they selected a club called Cyan. It was located downtown, surrounded by shops and restaurants. The walk there took no time. It was packed—typical of a Friday night. The crowd made Sam skittish, but Wesley seemed to grow three inches the second they walked inside.

The interior was more or less what Sam had expected: dark with strobing lights and loud music. There were booths lining the walls and an open space in the middle for dancing. On platforms, muscular men in their underwear gyrated for tips to the relentless bass. To the left was the bar, which Wesley made a beeline for with only a cursory glance at the oiled men.

Sam followed behind him, his anxiety ratcheting up as several of the patrons—all men; no women in sight—looked him up and down. Red-faced, he stared at his shoes, leading him to nearly plow into Wesley when he stopped.

Wesley pressed his mouth to Sam's ear. "What do you want? First round's on me."

"Anything." Sam could barely hear his own voice over the music. "Beer. And water. Water, water, water."

Wesley turned to the bar and signaled a bartender. One appeared as if by magic and smiled flirtatiously at Wesley before taking their order. Jealousy twanged in Sam's chest.

When he'd finished, Wesley faced him again. "You gotta make eye contact. You're always looking away, so people skip over you."

Sam blinked. "How'd you know I was thinking about how I never get served as quickly as you do?"

"What? No, I was talking about picking up guys."

"Uh. Why?"

"Because there's one staring at you right now, and you haven't noticed because you don't make eye contact." Wesley jerked his head to the right.

Sam glanced over, and sure enough, a guy was watching him from down the bar. When Sam caught his eye, he smiled and waved. Sam wrenched his head away, cheeks flaming. "Oh my God."

"Go talk to him."

"*No.*"

"Come on. It won't kill you."

"You don't know that."

The bartender appeared then with two beers, two waters, and of course, two shots. Wesley downed his without flinching and handed the other one to Sam. "Here, liquid courage."

After dutifully swallowing it, Sam voiced his thoughts aloud. "You know how I've told you before that being social makes me tired? If I go talk to that guy, for all I know, I'm going to need a nap after, and then the night will be over."

It was true. Funnily enough, Sam liked people. Despite his inability to talk to strangers without swallowing his own tongue, he was no misanthrope. But he needed controlled doses. Social interaction drained him, and some people were more draining to be around than others.

"Damn, I forget about your introvert problems." Wesley's mouth scrunched thoughtfully to the side. "Am I tiring to be around?"

Sam shook his head. "Not at all. That's one of a bajillion reasons why I'm glad I have you in my life. You're one of few people who doesn't Nosferatu all my energy away. In fact, most of the time I find you energizing. Like the sun."

"Aw, that's adorable." Wesley touched his cheek, pretending to pinch it. "That makes you a flower."

"Yeah, a shrinking violet."

Wesley laughed. "I still think you should say hello. It'd be good practice if nothing else, and probably free booze. You don't think he's cute?"

Sam peeked over again. Thankfully, the guy was looking a little to Sam's left. And yeah, he was cute, but not Sam's type. He was fair-haired, for one thing, and Sam had always preferred brunets. Plus, he was too tall. Kissing was way easier with men who around his same height.

"I dunno. He's too . . . blond." He glanced back at Wesley and found him grinning. "What?"

"He's too *blond*? What a sad excuse."

"It is not!"

"Is so. Next you'll tell me his name is Robert Paulson."

Actually, the more Sam thought about it, the odder it seemed. Michael had light hair too. So did Sam, for that matter. Since when did he discriminate against his fellow flaxen-haired fellas?

"Well, I like blonds just fine." Wesley ruffled Sam's hair. "You know, it won't kill you to—"

"Hi." It was as if their words were an incantation that had summoned the guy over to them. He was now by Sam's side. "How are you two doing tonight?"

"Fine." An easy smile found its way onto Wesley's face, without a hint of self-consciousness. "How are you?"

"Great. I'm Bret." He mirrored Wesley's smile.

"I'm Wesley, and this is my friend, Sam."

Sam managed to wrench his eyes up from his shoes and give a little wave. "Hi."

"'Friend'?" Bret glanced between them. "So, you two aren't together?"

Sam and Wesley exchanged knowing looks.

"No," Wesley answered. "We get that a lot. We're best friends."

One of Bret's eyebrows rose. "And you're both gay?"

"Uh, yeah," Wesley said. "Is that not allowed?"

"No, I'm surprised is all. Two gay guys at a gay bar together, and they're not hooking up? You don't see that every day. Or have you hooked up?"

Sam's blush came back full force. "That's kind of personal."

"Sorry! I talk too much." Bret was now studying them like they were science experiments. "I suppose I shouldn't be so shocked. Most of my friends are gay too. But they're all catty queens I can't stand half the time." He laughed.

Sam laughed too, reflexively, but the line of questioning had made him uncomfortable for more than one reason. It raised the question of why they weren't together, and for once, Sam's brain struggled to come up with an answer. Usually, one or both of them was seeing someone and could point to that as an easy excuse, but at the moment, they were both single.

Don't be ridiculous. Things are great the way they are.

He made the mistake of peeking to his right. Wesley was looking back at him, his brow pinched in thought.

Bret's gaze vacillated between them like a rotating fan. "I really am sorry. I said way, way too much. It's my fatal flaw." His eyes landed on Wesley. "I'd love to make it up to you. Would you care to dance?"

Wesley frowned. "I thought you were checking out my friend here."

"Hey, you're both hot. Can't blame a guy for having wandering eyes. But no, I was trying to make eye contact with you." Bret smiled. "Dance with me? Please?"

I should have known. Of course he was watching Wesley. Wesley's so . . .

Sam wasn't sure where that thought was supposed to go, so he let it drift off. He touched Wesley's arm. "It's okay. Go with him. I'm much happier on the sidelines."

Wesley shifted his weight back, frowning. "You sure?"

"You said you wanted to dance. Here's your opportunity."

Wesley hesitated, but when Bret grabbed his arm and dragged him onto the floor, he didn't resist. Although he craned his head back at Sam until they disappeared into the crowd.

Once they were gone, Sam pulled out his wallet, turned to the bar, and made aggressive eye contact with the bartender until he got his hands on another shot.

If I didn't know any better, I'd say that exchange upset me.

Sam concentrated on alcohol and not thinking, the former facilitating the latter. When Wesley failed to return after the song ended and switched over to another semi-identical one, Sam started to get bored.

What would Wesley do if you were dancing and he was alone?

That was easy. He'd have already made friends with half the people at the bar. He'd be asking the locals where the after-party was, and he'd probably have a guy eating out of his hands.

Allegedly, Sam was capable of doing those things as well. Hell, as he looked around the bar, more than one man caught his eye and flashed a flirty grin. The difference was, Sam was already with the only person he wanted to talk to. Too bad Wesley wasn't here with him.

Right on cue, the song ended, and Wesley appeared. He was sweatier than he'd been a moment ago, his hair in disarray. Sam felt another odd twinge, though he couldn't say what it stemmed from.

"Hey." Wesley gave him a crooked smile. "Sorry I was gone for so long. That dude was relentless."

"Where'd he go?"

"I dunno." Wesley shrugged. "Off to seek new prey, I guess."

"He decided he wasn't interested after all?"

Wesley reached into his pocket and pulled out a crumpled napkin. On it, someone had scribbled a phone number. "No, he was interested. I wasn't." He tossed the napkin into a trash can at the end of the bar.

Sam eyed him. Wesley wasn't a player or anything, but he was no stranger to hookups. He'd only ever had one "serious" boyfriend back in college, and that'd lasted all of three months. Sam hadn't even met the guy, which really said it all.

"Any particular reason?" he asked.

"I'm not in that sort of mood." Wesley retrieved his beer and took a long drink. "Besides, I couldn't leave you here all by yourself."

"Thanks for that. Though this wouldn't be the first time you met someone while out with me. It's not like I don't know the drill."

Wesley finished his beer and signaled for another one. After, he turned to Sam, eyes uncharacteristically serious. "I actually think we should discuss that. Protocol, so to speak, for while we're on this trip."

Sam raised a brow. "'Protocol'?"

"Yeah. Like, what we should do if one of us meets a comely stranger. We're going to be out and about every day for two weeks. We'll probably end up in bars and clubs on occasion. There's always a chance one of us will click with someone."

"Ah. I guess you're right." Sam swallowed and discovered his mouth was dry. He fingered his beer bottle, picking at the label. "So . . . what do you think we should do?"

Wesley paused, seemingly thinking. "I don't think we should hook up with anyone, honestly. Stick to flirting, and call it a night. It's not like either of us is going to meet our soul mate on this trip."

Apparently, Sam's heart thought it was participating in some sort of marathon. It matched the tempo of the pounding music all around them. "Really?"

"Yeah. If we go off with strangers, we could get murdered, and bringing them back to our room is dangerous too. Plus, it's kinda inconsiderate. We're a little old to be putting socks on doorknobs, you know?"

The relief that flooded through Sam caught him by surprise. He took a drink to give himself a moment to recover. "I agree."

"You do?"

He nodded. "Imagine if someone robbed us. We'd be screwed. I don't want to wake up in a bathtub full of ice either. And I especially don't want to . . ."

Sam trailed off as a new image entered his head: him, waiting outside of their hotel while Wesley had sex with a strange man inside. His guts tied themselves into knots.

"Sam?" Wesley gave him a once-over. "You okay?"

"I think so. I got this weird stomach pain all of a sudden." He shot an accusatory look at his beer. "Maybe this place has some health-code violations?"

"The reviews online said it was great." Wesley studied his face. "I think you hit a wall. You know what my solution for that is."

Sam laughed. "More drinking."

"You got it! Let's do shots."

Despite his better judgment, Sam let Wesley order for him. He downed the liquor as it was handed to him, and then he did the worst thing imaginable. He stopped drinking water and started drinking cocktails. Before long, he was pulling Wesley onto the dance floor. The two spent the night trying and failing to remember how to do the macarena and fending off advances from increasingly intoxicated men.

When asked later, Sam wouldn't be able to explain the binge. He chalked it up to DC having that effect on people and then buried himself in sweet, sweet avoidance. Also known as vodka.

He had vague memories of checking his phone only to be horrified at the time. Then there was a fuzzy section where there'd been warmth against his side, something heavy slung across his shoulders, and the smell of Wesley's cologne.

Thankfully, the end of the night was a little clearer. They got back to the motel, and as exhausted as Sam was, he fell facedown onto the nearest bed without taking off his clothes. Wesley collapsed next to him, despite the fact that there was a second one not three feet away, but Sam was too drunk to care.

Next thing he knew, he woke up to sunlight seeping through his closed eyelids. With a groan, he attempted to flop over but only made it part of the way. A leaden arm had been slung over the small of his back.

"Wesley." Sam could only get one eye open. "Wake up."

He received a grunt in response that had distinct tones of *absolutely not*.

Sam shook his shoulder as gently as he could, for both their sakes. "Come on, wake up. What time is it?" He squinted at the digital clock on the nightstand between the beds. A second later, his eyes flew open. "Holy shit!"

"What?" Wesley finally lifted his face from the bed. There were lines from the blanket impressed into his cheek. "What's wrong?"

"It's one in the afternoon. We overslept, big time."

Wesley's head dropped back down. "It'll be fine. We're not on any sort of schedule. Go back to sleep."

"Wes, we missed checkout. If we don't hurry up, they're going to charge us for another day."

That got Wesley's attention. Groaning, he flipped himself over like a pancake and nearly fell off the bed. A second later, he pushed himself up on his elbows. "Fuck. How did we sleep so late?"

"We stayed at the club until it closed, and then you insisted on getting chili dogs from that all-night diner." Sam rubbed his stomach. "Which was a *terrible* idea. I've never been so acutely aware of the fact that I'm not a teenager anymore. Eating in the middle of the night is a bad idea."

"I thought it would soak up some of the tequila." Wesley wobbled to his feet and shuffled in the direction of his suitcase. "Well, the good news is, we never unpacked. We can grab our shit and go."

"Yeah." Sam heaved himself to his own feet. "Lemme brush my teeth and use the bathroom. My mouth tastes like feet."

"Can I please go first? I'll be fast. I'm about to burst." At Sam's nod, Wesley stumbled into the bathroom and shut the door.

While Sam waited for him to reemerge, he brushed his teeth in the separate sink-vanity area. His eyes were bloodshot, and his hair was flat on one side of his head. He'd seen better days.

A thought drifted to him through the haze of his hangover. It took him a minute to figure out its significance. "Your arm was around me when I woke up."

"What?" The door opened. Wesley had a little plastic cup in his hand, presumably to fill with water from the sink. "You talking to me?"

"Kind of." Sam opened his mouth to follow the statement with something, but he had no idea what. He ended up closing his mouth again and staring off into space.

"I'm finished with the bathroom if you want to use it." Wesley grabbed both of their bags, stumbling slightly under the weight. "I'll load these into the car and get us checked out. Meet you out there in a few?"

"Okay."

When Wesley opened their door, light from the sun stabbed into Sam's eyes. He shut them reflexively and didn't open them again until he heard the door close. The silence rang. It was the first alone time he'd gotten since they'd left for the road trip. And it felt . . . odd.

I love alone time. I usually think it's necessary for my mental health. So, why does it feel like Wesley took something with him when he walked out the door? Something I need?

Sam had no clue. Maybe this was what happened when people spent too much time together. Or maybe things were changing. That thought sent a thrill down his spine, and he couldn't say if it was excitement or pure terror.

CHAPTER FOUR

Wesley managed to charm the lady at reception into not charging them for missing checkout, thank God. He endured her cheerful lecture about punctuality as he turned in their card keys, signed the bill, and helped himself to a handful of the plastic-wrapped mints set in a fishbowl on the counter.

Popping three of them into his mouth, he got out to the parking lot and retraced his steps to the car, where he'd already stowed their luggage. He opened the trunk and fished in his suitcase for a fresh shirt. He'd remembered too late that he was now sans a room key. He could knock and have Sam let him in, but every movement was painful. Holy shit, he'd kill for a Bloody Mary to take the edge off right now.

His stomach lurched at the thought. Maybe a mimosa instead.

He took a quick peek around. The parking lot was empty. Surreptitiously, he slipped his shirt off. It only took a second, and the sun felt good on his bare back. Unlike yesterday, it seemed they were in for a beautiful summer day.

Wesley had just caught his head in the armhole of a clean shirt when he heard someone clear their throat nearby.

"Please be Sam." His voice was muffled by the fabric. "Or an executioner. I'm flexible."

"It's Sam." The familiar voice was tinged with mirth. "Do you and the car need some alone time? I know you're fond of it, but this is a bit much."

Wesley corrected the shirt and pulled it on. Sam was standing a few feet away, his eyes somewhere in the vicinity of Wesley's navel. Suddenly, his gaze snapped back up in a way that seemed almost guilty.

Wesley shrugged. "We're in a hurry, right? I figured it'd be easier to change out here." He looked Sam over. He was also still in his clothes from last night. "You wanna use the back seat?"

Sam shook his head and wandered over. "I'm not that shy. No one's around." He shucked his shirt and draped it over the lip of the trunk before bending over to dig in his bag.

Wesley's eyes slid down Sam's back of their own accord. Sam had a nice back. Always had. He was much better about remembering to work out regularly than Wesley, though Wesley was naturally leaner. Sam's shape was phenomenal, though. Broad enough in his shoulders to exaggerate the difference between them and his narrow waist.

Distracted by his own thoughts, Wesley almost didn't notice when his eyes kept sliding down, as if guided by the ridge of Sam's spine. They took a brief detour at the muscle indents visible above his jeans before snagging on his underwear band. It'd peeked out when Sam had bent over. It'd be nothing to slide a finger under it. Or a hand. All of a sudden, Wesley had the strangest urge to reach out and—

"All right." Sam straightened up, yanking a fresh shirt over his head. He shook his hair out of his eyes. "We've got to decide where we're going and get there fast, or today's a total waste."

Wesley blinked several times, scrambling to collect himself. "Uh, yeah. I mean, no day is a waste if we're together."

"That's sweet. But seriously, we should head out. Any ideas for where you want to visit next?"

"Pull up a map, and let's see what's between here and New Orleans." Wesley hustled over to the driver's seat and got in.

Sam followed suit. After typing for a moment, he held up the screen of his phone. "There aren't a whole lot of major cities, but Charlotte's six hours away, and I hear the Carolinas are beautiful."

"Six hours means we won't get there until after dark." Wesley bit his lip. "I suppose we could call today a loss and try to get some distance in? We could cut west and hit up Nashville. How far away is that?"

Sam typed some more. "Ten hours. I don't think I can handle being in a car that long."

"You can stretch out in the back."

"And make you drive the whole way yourself? No way. What if we go to Charlotte tonight, spend tomorrow recovering there and checking out the city, and then start anew the next day? We can do Atlanta and then New Orleans."

"Sounds like as good a plan as any." Wesley unclipped his sunglasses from the visor and slipped them on. "God, my head hurts. Let's stop somewhere for water and painkillers. We need gas anyway."

"And food." Sam's stomach chose that moment to grumble. "*Not* chili dogs. Or anything resembling chili dogs. In fact, I need to eat something green."

"Maybe we can hit up a farmer's market or something. We should put together a plan for buying ingredients and eating a few meals in, or this is going to get way expensive."

"Good plan. I made that Instagram, by the way. I called it 'theramblingboysadventure' after Grandpa." He patted the dashboard. "I also posted our New York and Philly photos on Facebook."

"Are we internet famous?"

"Not yet, but we got a handful of followers overnight, and all our friends are super jealous we're getting to travel. Maggie thinks we're going to get drunk-married in Vegas and decide to stay that way."

Wesley forced a laugh, but for some reason, their oldest joke wasn't all that funny to him right now.

He guided them back onto the interstate, and they discussed plans. Sam participated in the conversation well enough, but his tone had a sharp edge. When Wesley referred to Discovery Place—Charlotte's famous science museum—as Discovery Cove, Sam corrected him with none of his characteristic gentleness.

Is the hangover making him grumpy, or does he blame me for our late start? Wesley's stomach dropped down to his feet. His pulse was already elevated, as it always was after a night of drinking, but now it was racing.

"Hey, Sam?"

"Yeah?" He was staring out the window. The ever-present trees slid by, looking like strokes of green paint. But now huge mountains loomed in the distance, their glistening peaks blending with the filmy clouds. Wesley had noticed other changes from state to state, like how much tax was, and the names of chain stores, but watching the landscape slowly shift was fascinating.

He forced himself to focus. "Did I do something to piss you off?"

Sam jerked his head toward him. "What? Why would I be pissed?"

"Well, I was the one who suggested we go out. We got drunk and overslept because of me."

The smile that swept over Sam's face was as warm and pleasant as the morning. "Wes, come on. You didn't force me to go out. If I remember correctly, I was the one who suggested that last round of shots. If anything, I'm mad at myself for overdoing it. I'm usually more responsible than that." He paused. "I have a lot on my mind."

"About your family?"

Sam's face blanked. Had he actually been thinking about something else? But then, he nodded. "They've been in my thoughts this whole time, to be honest. I don't want to dwell on something I can't control, but it's like a giant is walking behind me. I can see his shadow, and I know he's going to grind me under his heel, but I can't outrun him. All I can do is wait for it to happen."

Wesley had been afraid of that. One of many reasons he'd wanted to travel was to get Sam to focus on the journey, not the destination. Take his mind off things. It seemed Wesley might have achieved the opposite: he'd given Sam two whole weeks to work himself into a froth.

Having met Sam's parents on a number of occasions, he couldn't say he blamed Sam. They were kind but austere people. Not the sort to end phone calls with "I love you" or send birthday cards every year. They also weren't made of money. The wedding Sam had cost them wouldn't be last on their list of reasons to be pissed off.

His first instinct as a best friend was to provide comfort in the form of platitudes and assurances. Wesley's throat burned to tell Sam that magically, one day, everything would be okay. Good intentions would shine through, and all the people involved, despite their plethora of flaws, would find it in their hearts to forgive each other. Good would win, evil would lose, and everyone would live happily ever after.

But Wesley wasn't a starry-eyed teenager anymore, and the harsh realities of the world had added some gray clouds to his sunny outlook. He also had the undeniable and somehow implicit understanding that this was something Sam had to do for himself. Needed to. Like how old trees needed to die to make room for new ones. It was sad, but necessary.

Instead, Wesley resolved to do the one thing he could do better than anyone else: insert some fun into Sam's life. Be the balloon clutched in his fist. Give him memories that would shine through the bad times.

"I'm sure everything is going to work out," Wesley ultimately said, eyes on the road.

Sam didn't reply, and they fell into comfortable silence. Until Wesley's phone rang. He handed it to Sam to check while he focused on driving.

Sam held it up. "It's your dad. Should I answer?"

"No!" Wesley bit his tongue, quite literally. "I mean, not right now. I'm in the zone. Hit reject."

Sam did so, though he surveyed Wesley in a way that said his outburst hadn't gone unnoticed. A snippet of a scene played out in Wesley's head, one he'd been keeping a tight lid on so far.

"We're worried about you. Your mother and I think you—"

Sam interrupted the memory, thank God. "Something going on between you and your folks?"

"No," Wesley lied, guilt heavy on his tongue. "Dad gave me shit for taking the car on a long trip, but he'll get over it."

He hated keeping things from Sam, but it was necessary. No point upsetting Sam over what his parents had said. Nothing was going to spoil this trip. Nothing.

"I love driving," he said, apropos of nothing.

"Why?"

"The freedom. The escape. We could go anywhere right now, so long as there's gas in the tank."

"I love it too, but for different reasons." Sam's expression was dreamy. "It's so visceral. Speeding down the road faster than any human could run. The smell of gasoline, rubber tires, and hot asphalt.

Rolling the windows down and feeling the wind in your hair. Never running out of sky ahead of you no matter how far you go."

Wesley reached over and patted his knee. "That's the spirit."

With Wesley speeding like a demon and them only stopping when they had to, it still took them a little over seven hours to get to Charlotte. They were treated to a beautiful sunset—one that made Wesley's head throb—and now night was settling over the city. It seemed small and rural compared to the ones they'd visited before. Bigger than Williamsport by a lot, of course, but *nothing* compared to Philadelphia or New York.

"That's one cool thing about this trip," Sam commented as they pulled into the parking lot of the hotel they'd booked. "I can now make the statement, 'DC had awesome museums, but the food in Philly was way better.' It's nice getting out of our little corner of the world and seeing what other cities have to offer."

"By the time we're finished, we'll be able to make a top-ten ranking of American cities. We could write a travel book."

"Yeah, right." Sam laughed. "Like anyone would want to read a book about us."

They checked into their room, which was apparently the last one available.

"The farther south you go, the harder it's going to be this time of year," the clerk said after they informed her they were on a road trip. "And if you're going to Florida, book in advance. People and birds are on opposite schedules. Everyone migrates south for the summer. This is our busiest season."

They thanked her and left to find their room. The hotel was a chain with four floors that all looked the same. The generic carpet and beige walls made Wesley feel like he was in a mall. Inoffensive music played in the elevator, and bland art on the walls lessened the esteem of the word "decoration."

As soon as they got to the room, Sam threw his suitcase onto the nearest bed and riffled through it, pulling out some clothes. "We should start booking our hotels in advance."

"You think so?" Wesley set his suitcase down next to the other bed and flopped onto the ugly floral duvet. The mattress creaked, but the pillow his head landed on was perfectly fluffed. His eyes closed automatically.

There was a fumbling sound, followed by rustling. It sounded like Sam was pulling shit out of his luggage. "Yeah, if what that lady said is true, we could wind up not being able to find anywhere to stay. Remember what you said about sleeping in the car? I'd like to avoid that. Neither of us is small."

"That's true. We know what cities we're going to next, so we can call ahead." Wesley flopped onto his side and opened his eyes. As soon as he did, he froze.

Right in front of him, Sam stripped off his jeans and underwear and changed into fresh ones. His bag was blocking most of the view, but the curve of his hips showed around the side of it, and when he bent over to pull on his boxers, the swell of his ass was unmistakable.

Sam changing clothes was in no way a significant event. Wesley understood that. It was a miracle they'd avoided it so far, considering they were in such close quarters. They'd lived together for four years as well. It wasn't as if this was the first time Wesley had seen Sam naked.

So, why was it that Wesley couldn't stop staring? He could feel himself doing it—his eyes trailing up Sam's torso in a way that had to be obvious—but he couldn't help himself.

What the fuck is going on with me lately? I'm acting like I've never seen Sam before. Or like I'm seeing him for the first time.

Thankfully, Sam didn't seem to notice. He finished buttoning his jeans—they were tight, of course, in precisely the way Wesley liked—and ran a hand through his thick hair. It moved like wind rippling through wheat. "So, what now?"

Wesley glanced at the nightstand and was surprised to find it unadorned. He surveyed the room and finally spotted a clock on a desk by the singular window. "Damn, one of these places finally did something different. Anyway, it's too late to go to any attractions. We could grab dinner, but I'm not all that hungry."

"Me neither."

"In that case, I propose we paint the town red."

"Seriously?" Sam took a seat on the other bed, across from Wesley. "How can you even *think* about partying after how drunk we got last night?"

Wesley shrugged. "It's a Saturday night. Going out is the logical course of action."

"You know, there are people who don't spend every weekend getting plastered."

Embarrassment seeped into Wesley like cool water. "I know, but we're on vacation."

"What if we sleep in again tomorrow, and we lose another day?"

"I'll set an alarm. And we'll agree not to do any shots tonight."

Sam's mouth turned down. "I don't know. I haven't felt well all day, and I'm not looking forward to being hungover again tomorrow."

He had a point, but there was no way Wesley was going to waste a perfectly good Saturday by staying in. In his head, he was already three blocks over, looking for the nearest bar. "If you want to stay in, that's cool with me. There's no rule that says we have to spend this whole trip glued to each other's sides. Actually, it might be good for us to split up. Get some time apart. And that way, one of us will be sure to wake up on time tomorrow."

If the corner of Sam's lips lowered any more, they were going to slide right off his face. "I'm not letting you go out in a strange city alone. Especially not if you're going to be drinking. You could get lost."

Wesley laughed. "I'm not a dog."

Sam picked a pillow off his bed and tossed it at him. "You're right. Dogs need much less looking after."

"Hey, you're the one who looks like a damn golden retriever with that hair of yours." Wesley lobbed the pillow back.

Sam gasped, grabbed the pillow, and chucked it right at his face. "I do not!"

The pillow caught Wesley square on. "That's it. You asked for it."

Bellowing a war cry, Wesley launched himself at Sam. They fell onto the bed together in a tangle and immediately wrestled for dominance, like they had a dozen times before. Sam pressed a forearm against Wesley's neck just hard enough to make him breathless, while Wesley pinned Sam's free hand and tried to get an arm under him. He almost succeeded, but then Sam flipped them over, landing on top of him. Wesley only allowed that for a second before he muscled them over again, straddling Sam.

Within seconds, Sam was giggling, and it wasn't until Wesley felt Sam shaking under him that he thought about their position. It was as if he'd stepped out of his body and could see them from a different perspective. Lying on a bed, limbs tangled, bodies pressed together. They were breathing faster, faces flushed, and everything was so . . .

Hot, his brain supplied. *This is kind of hot. Jesus, am I turned on right now?*

Before he could process the thought, Sam suddenly stopped giggling. He looked up at Wesley from inches away. For a second, Wesley's mind went blank, but then Sam's eyes seemed to darken. It took Wesley a second to understand: his pupils had dilated.

He was off Sam in an instant. With the way he flew to the other side of the room, it must've looked like he'd been shocked.

Sam sat up on the bed, brow furrowed. "Whoa, dude. Are you okay?"

"Fine." Wesley struggled to catch his breath. There didn't seem to be enough air in the room.

"Did I hurt you or something?"

"No. Really, I'm fine." Wesley turned away and walked toward the bathroom, pretending to fix his hair in the mirror. "I was thinking about how late it is. We should get going." He snuck a peek at Sam.

Sam was frowning again. "Okay. Let me grab my stuff. I'll look up bars on my phone."

He got up and went to his bag, giving Wesley a much-needed respite.

Seriously, what is going on with me?

As he struggled to get his pulse under control, he thought back. It'd been a while since he last had sex. Not since he'd dated that guy he'd worked with. And he hadn't touched himself since the day before they'd left for this trip.

That was it, he decided. He was a little pent up from lack of release. He'd jerk off in the shower tomorrow and be fine. Maybe at some point, when he was drunk enough, he'd suggest to Sam that he do the same. There was no way Wesley had imagined that flicker of heat in Sam's eyes when Wesley had climbed on top of him. He must be feeling the same, and they were feeding off each other's hormones.

That thought made his heart race anew.

He shook his head. "You ready?"

"Yeah. You want to change clothes?" Sam wet his lips.

Wesley might've been imagining it, but he thought he heard something like muffled alarm bells in his head. "I'm good as is. Let's head out."

They found a sports bar a mere block from the hotel. True to his word, Wesley didn't order any shots, but he did down his fair share of beers. Sam relaxed once he had a couple of drinks, and after a while, it seemed as if their disastrous start to the day had been forgotten. They stumbled home around midnight and went to sleep in separate beds.

The next day, Sam's alarm woke them at nine sharp. With great reluctance, they hauled themselves up. Wesley had said in the past that hangovers accumulated like dust. Today proved him right once and for all. The dust was in his brain, making everything foggy. His head didn't hurt, though, probably thanks to the lack of hard liquor. With sunglasses and lots of water, he'd muddle through the day.

Their hotel had a continental breakfast, so they gorged themselves on free bagels and yogurt. Sam looked up attractions while nibbling on a distracting banana. It was Sunday, so a lot of the local museums were closed. Wesley thought he did a decent job of pretending he was disappointed, but judging by the wry look Sam gave him, he wasn't going to win an Oscar anytime soon.

Google informed them that there were several popular parks nearby. The weather was mild, and neither of them had worked out since the start of the trip, so Sam suggested a long walk. Wesley would have preferred to stay indoors—preferably somewhere dark, where he could get a Bloody Mary or three to make himself feel more human—but when Sam grabbed his hand and dragged him out the door, he didn't have the strength to complain.

The first park was beautiful, all green grass and sprawling stone paths. There were mossy trees everywhere, under which they stole brief breaks in the shade. On the far side, they discovered a wooden stage. A folk band that consisted of two acoustic guitar players and an energetic woman with a tambourine performed while couples sat in the grass. Wesley and Sam hovered on the periphery and watched.

It wasn't until Wesley saw one of the couples kissing in the sun that something occurred to him. This whole trip was sort of romantic. The kind of thing newlyweds would do. Friends might steal away for a long weekend together, but two whole weeks? People didn't do that.

Something nudged his side. He looked over.

Sam was studying him. "You're uncharacteristically quiet."

Briefly, Wesley considered voicing his concerns aloud. Being totally direct. But what if this was all in his head, and he weirded Sam out? He might've imagined the heat between them yesterday. Or he really was just horny and expressing it in inappropriate ways. What were the odds that after five years of platonic friendship, he would develop an attraction to Sam?

Then again, they'd never been in such close quarters for so long before. Even in the dorms, they'd had class and studying and other friends keeping them apart.

There had to be a reason why sharing a bed with Sam seemed so natural to Wesley. If they told their friends back home they'd done that more than once, everyone would tell them to get married already. Again.

Actually, Wesley felt closer to Sam right now than he ever had before, and not just physically. They'd been sharing new experiences together, exploring exciting cities and having a blast. They were the only two people who were ever going to have *this*.

What did that mean? Did it have to mean something? He supposed so, but he'd never been the big thinker of the two of them. Maybe Sam would figure it out and then explain it to him later.

"It's nothing," he answered as neutrally as he could manage. "I'm just hungover. I think I'll have a beer with lunch, and that'll fix me right up."

Sam smiled. "Sounds good to me. I'm actually hungry now if you are."

Maybe Wesley would make a decent actor after all. "Sure. Lead the way."

There were more parks scattered around the city, which made it scenic but also a nightmare to walk around. Everything was so spread out. Wesley actually felt like he got a decent workout as they meandered through the streets.

After lunch, they found a farmers' market and bought the first vegetables they'd had that hadn't come on a burger. Sam ate a raw red bell pepper like it was an apple while Wesley made fake gagging noises. Wesley bought a whole sack of oranges, joking that it would keep them from getting scurvy on their long voyage. As they walked, Wesley carried the goods. Sam peeled one and split it between them, feeding Wesley individual sections.

It ended up being a damn good day. The only thing that would have made it better was if Wesley's head stopped hurting. Weren't hangovers supposed to get *better* with time? He should've ordered a second beer at lunch, but Sam had been eager to see as much as they could. Tomorrow, they'd set sail for Atlanta.

Sam, for his part, seemed perfectly fine. When they got back to the hotel, he flopped onto his bed. "What do you want to do tonight? Watch bad cable and chill? Or we could call a Lyft and go to a grocery store. Get some supplies to go with our veggies. If reception has a hot plate we can borrow, we can attempt to cook."

"I was actually thinking we could make it a threepeat." Wesley refilled his water bottle from the sink and took a big gulp. "I saw a funky bar on the walk back. It had board games and shit. I bet I'd kick your ass at drunken Connect Four."

Sam groaned. "Dude, you are some kind of tank. I don't know how you can drink the way you do and still function."

"Hey, it's not like I'm like this all the time," Wesley argued, knowing perfectly well that he was. "We're on vacation. We should live it up while we can."

"Uh-huh." Sam chuckled. "You have an amazing ability to pull reasons to get wasted out of thin air. You were the same way in college. 'Come on, Sam, it's spring break' or 'It's Friday night' or 'It's national Talk Like a Pirate Day. Bottoms up, matey!'"

"It's a gift." This conversation was making Wesley antsy. "You know, college wasn't that long ago. You talk like you've forgotten what it's like to show up for exams after a late night and still ace them. That was *your* gift."

"Yeah, but we're too old for that now."

"Says who?" He edged for the door. "Are you in or not?"

"I don't think it's a good idea, honestly. It's Sunday, for one thing. It's expensive for another. And as fun as today was, I would have gotten a lot more out of the city had my head not been in a fog. Besides, you know the old saying: 'You're not an alcoholic so long as you're in college.' Well, we're not in college anymore."

That was true, and if Wesley woke up late tomorrow, Sam might not be as charitable as he'd been in the past. Then again, Wesley hated to waste a perfectly good evening in the hotel.

It's one night. You're not going to miss out on anything if you stay in the hotel for one night.

"You're right." Wesley flopped onto his bed. "My liver could use a day off. It's been working overtime lately. And making fun of crappy cable is always a blast."

Sam's smile was sunlight bright. "Awesome. I'll grab the remote."

After he'd retrieved it from the cabinet that housed their TV, Wesley expected him to return to his own bed. Instead, he made Wesley budge over, and they watched TV with their shoulders and knees touching.

They ended up ordering a pizza, and a little after midnight, Sam's eyes started to droop. He roused himself long enough to crawl into his own bed, and then the only sound Wesley heard from him was level breathing.

Wesley took a long time to fall asleep. Thoughts drifted around in his head like dandelion seeds. One in particular stood out: he'd spend his life exactly like this if he could. Traveling. Laughing. Finding fun in unexpected places. So long as Sam was by his side, the adventure would never end.

CHAPTER FIVE

Sam woke to the sound of running water. He opened his eyes and was hit by the disorienting sensation of not recognizing where he was. Blinking at the unfamiliar art on the walls, the generic carpeting, and the second bed to his right, he struggled to piece it together.

Then it hit him. The hotel. The trip. Wesley.

Relieved, he sat up in bed. His own bed. He didn't remember making the transition—he must've passed out the second his head hit a pillow—but it was a good thing he had. He was pretty sure falling asleep in Wesley's bed when they *weren't* drunk would be crossing a line. One of very few lines they had left; every day obliterated a new one.

Gingerly, he stretched his neck. There was no answering stab of pain from his temples. In fact, his head felt great. Clear and pain-free for the first time in two days. No trace of the hangover that had clogged his brain with cotton.

He reached for where his phone was charging on the nightstand and checked the time. It was nearly eight in the morning. His alarm hadn't had a chance to go off yet. Today was off to a damn good start.

"Atlanta, here we come," he murmured to himself.

A dark, wet head poked out of the bathroom door. "Did you say something?"

Sam startled. He'd been so lost in thought, he hadn't noticed the sound of the water had shut off. "No, sorry. How was your shower?"

For some reason, Wesley's face reddened. "What do you mean?"

"I'm hoping the water pressure here is better than it was at the last place."

"Oh. Yeah, it's great. Very refreshing."

"Good. I feel so much better today than I did yesterday. You?"

"I think I still have some recovering to do." He exited the bathroom, fully dressed. One of the hotel's white towels was wrapped around his neck. As he spoke, he ran it over his wet hair. "I woke up all sweaty. Hence, the shower. But I definitely feel better than I did last night." He took a seat on the bed and tossed the towel to the side. His hair was sticking up in all directions, like he had half a sea urchin on his head.

Sam tried and failed to smother his laughter.

Wesley frowned at him. "What?"

"Nothing. I'm going to shower too. Maybe it's because we've been in it for so long, but I noticed yesterday the car was getting a little funky."

"Bound to happen." Wesley shrugged. "We've been spending our days walking around in the sun, getting all grimy. And then at night if we go out, we end up reeking like a bar. I'm almost out of fresh clothes too. Gonna have to start wearing whatever smells best. Though personally, I kinda like the manly, musky scent of two young bucks in their prime."

Sam crinkled his nose. "We'll find a laundromat or see if the next place we crash at has laundry service. There are certain stages of 'comfortable with each other' that I'd rather not reach."

Wesley laughed. "So, no leaving the bathroom door open while I pee?"

"*No*, or you really will have to marry me. You break it, you buy it." Sam stood up. "I'll hurry so we can get an early start."

"Can we stop for a real breakfast today? Not microwavable burritos or some shit? I'm *starving*. Have been since last night."

"That's strange." Sam nodded at the empty pizza box they'd folded into the trash. "You ate most of the pizza."

Wesley shrugged. "Must be the excitement. Or maybe all the walking around we're doing."

"That's probably it. Breakfast sounds great. I'll be right back."

Sam showered, brushed his teeth, and, in the spirit of feeling refreshed, took the time to run some product through his hair. When he exited the bathroom, a towel cinched around his waist, he caught himself whistling a song they'd heard on the radio the day before.

Wesley was on the bed right where Sam had left him. "I checked Google, and there's a breakfast place on the way to—" He glanced over and stopped short. His eyes skittered once down Sam's torso before snapping up to his face. Like earlier, he turned red.

"What?" Sam looked down at himself. "Oh God, it's not a spider or something, is it?" He brushed both hands down his chest and stomach.

"No!" Wesley's voice was pitched too high. "I was just, um, surprised. You were fast."

"Oh. Okay." Sam frowned. "Wait, that doesn't make any sense."

"Are you finished with the bathroom?" Wesley jumped to his feet. "I just remembered something I need to do."

"Um, yeah, I guess." Sam had to scramble out of Wesley's way as he bolted past him.

Right before he closed the door behind him, Wesley paused. "Hey, will you do me a favor and check the local news station? It's channel eighteen."

"What?"

"Just turn on the TV please. Will you?"

"Uh . . . sure?"

Before Sam could question him further, Wesley slipped inside the bathroom and shut the door with a firm *thud*.

Sam stared at it before shaking his head. *What was that all about?*

True to his word, Sam turned on the TV and flipped it to the news. He listened with one ear while he dressed, gathered his belongings, and checked the room for anything they might be forgetting.

About five minutes passed before Wesley reemerged again, smiling. "All right, let's get this show on the road."

"Excellent. There's no traffic, by the way."

Halfway to bending down to pick up his suitcase, Wesley stopped. "What?"

"On the news. The traffic report said the roads are clear. That was what you wanted me to listen for, right?"

"Oh. Right." Wesley didn't quite look him in the eye. "Yeah, that and the weather."

"Ah. They didn't get to the weather. We'll have to check on our phones."

"No worries. I'm sure it's fine."

They did one final sweep, shut everything off, and closed the door behind them. After breezing through checkout, it was back into the car. To Sam, it was oddly starting to feel like returning to home base.

"You booked a hotel, right?" Wesley asked as he settled into the driver's seat. His hair was still wet, but the spikes had calmed into artful peaks.

Sam resisted the urge to smooth them. "Yup. I found a cute place near everything. I borrowed your credit card, by the way, since I paid for the last place. It's back in your wallet now."

"Fine by me. What all is there to do in Atlanta?"

"From the looks of it, *tons*. There's Six Flags, the aquarium, World of Coca-Cola, and free shit like parks and museums. We could go see where MLK was born too."

"That all sounds awesome." As Wesley turned the key in the ignition and shifted gears, his hands shook. It was so slight, however, Sam wondered if he was imagining it.

Breakfast consisted of eggs and bacon from a little mom-and-pop place where their waitress spoke with a Southern twang and called them "sug." There was a tourist trap next door that sold snow globes, rock candy, and terrible T-shirts. Wesley insisted they check it out before leaving. Sam took his favorite picture of the trip so far: Wesley holding a shirt up to his chest that had a kitten fighting a velociraptor with a lightsaber.

He had every intention of buying it too, but then he checked his bank balance on his phone and groaned. "Not as bad as I was expecting, but still pretty bad."

They headed back to the car and followed the signs for the highway.

Wesley got them pointed in the right direction and then asked, "Is there much nightlife?"

"Where?" Sam blinked. "Oh, in Atlanta? According to Google, definitely. It might not be hopping, since it's a Monday and all, but if we wanted to take in a show or something, I'm sure we could."

"When you mentioned World of Coca-Cola earlier, it gave me an idea." Wesley had put on his sunglasses, making his face hard to read. "Remember that craft beer we had back in Washington?"

"The apple beer? It was really good."

"Yeah, and we had some in Charlotte, and that pitcher back in New York, though it wasn't anything special. I was thinking, we should try a local beer in every city we hit. See how they change from place to place. I'm sure not everywhere will have a craft-beer scene, but I know Atlanta does. We can make it our thing."

"Sort of like getting your passport stamped, only more adult." Sam laughed. "I like it. I'd be down for that. One beer in every city."

Wesley nodded. With his hair wild and his sunglasses hiding his eyes, he could have been the stoic lead of a daytime drama. Sam voiced this out loud.

That got Wesley's lips to curve up. "It's funny you should say that. When we first left Pennsylvania, I imagined us in a buddy-cop movie."

"Nice. I can see that. Or the stars of a sitcom. Maybe one about two roommates who get in and out of zany antics together."

"Only one problem with that." Wesley peeked away from the road briefly to flash him a smile. "We get along too well. Everyone would think we were totally boring and domestic. It'd just be us feeding each other orange slices and not fighting."

"Touché."

They fell silent. Sam stared out the window for a few minutes at the fluffy clouds overhead, waiting for Wesley to suggest a game or tell a joke. When he didn't, Sam didn't try to force conversation. If Wesley had felt chatty, there'd be no stopping him, so he must be in a rare quiet mood.

Instead, Sam reached into the back seat, where he'd stowed his bag. After a few minutes of rummaging, he pulled out one of the books he'd brought and opened it to his "bookmark": a postcard his sister had sent him shortly after he'd left for college. It pictured one of Montana's mountain ranges, and on the back it had five words scrawled in Jessica's bubbly hand: *In case you're missing home.*

He'd never missed Montana, but he'd missed her almost every day. No matter what happened when he got home, at least he'd get to see her again.

Wesley voice broke into his thoughts. "You know what that reminds me of?"

Sam looked up. "What? The postcard?"

"No, the book. Remember when we drove back from our Jersey beach trip?"

Sam thought back. "Not really. I know we left late because we spent all day partying, and we had to wait to sober up before we could drive. You volunteered, so I gave you my keys. That's about all I remember."

"You were reading then too." The skin by Wesley's eyes crinkled—or the one Sam could see did. "I wouldn't let you turn any lights on, so you spent the whole trip angling pages to the moonlight and catching little snippets every time we passed a streetlight. You were determined. I asked why you didn't wait until we got back, and you said, 'I have to *know*!'"

Sam laughed. "I can't believe you remember that."

Wesley cleared his throat. "Of course I remember. I remember everything about that trip."

"Why?"

There was a pause.

Sam tried again. "Is it embarrassing? C'mon, you can tell me."

Wesley sighed. "Traveling is my relationship litmus test. It works on everyone: friends, family, lovers. If you can travel with someone without ripping each other's throats out after a couple of days, it's meant to be. That trip we took to the beach was what convinced me."

"Convinced you of what?"

Wesley turned his head to glance at him. "That we were going to be in each other's lives forever. No matter what."

Sam swallowed. Was it possible for a heart to race and skip at the same time? If Sam had been hooked up to a monitor, he might have wowed the medical community. Something clicked in his head, and pieces from the past suddenly fit themselves together.

Wesley telling goofy stories from their past. Sleeping next to Sam. Wrestling with him. Looking into his eyes from inches away, firm and heavy on top of him. For a second that had flitted by too quickly for him to grasp onto it, Sam had felt . . . something. A stirring he hadn't acknowledged, because for some reason, it'd terrified him.

Before Sam could make sense of it, Wesley snorted and focused back on the road. "Jesus, dramatic much? Sorry, that was the bad cable from last night talking."

Sam chuckled, but there was no real mirth behind it. He wasn't sure why Wesley's declaration had rattled him, but something had gotten knocked loose, and now it was all Sam could think about. He tried to get into his book, but he ended up spending the four-hour drive reading the same paragraph and sneaking peeks at Wesley.

When they got into Georgia, the terrain changed. It was less mountainous but much hillier, reminding Sam of a dry Pennsylvania. The next big surprise happened when they stopped at a little diner to grab some sandwiches to go. When they walked in, Sam's nose filled with the sharp smell of cigarette smoke. He looked around for the source and was stunned to see that several people sitting in the booths were smoking. He could feel himself staring, but he was frozen in place. It wasn't until one of the smokers eyed him curiously that the spell shattered.

They ordered their food to go, and as soon as they were outside, Sam said, "Was that legal?"

"What?" Wesley was already digging into the paper bag they'd been given. "The indoor smoking? Yeah, you can do that here."

"In restaurants?"

"Pretty much everywhere, I think." Wesley set the bag on the hood of the car to better riffle through it. "My cousin used to live here. One time, when he came up north to visit, we went to see a movie. He lit up in the middle of the damn theater. Gave me a heart attack, and I ruined a perfectly good cherry slushy when I hastily put it out. But he thought he hadn't done anything out of the ordinary."

"Wow. I knew you could smoke in bars in some places, but restaurants? I thought that only happened in old movies."

"Better get used to it. It's the same in Alabama and Texas. We have to drive through them to get to the Pacific Ocean."

"Huh. How do you know that?"

Wesley lifted up his sunglasses and winked. "I may not know the names of famous Russian dances, but I have my own useless trivia."

An hour later, they made it to Atlanta. Having seen so many big cities in a row, it wasn't the skyline that impressed Sam, but rather, the people. Atlanta was *alive*. Everywhere Sam looked, people were smiling as they strolled down the streets. Talking. Laughing. Singing, in the case of a group of young girls in school uniforms who crossed in front of them at a red light. One of them caught Sam staring and winked at him.

"I love this city," Sam announced.

Wesley glanced at him. "It's been five minutes."

Sam nodded. "I know. I already love it."

They got to their hotel, which looked like an old, converted bungalow. Their room was cozy, with twin beds and antique furniture. It was decorated like an old woman's tea room: embroidered pillows on the beds, rose duvets, and needlepoint on the walls.

It was a marked difference from the generic art and sameness of the previous hotels. They had to share a bathroom with the whole floor, but after the nightmare hotel from New York, that was nothing new.

"We should ask if this place has a laundry room," Wesley said. "It looks like it will."

"I think they do, and there's a kitchen. I read online that guests are welcome to cook."

"Sounds like we get to nest for a bit."

They balanced chores with fun. They found the laundry room—a closet with one old machine and a battered dryer—and timed out a load of clothes. While it washed, they toured the botanical garden down the street. While it dried, they went to the aquarium.

After, they found a corner market and bought pasta and fresh vegetables for dinner. Cooking together in an unfamiliar kitchen led to mishaps, laughter, and Wesley chasing Sam around with a handful of flour. By the time evening rolled around, Sam was ready to see another side of the city.

Back in their room, he separated his laundry from Wesley's and folded the former. "How about we find ourselves a craft beer tonight?"

Wesley was lounging in bed, as per usual. At that, he rolled onto his side to face Sam. "Hell yeah! Where should we go?"

Sam shrugged without looking up from the laundry. It was easy to pick out his more understated clothes from Wesley's bright colors and ripped jeans. "I'm not sure. Ask the internet."

Wesley had his tablet on the mattress next to him. He turned it on and typed with both hands, fingers making gentle drumming noises.

"There are a lot of gastropubs and breweries, but they close pretty early."

"How early are we talking?"

"Nine seems to be the average."

"That's plenty of time. We only need to have one beer."

Wesley laughed. "It's never *one* beer. Let's go somewhere we can actually chill for a while." He scrolled down a list of search results. "Here's a place. The Peach Tree. They're open until two, and apparently they have the best homebrew in the city. Kinda out in the middle of nowhere, though."

"We could take a cab."

"Too expensive."

"Lyft?"

"Less expensive, but it would still be a good chunk of change. This bar is on the outskirts of the city." Wesley rubbed his chin. "Well, shit. It looks like this is the only place with local craft beer that's also open late. They do small batch brewing too, so there are all sorts of flavors and combinations specific to Atlanta. Damn."

"Why don't we go to a closer craft place, get our beer, and then we can find something else to do?"

"Yeah, I guess that would be best. It's a shame, though. The reviews for the Peach Tree are *amazing*. It must be great to be so popular while located in the middle of nowhere. I hate to miss out."

A rare burst of spontaneity swept through Sam. "Then let's go."

"How will we get there, though? It's too far to walk."

"I'll drive. I can have my one beer and then find other ways to entertain myself."

"Are you sure? Their website had a menu, and I want to try, like, eight of them."

"I'll get a flight. Or I'll take one sip out of each of your beers." He winked.

Wesley's face lit up. "You sure you don't mind?"

"No. This is actually a good development. I have no desire to get drunk again after the weekend we had."

"Hey, like I said before, we're on vacation. Not that I don't appreciate your sacrifice." Wesley swung his legs over the side of the bed and glanced at the laundry. "Uh, Sammy?"

"Yeah?"

"You realize you've been folding my laundry too, right?"

Sam looked down. Sure enough, their clothes were now in two neat piles. "Damn. I was trying to avoid that so I wouldn't feel like a maid."

"You're going to make such a good husband someday."

Wesley's tone was teasing, but for some reason, it made Sam's face hot. "So, when do you want to go?"

"The sooner, the better. You want to change into something clean?"

"No. Judging by earlier, our clothes are going to smell like smoke by the end of the evening. Might as well sacrifice the ones that have already been through a day of travel."

They drove out to the Peach Tree, which was in fact a hell of a trek. The thick trees surrounding the squat building might have obscured it from view were it not lit up like a sky full of fireworks. Sam had never seen so many string lights. They lined the roof and wrapped around the trees.

What the building lacked in height, it made up for with several additions that looked like differently colored patches in a blanket. The biggest tree in the vicinity was loaded with peaches—probably the source of the bar's name.

There was no set parking lot. Cars were scattered wherever there was room between the trees. Sam managed to find a spot, though it was way far out. Silvery light filtered through the leaves in a way that probably should have been eerie, but Sam loved how it pooled on the ground like puddles of mercury.

"They make peach moonshine," Wesley said as they got out of the car. "Don't think I'll try any of that though. Out here, they probably make it in old bathtubs."

"We're certainly not in Kansas anymore."

"I have it on good authority that partying in the woods is a time-honored Southern tradition." Wesley headed for the front door. "Come on, I can hear the beer calling to me."

They closer they got, the louder the sound of music and voices got. There were people hanging out on the porch, but no one paid them any mind as Wesley opened the front door for Sam.

The inside was as eclectic as the outside. Each addition was a themed room, ranging from tropical island to disco. There were bars in every room, and as predicted, there were ashtrays set out, though Sam didn't smell any smoke so far. It wasn't overly crowded, despite the number of cars outside. The night must still be young.

Wesley headed for the bar right ahead of them, head turned back toward Sam. "You want a beer, or are you going to try some of mine?"

"I'll try yours. Unless they have flights. In which case, you know what I like."

While he waited, Sam surveyed the room. Unlike the gay bar they'd gone to, this one had its fair share of women. It was nice to get out and be around different people after almost a full week with Wesley, even for Sam.

Wesley returned with a pint glass and a plastic cup full of water. He handed the latter to Sam. "No flights, so it looks like we're sharing. I went with their famous peach beer to start. According to the bartender—who was *cute*, by the way, and possibly gay—it's their best seller." He took a sip, swished it around in his mouth, and then swallowed, smiling. "Delicious. Try."

Sam did and immediately agreed. The beer was a perfect mixture of sweet and hoppy. The peach flavor came through without being overpowering. He handed it back to Wesley. "Good choice."

They spent the next hour or so talking, laughing, and introducing themselves to some friendly locals. According to them, the Peach Tree was a not-so-well-kept secret in Atlanta. It was too eclectic to become a tourist destination for now, but they all lived in fear of it blowing up and getting commercialized.

While they talked, Wesley finished his beer. He turned to Sam. "You want to pick this time?"

"Sure, thanks."

Sam wove through the steadily increasing crowd to the bar. One look at the guy working behind it confirmed what Wesley had said: he was cute. White, tall, probably in his early twenties, with big brown eyes and full lips. Sam hated to stereotype, but he had pink hair and was wearing a crop top. So yeah, probably queer.

When Sam approached, he expected to wait as he always did, but to his surprise, the bartender came right up to him, flashing a radiant smile. "What can I get you, hun?"

"Um." Sam looked up at a menu written in colorful chalk above the bar. "What do you recommend?"

"Our strawberry wild ale is delicious. Fair warning, though: it's a sour."

Sam frowned. "I've never had one before. Are they good?"

"They're an acquired taste. Maybe you could get your cute boyfriend to stick his finger in it and sweeten it up."

Sam stared at him blankly for a moment before understanding dawned on him. "Oh, he's not my boyfriend."

"Really?" The bartender leaned on the counter, eyes sparkling. "I saw you drink from his beer earlier."

"Yeah, but we're just friends." He paused. "I'm surprised you noticed that in a crowded bar."

"I was watching you." The bartender's smile was impish. "So, you're single?"

Is he . . . flirting with me?

"Um, yes?"

"You should stick around until my shift ends. I'll buy you a drink."

Okay, yeah, that's flirting.

Blood rushed into Sam's face. He prayed it was too dark for anyone to notice. Looking at the handsome bartender, it was impossible not to feel a twinge of arousal. It resonated in his belly, sure as if he'd plucked a string. Distantly, it occurred to him that he hadn't hooked up with anyone in months.

He glanced toward where Wesley was sitting off to the side with their new acquaintances. Sam expected to find him in the middle of a story, as he usually was, but instead, Wesley was watching him. The second their eyes met, Wesley looked between him and the bartender. Sam couldn't be certain in the dim light, but he thought Wesley's expression tightened.

A strange mixture of emotions trickled through Sam. Some of the arousal from before—or was this new arousal?—and guilt. What did he have to be guilty about?

You made an agreement with Wesley. No hooking up. He must think you've forgotten. When you get back, you'll have to assure him you'd never break your promise. Although, you were totally considering it.

Realizing he'd never replied, Sam cleared his throat. "Um, that beer you recommended sounds fine."

"Uh-huh." The bartender followed the line of Sam's gaze and giggled. "'Just friends' my ass." He plunked a beer bottle in front of Sam and popped off the cap with an easy wrist flick. "No charge, hun. Think of it as an early wedding present."

Sam had no idea how to respond to that, so he about-faced and scurried away like the frightened bunny he was. When he reached the table, Wesley opened his mouth—ostensibly to ask what'd happened—but Sam only paused long enough to drop off the beer. "I'm going to get some air. Be right back." He made a beeline for the nearest exit.

The second Sam hit the night air, he took a deep breath. His head cleared, and his heart slowed from a gallop to a trot. Movement out of the corner of his eye caught his attention. A group of people were hanging out on a little patio area attached to the side of the bar. They weren't looking his way, but their presence made Sam acutely aware of himself. He'd be hard-pressed to find privacy out here. But then, Wesley had given him the keys.

Sam backtracked to the car, slid into the front seat, and after a second of deliberation, lay down with his hands on his stomach, legs folded so he'd fit. With the door closed and tree limbs visible through the windshield, it felt like he was closed off from the world. It was the first real privacy he'd had in days, besides when he showered and slept. In the newfound quiet, his thoughts blared.

What was that in there? That look Wesley gave me? I'm no expert at reading people, but he seemed . . . jealous.

Sam squirmed with discomfort, both from uncertainty and the fact that he was still aroused. It was weird for him to get an itch like this. He hadn't gotten off since before they'd left, but he'd never been the sort to masturbate regularly.

It had to be because he was in close quarters with another guy. His hormones didn't care that it was Wesley. They smelled sweat and cologne, and that was all they needed. With both of them getting hit on left and right and an embargo on sex, tension was bound to mount.

While he'd been thinking, one of his hands had inched lower of its own accord. He considered stopping its downward journey, but he was getting hard, and his body *ached*. It'd probably take him no time to come. Hell, getting to palm himself through his jeans would be a relief after being so touch-starved.

Biting his lip, he slid his hand between his legs, and—

Someone knocked on the glass. Sam jumped and banged his head on the door behind him, yelping. A second later, a back door opened, and Wesley's head popped in. "There you are."

Sam flushed from head to toe, heart pounding. "Wesley."

Holy shit, I was about to masturbate in my best friend's car. What the hell is wrong with me? And what would have happened if he'd showed up a minute later?

Wesley slid into the back seat and closed the door behind him. "What are you doing in here? I've been looking all over. Some people on the porch said they saw you head into the woods. I thought some Blair Witch shit had gone down."

"No, nothing like that." Sam swallowed. "I was stealing a minute for myself."

"Oh, sorry. Want me to leave?"

Sam almost said yes. Wesley's sudden appearance hadn't chased away his libido. He could still feel his cock rubbing inside his jeans every time he moved. "No, it's okay. I can't kick you out of your own car."

Wesley lay down the same way as Sam, only he propped his feet up on the closed window. For a moment, it was quiet except for their breathing. Then, Wesley's voice drifted over the backrest that separated them like a wall. "What happened with the bartender?"

"Nothing. He's definitely interested in men, though."

There was a pause. "Did he flirt with you?"

"Yeah, but I didn't flirt back."

"Why not?"

Was that relief in Wesley's voice?

"We have that rule, remember? No bringing guys back to the hotel. Besides, where would that have left you? You'd have to wait out in the parking lot for us to finish. Awkward."

Wesley fell silent again. Sam yearned to see his face, but he was also grateful for the partition between them. The last thing he needed was for Wesley to read him, as he so often did. What if he could tell

Sam was aroused? Or worse, that his presence had made Sam hotter for some reason?

What the hell is happening to me?

"I would have lent you the car if you'd asked."

Sam startled. "What?"

Wesley's fingers skimmed the top of the backrest briefly before disappearing again. "You could have brought him here, or any other guy you might've hit it off with. Don't tell my dad, but this car's no stranger to fogged windows."

Fuck. Now Sam was picturing Wesley having sex in this car. That image wasn't going to make his erection go away anytime soon. His brain screamed at him to suggest they go back to the bar before things got weird, but his tongue refused to form the words.

Wesley drew a shaky breath, and the sound ricocheted through Sam. "Or hell, the bar had bathrooms. You could have dragged him into one, locked the door. You wouldn't be gone longer than fifteen minutes if you did it right." His voice lowered. "Nothing fancy. Just a quick and dirty fuck."

Sam had already been plenty turned on, but the obscenity of that zinged right up his spine. When he spoke, his voice was rough. "Why would I do that though?"

"Come on, Sam. Hot guys don't stumble into our laps every day. If I'd been in your shoes, I'd . . ."

Sam's mouth had gone dry. "You'd what?"

Silence. A long, drawn-out breath. Then, "I would have waited until closing time—until everyone else had left—and then I would have cornered him behind the bar, dropped to my knees, and sucked his cock. Bet I could get off from hearing him moan alone."

Before Sam could stop himself, a small, needy sound escaped from him. *Why is that so hot?*

Rustling came from the back seat. Maybe Wesley was untucking his shirt, but Sam's brain was too muddled with arousal to be sure.

Suddenly, Wesley laughed. "So, are we going to pretend we're not both hard right now?"

His words, said with the air of someone trying to lighten the mood, punched Sam in the gut. Wesley was turned on by this too. They were inches from each other, separated only by a car seat.

That should have killed Sam's boner, but if anything, it excited him. It gave this the most dark, delicious sense of being utterly forbidden.

He didn't answer Wesley's question. Didn't think he could, honestly. If asked later, Sam wouldn't be able to pinpoint what prompted him to say what he said next, but he suspected his dick straining in his jeans had something to do with it. "The bartender. Would you get him off with your mouth or fuck him?"

Wesley didn't hesitate. "If he wanted me to, I'd definitely fuck him, but honestly, I wouldn't mind getting bent over that bar myself. I like feeling a guy's weight on me. Bonus points if he holds me down, just on the right side of too rough."

Fuck. Sam wanted to touch himself so badly, but there'd be no way he could hide what he was doing. Hell, merely having this conversation had crossed several lines they'd never touched before. And Sam couldn't blame it on alcohol. Neither could Wesley, with his not-even-two beers.

This wasn't them being drunk and reckless. This was something else. A bad idea, for one thing. But Sam was hard to the point of pain, and it'd been so long—way too long—since he'd been turned on like this. For once in his life, he didn't want to plan. He didn't want to play it safe. He wanted to do something for no reason other than it felt good.

He took the plunge. "If you fucked him, is that how you'd do it? Would you bend him over the bar and take him from behind?" Sam could picture it a little too well for someone who'd never seen Wesley in a sexual situation before. Although, in his mind, the guy Wesley had bent over the bar wasn't the bartender. It wasn't anyone, really. A random guy who was moaning helplessly while Wesley fucked him hard.

I'm going to burst out of these pants soon if something doesn't give.

Wesley seemed to have the same idea. In the near-silence of the car—broken only by their heavy breathing—Sam heard the click of a zipper sliding down.

Fuck. Fuck me. He's— Oh God.

Sam's brain cut to white noise, overloaded by the surge of arousal that swept through him. Panic followed in its wake. This didn't count as hooking up, did it? This wasn't serious, right? This was scratching an itch they both clearly had.

Don't think. Act.

Sam finished sliding his hand between his legs like he'd been trying to earlier. The second he brushed his dick, pleasure crackled through him. It was so much more intense than he'd anticipated, and he whimpered.

There was no way Wesley hadn't heard that. He had to know what Sam was doing. With bated breath, Sam waited for him to speak.

But he didn't. There was dead silence for one interminable moment. Then, Sam heard fumbling and a small, raw groan of pleasure. There was no mistaking it. Wesley was touching himself too.

I can't believe we're doing this. But also, it seems . . . natural.

They'd shared so much over the years. Why not share this too?

Sam needed to know for certain. "Wesley, are you . . ."

Wesley cut him off, voice deeper than Sam had ever heard it. "I'm sorry, but I'm crazy horny. Can we please— Tell me about the guy. If you were with him, what would you do?"

Dirty talk was not Sam's forte. Hell, talking in general wasn't. But not being able to see Wesley made it easier. "I'd bring him out here to the car. It's private, but there's still the risk of someone seeing us. We'd be frantic to get off fast, and it'd make the whole thing that much sexier."

Wesley let out a ragged breath. A second later, Sam heard the unmistakable slick noise of a fist working a wet cock. For it to sound like that, Wesley must've been dripping pre-come.

Sam's mouth watered. He finally broke down and scrambled for his jeans. The button and zipper practically sprang open on their own. His dick bobbed up, bringing his boxers with it. Sam reached into the front slit and ran his fingers down his length, not sure how much sensation he could handle. That light touch alone made his vision blur.

"Keep going." Wesley's feet were still propped on the window. They moved apart, like he'd spread his thighs. "Don't stop."

God, I'm not going to last.

"He'd be aggressive, and I'd love it." Sam had to work up the spit to keep talking. "He'd pull me into the back seat and push me down, climbing on top of me. He'd kiss my neck one second and then bite it the next. When it came time to fuck, he wouldn't ask me how I wanted it. He'd arrange me on all fours, grab a handful of my hair, and pound into me."

"Holy fuck." Wesley moaned, low and throaty.

Sam pushed his underwear down enough to get his cock out. He was so hard he couldn't see straight. Burning hot too, and wet. Wrapping a hand around himself, he pumped fast and tight. He was close already. He pictured that a random attractive guy was touching him. One with dark hair. For some reason, his brain thought that detail was important.

He must've made more noise than he'd thought, because Wesley grunted. "Whoa, easy. Slow down. Like this." The slick sounds became more pronounced.

Sam obeyed, matching Wesley's pace. The filthiness of it caught up with him a second later. They were masturbating together, at the same time, to the same pace, and now Wesley was telling him what to do. It was obscene, and inappropriate, and *hot*.

A thought drifted into Sam's head like a cloud floating past: Sam had never had sex this good in his life, and it wasn't technically sex. If Wesley could make masturbating feel this intense, what would fucking him be like?

"Yeah, that's it." It was hard to tell if Wesley was talking to Sam or himself or both. "Just like that. So good. Give the head a squeeze."

Sam did, and suddenly, he was right on the edge. He'd bitten his lip nearly bloody trying not to moan, but now he couldn't help himself. With every stroke, he cried out, pleasure coiling tighter and tighter in him.

"Good, Sam. Faster now." Wesley's hand sped up.

Sam matched it, and as he did, he had to fight back a mental image of Wesley fucking his own fist. It was so difficult not to picture him while they were synced up like this. It was like—

It was like Wesley was getting Sam off by proxy.

That shouldn't turn me on, Sam thought as fresh arousal burst through him.

"Are you close?" Wesley sounded like he was talking through gritted teeth. "Please be close." It was the first real out-loud acknowledgment of what they were doing.

Sam nodded and then remembered Wesley couldn't see him. "I'm there. I'm so— Oh God, Wesley, I'm gonna come."

The admission was still ringing in Sam's ears when Wesley *moaned*, loud and luxurious. "Fuck, Sammy, I'm there too. I'm coming."

The nickname, which Sam always associated with Wesley and affection, was almost unbearably intimate in this context. It tipped Sam over the edge as surely as if Wesley had touched him.

As Sam started to come, his body convulsed, and on reflex, he grabbed the top of the seat for purchase. Only when he did, he didn't feel leather. There was something else already there. Something warm and soft.

Oh fuck. Wesley's hand.

Sam came so hard, he saw stars. With Wesley's moans in his ears, and their hands touching, it was impossible not to picture Wesley orgasming. He gave into it, dissolved into it. Wave after wave swept through him, wrecking him. Pleasure brighter and sharper than any colors he'd ever seen burned behind his eyes like an afterimage.

He had no sense of how long his orgasm lasted or how long it took him to come back down to Earth, but when he did, he was panting, sweaty, and starting to cramp.

He forced his eyes open. The windows were completely fogged over. So was the windshield. Christ.

Sam's hand was still on Wesley's. He was almost afraid to move it. "Uh, Wes?"

Wesley slid his hand out from under Sam's. Sam heard rustling, and then a napkin appeared over the separator. "Here, I grabbed a handful of these from the bar."

"Thanks." Sam took it, right as panic shot through him.

Jesus, what have we done?

Now that he wasn't turned on to the point of irrationality anymore, awkwardness settled on him like cold dew. Upon looking down at himself, he swallowed. He'd made a *mess*. Had he ever come this much in his life? Was it because he'd waited so long?

It's because of who you were with.

He shoved that thought into an empty room in his mind, shut the door, and padlocked it. While he cleaned up, he ran through a list of things he could say. Excuses he could make. Or would it be better to act like nothing had happened?

Shit. He had no precedent for a scenario like this. How had they ended up here? After all this time?

A traitorous voice in his head spoke out. *Maybe you never got the chance before. You were strangers when you first roomed together, and then you got engaged to Michael. But there's nothing stopping you now. You're both single, and you threw yourselves into this sexy petri dish together. The real question is, why fight it?*

Oh God, Sam was going to need bigger padlocks.

He was working up the nerve to say something—he wasn't sure what yet, but something—when Wesley beat him to the punch.

"Well, I for one feel better." Wesley laughed, but it sounded forced. "I'll see you back inside, Sammy."

Before Sam could so much as twitch, Wesley flung open the door by his head. Cold air rushed into the car. Wesley climbed out and slammed the door behind him so quickly, Sam didn't see so much as a flash of his face.

CHAPTER SIX

It wasn't often that Wesley found himself at a loss for words, but as Sam and he stood at the bathroom sink together the next morning, brushing their teeth, he was grateful for the excuse not to talk.

Wesley kept his eyes glued to the porcelain. He hadn't made eye contact with Sam in twelve hours, and the sunlight streaming through the windows behind them made him wince. With good reason. He'd really overdone it last night. Also with good reason.

As he rinsed out his mouth, he replayed last night's inauspicious end for the umpteenth time. After the "incident," as he was calling it in his head, he'd gone back to the bar and pounded shots until his thoughts had glazed over. Sam had shuffled in eventually, and they'd spent the night pointedly not talking about it. Then they'd driven home and gone to sleep in separate beds. Or at least, Sam had slept. Wesley had stared at the ceiling, trying to figure out what the hell had come over him.

It hadn't been alcohol; he'd been dead sober at the time. Close as he could figure, it'd been some sort of fever, an itch that had *demanded* to be scratched. He'd gotten swept up in it, how good it'd felt, how much he'd wanted it. But after, there'd been nothing but awkwardness, confusion, and . . . need.

That was the thing. If this were a one-time deal, Wesley could write it off. Make excuses, or straight-up ignore it. But the fact was, last night wasn't the first time Wesley had touched himself while thinking about Sam.

Earlier that day, he'd jerked off in the shower as planned. It was supposed to take the edge off the monstrous horniness that kept creeping up on him. And it had. Right up until Sam had come out of the shower wearing nothing but a towel.

Wesley hadn't masturbated twice in one day since he was a teen and had first discovered it. But at the sight of Sam's well-shaped torso—beads of water rolling down his skin—the fire he thought he'd doused roared back to life.

The second time around, in place of the generic hot guys who usually starred in his fantasies, Wesley hadn't been able to get Sam out his head. His soft hair and hard body. His deep, dark eyes. The way he'd felt the other day when Wesley had pinned him down on the bed.

Wesley had come hard, and even *that* hadn't been enough. As soon as it was over, the itch had crept back up. Every time he looked at Sam, it sharpened. Maybe what'd happened in the car was inevitable. More importantly, it'd made Wesley realize something that rocked him to the foundation of his being.

He wanted to do that again.

"You finished with that?"

The question startled Wesley into looking up. In the mirror, he met Sam's eyes for the first time since last night. Sam was pointing to the travel mouthwash in Wesley's hand. His face was composed, but Wesley knew him well enough to recognize when it was *too* composed.

His tongue burned. Shit. He'd been swishing his mouth out for over a minute now. He quickly spat into the sink, wiped his mouth, and handed over the bottle. "Yeah, all yours."

Their fingers touched briefly, and Wesley swore he felt an honest-to-God spark. Snatching his hand away, he cupped some water into his mouth, and then retreated to his suitcase. He busied himself with packing while his heart attempted to win the Kentucky Derby.

The question he'd dodged earlier came blaring back: What did this all mean? Sam was his friend, and Wesley had never wanted him to be anything more. That was their whole schtick. They were two gay guys in an intimate friendship who had never hooked up. He must be hard up if he'd lost sight of that.

Although, that didn't explain why Sam had gone along with it. He'd been sober too, and at any point, he could have laughed and told Wesley to stop messing around. But he hadn't.

Was there a chance . . . Sam wanted this as badly as Wesley did?

"Are you excited?"

Wesley's head whipped around so fast his neck cracked. "What?"

Sam met his gaze in the mirror again as he ran gel through his hair, styling it into perfect waves, like an ocean of gold. "Today's the day we drive to New Orleans. The city you've been waiting for. Are you excited?"

"Oh." Wesley swallowed. "Yeah. Can't wait."

Can't wait to return to the car, the scene of the crime, and be trapped there with you. No way to escape.

This was going to be the longest day of his life.

Don't be ridiculous, scolded a voice in his head. *It's Sam. You know Sam. What do you think is going to happen?*

Wesley took a breath. Nothing. Nothing was going to happen. If all went according to plan, in a few hours, they'd be in a new city. They'd leave this awkward encounter behind them and move on with their lives.

Everything did not go according to plan.

Wesley rubbed his temples to soothe his aching head. "How much will it cost to fix?"

The mechanic—whose greasy coverall had the name *Rusty* stitched on it in faded red thread—grinned wolfishly at him. "The part's a hundred, and then there's labor. Won't take me but half a day to finish, though. Only got one car ahead of you."

"Half a day?" Sam's shoes squeaked on the tile floor as he stepped forward. "You can't have it finished any faster?"

Rusty's watery blue eyes drifted toward the murky windows. Outside, the sun was hanging low in the sky like ripened fruit. Between the breakdown and terrible cell phone reception, it'd taken them hours to tow the car here.

"Sorry, boys." Rusty shrugged. "Store's about to close for the night. But I can get to it first thing in the morning."

A *bang* made Wesley jump. The wooden sign outside the auto shop was swinging in the wind. His eyes traced over the letters painted on it: *Sunflower Auto.*

Most people would probably think that name was too flowery for the squat, dank shop in which Wesley now stood, but it made sense, considering they'd broken down in Sunflower, Alabama, a tiny town off the end of Florida's tail.

It had more churches than businesses and was the definition of Nowheresville. The dusty collection of rundown old buildings and trees they'd driven through barely constituted the term *town*. Thank God there had been a nearby mechanic. Wesley could only imagine how much it would have cost to have the car towed back to civilization.

What if we have to cancel the rest of the trip because of this? How can we turn around now, after all this?

"Excuse us for a moment, Rusty." Wesley took Sam by the shoulder and led him as far away as he could, which was all of ten feet. He spoke in an undertone. "Sam, I'm so sorry."

Sam shrugged. "It's not your fault."

"I was the one who swore the car was fit to drive, but here we are with a dry-rotted serpentine belt. I had no idea they were so loud when they snapped. Good thing my super manly shriek drowned it out."

Sam smiled. "That *was* pretty funny. But seriously, don't worry about me. I'm worried about you. We're going to be delayed getting to New Orleans by a whole day."

Wesley waved him off. "I've waited to get my hands on some beignets this long. I can wait a little longer." He turned back to Rusty. "Go ahead and fix it. What do you need from us?"

Rusty gave them a form to fill out: payment information, billing address, and a way to contact them when the work was finished.

"I wonder how much this is going to run us," Wesley whispered to Sam as he jotted down his cell number. "All the partying we've been doing has been taking a toll on my wallet. Maybe we can pull a *Crossroads* and win a local karaoke competition to scrape up the cash."

Sam laughed. "Or we can put it on a credit card. I know neither of us is rich, but we're not so destitute we can't swing a simple belt repair."

"Well, sure." Wesley scoffed. "If you want to suck all the fun out of it."

There was only room for one credit card number. Sam put on a brave face and wrote down his. Wesley tried to fight him on it—the car was his, after all—but Sam insisted. "I should have bought you that cat shirt. It would have brought us good luck. When we get to New Orleans, buy me all the jambalaya I can eat, and we'll call it a wash."

They asked Rusty if there were any lodgings nearby, and as luck would have it, the town had a single motel. Wesley couldn't imagine anyone visiting of their own volition, but he wasn't complaining.

"Be sure to check out the festival too," Rusty said as he opened the door for them on their way out. "Happens every summer. There's rides and good Southern cooking."

"We'll do that," Wesley promised as he made a mental note to do nothing of the sort. "Sounds like a *hoot*."

Sam grabbed him by the hand and dragged him away before he could say anything else. They found the motel easily. The town had one main street, and everything of importance was located on it, like the single bank, grocery store, and post office.

According to the old woman who worked at the derelict motel, the summer festival took place in a clearing on the outskirts of town. In Wesley's head, he immediately dubbed it *the murder field*.

"You boys should stop by," she said in a voice that creaked like wood. She handed over their room key, which was brass and looked older than them. "It's a real humdinger."

As they exited the front office, Sam nudged him. "Maybe we should check it out."

Wesley scanned the row of doors facing the parking lot until he spotted a brass number eight. "Hell no."

"Why not?"

"Because I'm not eager to get slow-cooked on a spit by the locals." He laughed. "Think about it. We're stranded in a small town in the middle of nowhere, with no wheels and spotty cell reception. Good thing we're not sorority girls, or we'd be dead already."

Sam rolled his eyes. "You watch too many movies."

Upon finding their door, he got it open with some key jiggling and shoulder action.

To his complete shock, the interior was nothing like the building's dingy exterior. The clean wood floors were freshly polished, there was a TV on a bureau, and the two beds had been covered in cozy quilted blankets.

"See?" Sam waved at the room as if it were evidence. "This place isn't so bad. I wonder what channels they get out here."

"We're going to find out, because I am so not leaving this hotel room until the car is fixed." Wesley plunked his suitcase onto the closest bed with an air of finality.

Sam's suitcase landed on the other bed as he squared off with Wesley. "Why not? I thought this trip was about making memories and trying new things?"

"Yeah, but those things don't include learning to play the banjo and eating fried opossum. I'd think you'd leap at the opportunity to not be around people."

"Normally I would, but I'm trying to break out of bad habits." Sam cocked his head to the side, eyes sparkling in a way Wesley didn't trust at all. "But if you want to stay in, we can do that. We can spend all night locked in this room. Together. Alone."

Wesley's heart started to pound. *What's he getting at?* "Fine by me."

Sam hesitated. "I'm sure we can think of some way to pass the time. Something we can talk about, perhaps."

Unease lapped at Wesley like a tide.

Is he . . . using the weirdness between us to get me to go to the festival? Fucking manipulative genius.

His phone buzzed, offering a welcome distraction. Welcome, until he glanced at the screen and saw that it was his mom texting him. Again. A frantic phone call from Dad wouldn't be far behind. If they stayed in the room, he'd have little to distract him from their nagging. And worse, Sam might ask who was blowing up his phone.

"All right!" Wesley threw his hands up. "You win. Let me change into something I don't mind getting burned alive in, and we can go."

"Don't you have a Burning Man shirt? Wear that."

"I hate you."

For once in his life, Wesley was happy to admit he was wrong.

The moment they got to the aforementioned clearing, it was obvious the summer festival was a much bigger deal than the tiny town that hosted it. The sinking sun painted the scene in bold strokes of gold and shadow. Lanterns had been hung from wooden poles placed around the perimeter, along with streamers and bundles of wildflowers. The smell of kettle corn, smoked meat, and fried dough permeated the air.

A handful of ancient rides had been set up, somehow still in working order. There was a wooden carousel, a line of tents boasting carnival games, and a creaky Ferris wheel that went up about thirty feet but was lit by big round bulbs that made it look magical.

Dozens of people were milling between the attractions, way more than they'd seen around town. Crafters sold handmade goods out of their trailers: jewelry, clothing, and furniture. Children jumped out of the backs of pickup trucks and sprinted around, giggling. Adults set low-country boils to simmer in huge pots over open flames.

Wesley took a deep breath, his mouth watering. "You were right, Sam. I'm glad we didn't miss this."

"Told you," Sam said without venom. "What should we do first?"

"I'd like to get my hands on a giant turkey leg and then kick your ass at ring toss."

"You can certainly try."

Wesley ate his body weight in meat and elephant ears. Everything was *delicious*. They threw baseballs at milk bottles until Wesley's arm burned. Sam beat him by a single point and spent the next ten minutes giving him cliché advice—like "keep your eyes on the prize"—in an old-timey announcer's voice until Wesley stuffed cotton candy in Sam's mouth.

When dusk asserted itself, old men sitting in rocking chairs brought out guitars and filled the area with gentle strumming. The music seemed to drift on the wind, filling the clearing. Wesley and Sam found themselves gravitating toward the Ferris wheel. It had eight carriages, all of which were constantly full.

"I wonder how far you can see from the top," Sam said.

"You wanna find out?" Wesley polished off his (fifth) corn dog and tossed the greasy waxed paper into a nearby metal can. "It'd be a great way to watch the sunset. Let's get in line."

There were three couples ahead of them, emphasis on *couples*. Wesley had expected the ride to attract children, but it seemed this one was a magnet for lovers. He studied Sam out of the corner of his eye. His hands were in his pockets, his chin tilted up at the purpling sky. There was the barest hint of a smile on his face. His expression was so peaceful, Wesley would have paid money to hear the cadence of his thoughts right then.

He plucked up the courage to ask, "What are you thinking about?"

Sam glanced over at him, the sunlight catching his eyes and turning them the color of molasses. "Nothing."

Wesley let his expression show his opinion of that response.

Sam chuckled. "Yeah, okay. I was thinking that the last person I watched a sunset with was Michael, but in a couple of minutes, that's going to change."

"Is that bad?"

"Not at all." Sam nudged him with an elbow. "I think I'm having a breakthrough, actually. I don't want to keep agonizing over a decision I've long since made. I can move on and leave the past in the past. Or at least, I can when I have you nearby, kicking my ass."

The last part was said teasingly, but the way he looked at Wesley— like he was something precious, or necessary—sucked the air out of Wesley's lungs.

He cleared his throat and scrambled for a joke. "You got all that from a sunset? Must be something in the water around here."

They reached the front of the line. Operating the ride was a bent man so coated in grime, it was hard to tell where the dirt ended and his skin began. He peered at them with milky eyes, lip curling up in a way Wesley didn't like at all. "You two waitin' on yer dates?"

Sam's brow puckered. "No. We want to ride together."

The man sneered. "You can't."

Wesley's temper flared up. "Why not?"

"It's fer couples and kids only. Won't look right, two men ridin' together." He turned his matted head toward the couple behind them as if that was the end of the conversation.

Annoyance blazed through Wesley. He opened his mouth to say something snide, but before he could, Sam took a step forward.

"Excuse me, but we are a couple."

The man's head whipped toward them, eyes huge. "What?"

Before Wesley could react, Sam took his hand and laced their fingers together. "This is my boyfriend, and since the Ferris wheel is for couples, that means we get to ride." Sam straightened his back, radiating confidence.

Wesley's mouth popped open at the same time the operator's did. The operator glared at Wesley. "Is that so?"

Wesley was looking at Sam, however. "Dude, what the hell?"

Sam seemed to shrink like a candle flame flickering in the wind.

But then Wesley gave his hand a squeeze and leaned toward the man, talking in a stage whisper. "I'm not his boyfriend, I'm his *husband.* We're newlyweds, and *somebody* hasn't gotten used to saying it yet. He's so going to pay for that later."

Sam fluttered his eyelashes. "Sorry, honey. Forgive me?"

They laughed while the man sputtered. The wheel finished a rotation and came to a stop. Wesley bypassed the man and opened the little metal gate leading to the ramp. "After you, hubby."

"Thank you, dear." Without letting go of his hand, Sam tugged him along.

They got into their carriage, which was little more than a metal bench with a floor, and lowered the rusted safety bar. The wheel started the second they were settled. No doubt the toothless jackal wanted to get them off the ride as soon as possible.

As it rose higher, Wesley forgot all about him. The view was stunning. The sunset colored the trees all around them pitch-black, like calligraphy strokes. The thick clouds were spun gold that blushed pink. It was so beautiful, Wesley almost didn't notice Sam was still holding his hand.

Wesley looked down at their twined fingers, heart thumping. As if sensing his gaze, Sam glanced down too. His eyes were bright with emotion.

"In case he's still watching us," Sam murmured, voice melding with the breeze.

There was no way the operator could see them from this vantage point, but Wesley didn't say a word. He wasn't one to complain about small blessings.

"Sam." Wesley wet his lips. "What made you do that? With the guy down there. You're not usually the sort to stand up to people like that."

Sam shrugged. "No one's going to force me back into the closet. I may not be the boldest or bravest at times, but I know who I am, and I'm not ashamed."

Five years later, and he still surprises me.

It was one of many things Wesley loved about him.

At the word *loved*, Wesley's breath caught in his throat. In that moment, he had a breakthrough of his own. Whatever had changed between them was changing fast, and Wesley couldn't stop it. It was like lightning, or an avalanche. Ignoring it wouldn't work either. With his heart skittering in his chest, it was impossible to tell where fear ended and exhilaration began.

As they reached the top, Wesley was certain they were going to keep rising. Up and up, into the golden sky. The idea should have frightened him, but with Sam holding his hand, grounding him, he wouldn't drift too far.

CHAPTER
SEVEN

B y the time they headed back to the motel, Sam was wired. Instead of wearing him out, all the excitement had injected itself right into his system, more potent than a shot of espresso. He was practically bouncing on the balls of his feet as he walked.

Wesley had been quiet ever since the Ferris wheel, however. Either he had something on his mind, or the festival had tuckered him out. If only Sam could osmose some energy over to him.

When they got back to their room, Wesley made a beeline for his bed and flopped onto it. Sam did the same, only he sat on the opposite mattress, facing Wesley.

"You tired, Wes?"

Wesley cracked an eye open. In the light of the single lamp on the wall, its blue color was bleached to nearly white. "Sort of. I've been thinking a lot lately, and you know how thinking makes my brain-place hurt."

"What have you been thinking about?"

Wesley shook his head. "Nothing I understand well enough to share." His head swiveled to take in the room. "What should we do now? Go to bed early like old men?"

"We could go out. For once, I'm in the mood for it."

"Hold up." Wesley made a T shape with his hands. "What do you mean 'out'?"

"You know. Out. Like, on the town. That thing you've been asking me to do every day of this trip."

"Dude, no. I was joking earlier, but now we really can't leave the room."

"What? Since when are we under house arrest?"

Wesley sat up. "You held my hand back at the festival."

Sam's face instantly heated. He'd been trying not to think about that. Taking Wesley's hand in the first place had been justified, but continuing to hold it for the whole ride . . . Sam had done that for the sheer pleasure of it. It'd been so different from when he'd touched Wesley's hand in the car. More intimate, which was so damn counterintuitive. When he'd finally let go, Sam had felt strangely empty, like he was missing something now.

He put on his best nonchalant expression. "So?"

"As fun as it was to show up that jackass carnie, you outed us to the whole town. I don't mean that in an accusatory way. You did the right thing. But you gotta admit, it was a risky move."

"Why, though?"

Wesley spread out his arms to encompass the room. "We're two gay guys currently stranded in Murdertown, Alabama. This state isn't exactly known for its tolerance. You know all those cute things we do because we're close, like feeding each other and drinking from each other's cups? No one in the big cities batted an eye, but I guarantee there were people who saw us holding hands at that festival and didn't like it one bit. You know how it is. You grew up in superconservative Montana. So please, can we stay put until we have our car back and can jet out of here if we need to?"

It wasn't often that Sam felt like he'd lost the logical high ground to his whimsical best friend, but Wesley had a point. Wesley knew it too, judging by the triumphant gleam in his eyes.

"It's weird to hear you being all cautious," Sam said. "That's usually my job. But yeah, we can stay in. This is going to so boring, though."

"Fingers crossed. Boring means nobody got murdered. Want to see what's on TV?"

"No, I'm too wired for that." Sam stood up and tried to pace, but the room wasn't big enough. He ended up in the tiny bathroom. A dish of flower-shaped soaps caught his eye. He could stand to wash his hands after eating all that sticky carnival food.

Over the flowing water, Wesley called to him. "Then what do you want to do?"

"I don't know. Something." Sam dried his hands off on a delicate, embroidered towel and wandered back into the main room.

He stopped at the foot of Wesley's bed. "I have all this pent-up energy and no outlet for it. I need to burn it off somehow."

As easily as a switch being flipped, tension sprang up between them. It felt like electricity, charging the air. He didn't dare look Wesley in the eye for fear that what he was thinking was written all over his face.

We're alone in this room with nothing to do. If we wanted to, we could—we could—

He couldn't make himself finish the thought. They hadn't talked about that night in Atlanta, and Sam was fine with that. If they never talked about it, he could go on pretending it was a one-off. He'd never have to acknowledge how much he'd been craving a repeat performance ever since.

But that was so wrong. He couldn't let his libido take over again. Not with his best friend. Sam *needed* Wesley, needed his friendship like he needed water and shelter. Jeopardizing what they had for sex didn't make any sense. It wasn't the sort of risky move Sam would ever make.

So why did he *want* it so badly?

His eyes dragged down Wesley's chest. He was wearing a tight green T-shirt and loose jeans. Sam preferred skinny cuts, but on Wesley, the jeans worked. They sunk down a bit on his waist, showing the band of his underwear, and the fabric clung to—

Sam jerked his head away. *Stop it. That's your best friend.*

Wesley cleared his throat. "I think I know what we need."

Eager for a distraction, Sam asked, "What?"

Without answering, Wesley rolled off his bed and grabbed his suitcase. After some fumbling, he produced a bottle of whiskey. "I've been saving this for a special occasion. It's the bottle Dad gave me for graduation."

"Wow, and you brought it along?"

"I had a feeling we'd have cause to crack it open. Getting stuck in the middle of nowhere with nothing to do is good enough for me. I also brought this." More rummaging, and he pulled out a deck of cards. "Wi-fi–free entertainment."

"Nice. That works out well. I haven't charged all my devices since Atlanta. We can give everything a rest for the night."

"Sounds good."

Sam hunted for free outlets while Wesley went in search of glasses. There weren't any, except for a small cup by the sink. With a shrug, they decided to pass the bottle back and forth, as they'd done many a time when they were lazy freshmen who didn't want to wash dishes.

They started out with poker, but with only two of them and nothing to wager, that got old fast. Wesley suggested strip poker, a joke that would have earned a laugh in the past. Now, it surprised Sam into tense silence. Wesley sputtered that he hadn't meant it, but Sam still spent a moment not looking him in the eye.

They tried gin next, and then rummy, but when Sam proceeded to win nearly every hand, a sulking Wesley insisted they play something else. They finally settled on a game of their own invention in which they both drew a card, and whoever had the lower number had to drink.

It wasn't the most intellectually stimulating, but as they worked their way through a quarter of the bottle of whiskey, Sam became increasingly thankful for the lack of cognizance needed to play.

"Let's make this more interesting." Wesley wasn't slurring, but his eyes were glassy. Sam had learned long ago that meant he was in the warm-fuzzy stage of being tipsy. "If you draw the low card, you do, like, a dare."

"What would we dare each other to do though?" Sam giggled. "We're stuck in this room."

They were sitting cross-legged on his bed with a pile of discarded cards between them. Wesley had the bottle in his lap, and one of his socked feet was tapping out a random rhythm against the duvet.

"Okay, good point." Wesley stroked his chin in the exaggerated way people only did in movies. "How about you have to answer a question? Any question, and you gotta be truthful. Like when we played Would You Rather in the car."

Sam scrunched his nose. "That was so mean of you. Though I stand by my choice. I wouldn't mind being sticky so much."

Something flashed across Wesley's face too quickly for Sam to register it. "Are you game?"

"Let's do a practice round." Sam reached for the deck and selected his card, holding it up for them both to see. "I got an eight."

Wesley grabbed his. "Three. I lose." He took a swig from the bottle. "Ask me something, or gimme a dare."

"Hm." Sam thought back. There was so little they didn't know about each other. After a moment, something he'd always been curious about popped into his head. "Why do you think you've never had a serious boyfriend?"

Wesley shrugged. "I dunno."

"You must have a theory. You're so funny and charming, and you're hot and all that. Guys should be falling all over themselves to date you."

Wesley's eyes seemed to glint as they considered Sam. "You think I'm hot?"

Sam swallowed. "I've told you before you're an attractive man."

"Attractive and hot aren't quite the same thing."

Grabbing the bottle, Sam took a swig without looking at him. "Hey, I'm the one asking the questions here. What's your answer?"

To his credit, Wesley paused for a few seconds before responding. "It's a lot of things, I guess. It's not like I've never met anyone I liked. I'd love to date someone for real. But . . . I dunno. I always told myself that if I was going to be in a serious relationship, I'd have to be stable first. Get my shit together. Stop being such a fuckup."

Sam studied his face. "What makes you think you're a fuckup? I've never heard you talk like this before."

Briefly, Wesley's expression contorted. Then, he reached for the bottle. "It's kinda why I wanted to come on this trip. I needed to get away so when I came back, it'd feel like a fresh start."

"I wondered about that, actually. My reasons for coming made sense, but yours seemed to be missing something. Obviously, you're always up for an adventure, but a two-week vacation from life isn't something you can go on for the hell of it. What drove you to—"

"Uh-uh." Wesley wagged a finger at him. "Your turn's over. You want another question, you gotta win another round." Wesley flipped a card over. "Ten of clubs. Top that."

Sam selected his card. "Can't. Got a four."

"Yes!" Wesley pumped a fist in the air. "I am victorious! Here's your question: If you could go back and change anything in your life, what would you change?"

"Yikes. Going straight for the hard questions, huh?" Surprisingly, it only took Sam a second to come up with his answer. "You remember when we met?"

"Course I do. First day of freshman year, I walked into my new dorm room for the first time and found this skinny blond guy sitting on what should have been *my* bed."

Sam chuckled. "It was first-come, first-serve. Not my fault you were late."

"But you can't just claim the top bunk! We should have drawn straws or done Rock, Paper, Scissors."

"It's been five years, Wes. Let it go."

Wesley grumbled to himself. "Fine. So, was that it? You'd pick the bottom bunk instead? If so, I gotta say, your life has been peaceful."

"Oh no. I was leading up to my answer. Did I ever tell you that when we first met, I thought we were going to hate each other?"

Wesley sat up straighter. "No way. Seriously?"

Sam nodded. "It's true. There I was on my first day of college, terrified and trying not to freak out, and in bounced this loud guy with the energy of a newborn puppy. You walked right up to me and started talking a mile a minute, and my poor little introverted heart sank. I thought we were total opposites and that we couldn't possibly get along. I spent the next week trying to keep my distance."

"You know, now that you mention it"—Wesley scratched his chin—"I remember you being kinda standoffish when we first met. I assumed you were shy."

"That was part of it too."

"So, what happened?"

"I got to know you." Sam smiled. "Or rather, you got to know me. You were so insistent that we bond, I couldn't resist. And I'm grateful. I discovered how funny and caring you are, and how even though you're an extrovert, you're not draining. I hate to think that if I'd stuck to my first impression, we might never have become friends."

"Perish the thought." Wesley winked. "This has been a lovely trip down memory lane, but I don't see how it answers my question. What would you change?"

"I'd get that first week back. I'd walk right up to you the second you entered our dorm and introduce myself. I know in the grand scheme of things a week is nothing, but I want every second of the time we have."

Sam didn't think what he'd said was all that groundbreaking, but after he'd finished, Wesley stared at him, eyes huge.

"What?"

"Nothing." Wesley swallowed audibly. "How are you feeling?"

"Good." Sam grinned. "A little tipsy. Not too bad. How about you?"

Wesley didn't answer. He took the bottle and set it on the nightstand, out of Sam's reach. "You swear you're tipsy and not drunk?"

"Yeah. I probably only had three drinks. Liquor hits me a little harder than beer, but I feel fine. Why?"

"I want to play one more round." Wesley mumbled something under his breath. Sam caught a few words. ". . . let fate decide . . ."

He shrugged. "Okay. I'll go first." He picked a card. "Jack. Beat that."

Wesley's expression was tight as he flipped over his card. He let out a breath. "King. I win."

"'Grats. Lay it on me."

Wesley paused again before looking down. "My question is . . . can I kiss you?"

Sam was lucky the bottle was nowhere near him, because if he'd been taking a swig just then, he would have spit it out. "What?"

Wesley's face was red, but he raised his eyes up to look at Sam directly. "Can I kiss you?"

For a long moment, Sam was silent. Then he asked a question that was equal parts silly and necessary. "Why?"

Wesley shrugged and gave a little laugh. Sam recognized that move: Wesley's classic playing-it-off behavior. Beneath that, he was radiating nerves. "It's been a while since I kissed anyone. Hell, it's been a while since I did anything with anyone. Except . . ." He trailed off, blush intensifying.

Sam's breath caught in his throat. *Oh God. Does he want to talk about that night right now? I don't think I can.*

Luckily, Wesley didn't finish his sentence. "I've been thinking about it a lot lately. This whole setup we have on this trip is kinda bullshit. We're out on the town almost every night, two single guys, meeting people, but we can't bring anyone back to the hotel? No sex for two weeks? No wonder I've been so . . . No wonder we . . ." He cleared his throat. "I want to try kissing. I think it'll be fun. Healthy even, for both of us. Release some of the tension. I know you've felt it too."

Sam's brain was doing its best to wrap itself around Wesley's proposal. "But it's us, Wes. It's *me*."

Wesley shrugged. "Who better?"

Those two simple words made a strange amount of sense. Sam couldn't think of anyone else he'd trust to kiss and not have it be a big deal. Definitely not any of his other friends. And technically speaking, Wesley and he had already done way more than kiss. That hadn't ended in disaster, so maybe this wouldn't either.

God, Sam was actually considering it.

"I don't know." His body heated up, and he couldn't tell if it was from embarrassment or arousal. Then Wesley's eyes dropped down to Sam's mouth, and Wesley licked his lips.

A shudder worked its way through Sam. *Definitely arousal.*

"It's not like we've never kissed before." Wesley's voice was getting soft and low. "Remember that one time in sophomore year? Billy Snyder told you that you were a terrible kisser, and you were so upset. I kissed you that night."

"That was a peck on the lips, and you only did it to comfort me." Sam's protests grew weaker with every second.

"It worked, though." Wesley was leaning closer one infinitesimal degree at a time. "I really think this will be good for us. Take some of the edge off. We can try it, and if we don't like it, we'll pretend it never happened."

That was so not going to work. Denial never did anybody any good. Sam couldn't seem to find it in himself to care though. Wesley had gotten one thing right for sure. Being out on the unfamiliar road was taking a toll on Sam. Strange towns, strange people, and sleeping in strange beds. It was lonely. Kissing someone, someone he knew and trusted, would be a huge comfort.

Not only that. Sam could pretend all day that he didn't want this, but he couldn't lie to his own body. As Wesley closed the space between them, excitement rushed through Sam like it'd replaced his blood.

"Okay." The word was out of Sam's mouth before his brain caught up with it. "Okay, let's do it."

The way Wesley's face lit up with eagerness made goose bumps pop up on Sam's skin. "Really?"

"Yeah." Nervousness tugged at Sam, along with desire he could feel in his teeth. He wasn't sure where this need had come from all of a sudden. Maybe it'd always been there, waiting to burst out. Had he been stamping it down all these years?

"All right." Wesley exhaled sharply. "Let me . . ." He touched the side of Sam's face, gently at first and then with more confidence. His fingers were rough but warm as they brushed down Sam's cheek to his chin. "C'mere."

Wesley had leaned as far as he could. Sam was going to have to meet him halfway.

With one final swallow, Sam did. Wesley's hand on his face helped ease him forward, eliminating the distance between them inch by inch. The closer he got to Wesley's face, the harder they both breathed. The first tickle of Wesley's air against his lips made him shudder. He hardly had time to process his jumbled emotions before their mouths met.

The initial brush was so light, it almost wasn't there at all, but Sam felt it. He felt it like a nearby live wire, a prickle of electricity in the air that told him something big was about to happen. It wasn't until Wesley tilted his head to fit their lips better together that Sam understood. That first touch was just the lightning. Next would come the thunder.

And come it did.

The kiss had a life of its own, and it was electric and deafening. One second, they were tentatively pressing their mouths together. The next, Wesley had wrapped a hand around the back of Sam's neck and was gripping him so hard it bordered on pain. Sam had expected some part of this to be awkward, for a voice in his head to scream, *What are you doing? This is Wesley.* That never happened. Instead, the realization of just whose mouth was on his flooded him with sharp pleasure.

Wesley kissed desperately, like he'd found water after days of thirst. Sam struggled to process all the new sensations. Wesley's mouth, soft and hot. His body, firm and hotter. His stubble scratching Sam's face in a way that should have hurt but added to the intensity. All of it combined into a powerful cocktail inside him.

Holy shit, this was the most terrifying thing Sam had ever done, and he couldn't believe he hadn't done it sooner.

In an effort to get closer, Sam moved to his knees. Wesley followed him up, and their bodies came together like a crash of cymbals. Their arms joined the tangle as they both tried to bridge some imaginary gap between them.

Wesley's tongue found its way into Sam's mouth. It rolled over his, letting Sam taste him. The new wet heat made Sam moan, and the sound seemed to spur Wesley on. He nipped at Sam's lip, earning a gasp, and then soothed it with his tongue.

Sam buried his hands in Wesley's soft hair, trying to get more of him, but it wasn't possible. They were skin to skin, or they would be if it weren't for their clothes.

Oh God, what would this be like if they were naked? So much better. Would that lead to sex? Would Wesley want that? He hadn't mentioned anything beyond kissing, but he had to be feeling what Sam was feeling, right?

Suddenly, it was all too much. Sam pulled away, panting for breath. Wesley let him, but his mouth moved to Sam's throat instead, like he couldn't stop kissing him. He mouthed Sam's jaw, skimmed over to Sam's ear, and there his teeth found Sam's earlobe. He bit down with exactly the right amount of pressure.

"Fuck, Wesley." Sam took a shuddering breath. "I can't think. The alcohol is making me dizzy."

"I don't think it's the alcohol." Wesley's voice rumbled in his chest. "Here, lie down." He guided Sam back, and Sam let him. The cards spilled off the bed as they changed positions: Sam lying against the pillows with Wesley on top of him. Fuck, that felt good. Sam had known it would. It'd felt good when Wesley had pinned him down before. Better than it should have felt.

Wesley was trembling. One arm supported his torso while his free hand shook its way to Sam's face. He cupped Sam's chin again.

This time, when their mouths came together, it was less desperate, less frantic, but much more potent. Wesley's mouth was open to him, inviting him in. The whiskey taste added honey and smoke to an already nuanced kiss.

With every passing second, Sam was filling up. He had no clue with what, but he was so full of *something*, he was going to burst. It was bigger than lust, deeper than longing, and so raw he was scared to poke at it too much.

This position was a mistake. Before, when they'd been kissing brutally, like a fight, he could pretend it was just hormones. But lying like this, with Wesley on him, between his legs, felt way too much like they were lovers.

I'm hard. Sam's heart hammered against his ribs. *Any second now, Wesley's going to feel it. What should I do?*

Before he could decide, Wesley pulled his mouth away with a soft sound. He shifted on top of Sam. For a moment, Sam's panicky brain thought he was going to rub their groins together. The only thing more frightening than Wesley finding out Sam was hard was Wesley being hard too.

To Sam's relief, Wesley didn't change positions. But he did slide his hand down Sam's face to his chest. His knuckles dragged over one of Sam's nipples, and even through a layer of fabric, that felt too good for words. Good enough that it took Sam a moment to realize Wesley's hand was still moving. Down his stomach to his hips, clearly heading for—

Holy fuck. Wesley's going to touch my cock.

The realization sent shock ricocheting through him like a gunshot. Two facts slammed into his brain simultaneously. One, there was no way this was ever going to be just kissing, and two, he wanted Wesley to touch him more than he wanted to keep breathing.

Sam's body acted without the permission of his brain. He shoved Wesley off him and scrambled away. He was across the room in three strides, face in his hands.

A moment of stunned silence passed. Then Wesley's voice sounded behind him. "Sam, what's wrong?"

Sam didn't answer. His libido was a swarm of angry bees buzzing in his ears, ordering him to go back to the bed. His brain, however, was jumping back and forth between panic and confusion. He'd thought they'd crossed a line that night in the car, but that was a pencil mark compared to the one they'd vaulted over tonight. In what universe was kissing scarier than getting off?

The universe where I kissed my best friend, and not only did I like it, I wanted to do more. This can't happen. We can't do this. If I lose him, I'll—

He heard the mattress creak behind him. Wesley must be getting up, probably to come over and see if Sam was okay.

Sam held a palm out without looking at him, fending him off. "I'm all right. Nothing's wrong."

"I don't believe you. Look at me."

Sam did. Wesley's hair was in disarray, and his lips were reddened. He looked sexy as hell.

Fuck, I did that. Why did I do that?

Sam didn't know what to think. No matter how nonchalant Wesley acted, to Sam this felt earth-shattering. Like a meteor heading right for them, ready to slam into their lives and obliterate everything.

He wanted to have sex with Wesley. There was no denying it now. He had the erection to prove it. But was that because Wesley was the only guy here, or because Sam wanted *him*?

It was impossible to tell while his emotions were dialed up to a hundred. He had so many feelings for Wesley, tangled up like fishing line inside him. He'd never had cause to examine them before. He'd decided how he felt about Wesley long ago and had never looked back. Now, this attraction was forcing him to stop and do a double take.

Where was the line between loving someone as a friend and wanting something romantic? Was it obscured by the lust washing over him, or had they passed it already? What did Wesley think this was?

I can't deal with this right now. I need time and sobriety to pull myself together.

"I want to go to sleep." He couldn't drum up the wherewithal to phrase it more elegantly.

"Okay." Wesley's expression flickered with disappointment. "Don't you think we should talk first?"

Sam studied him. "What's there to talk about? You said you wanted to kiss, right? We kissed. Is there something else you want to say?" He held his breath and watched for the tiniest flicker of emotion on Wesley's face.

Wesley's brow pinched together. "Well, yeah. Did you like it?"

Sam's heart throbbed. If he were smart, he'd say he hadn't. End this now. Forget about it. But he loved Wesley too much to lie to him. "Of course I liked it, Wesley. You felt that for yourself."

"I don't know what I felt. This is all new territory."

Did that mean Wesley hadn't liked it? Mustering all his bravery, Sam glanced down at Wesley's groin. Even his baggy jeans couldn't hide the hard-on he was sporting. The knowledge punched Sam in the gut.

Wesley made no move to cover himself or look away. He seemed totally unashamed. "Do you think we could do this again?"

Sam's throat closed. He had to swallow several times to coax it open. "I need to sleep on it. Things will be clearer in the morning." *Please, God, let them be clearer.*

"All right." Wesley paused. "We'll talk tomorrow."

His tone was somewhere between a promise and a warning.

"Good night." For the first time since they'd left on the trip, Sam grabbed his pajamas out of his bag and took them into the bathroom to change. He felt Wesley's eyes on his back until the moment he shut the door.

Once inside, he gripped the edge of the sink and stared at himself in the mirror. He didn't know what he was looking for. Perhaps some outside change to reflect everything that was changing inside him. But all he saw were kiss-red lips and the frightened eyes of a man who had no idea what he was doing.

CHAPTER
EIGHT

Rusty the mechanic called Wesley at seven the next morning, and by some miracle, Wesley was awake enough to answer. Not only was their car fixed, but Rusty had salvaged a used part for them. They weren't going to have to pay full price for a new belt. It seemed there was some truth to the tales of Southern hospitality.

After he hung up, Wesley eased himself up in bed. "The car's ready, Sam. As soon as we pick it up, we can get out of here."

A mumbled response came from the next bed over, too quiet for Wesley to hear. He blinked sleep from his eyes and peered at the bed to the left. The curtains were drawn, but enough light filtered in around the edges for his eyes to adjust.

Sam was sleeping on his stomach, face buried in a pillow. The sheets had fallen to his waist, and the shape of his back was distinct against the white linen. The way it peaked at his shoulders, sloped down to the small of his back, and then swelled again, was poetry.

Wesley tore his eyes away as moments from the previous evening flashed into his head. Sam's face getting closer as Wesley leaned in. His eyes, uncertain but full of trust. The perfect, smooth heat of his mouth, and what a relief and a torture it'd been to finally be with him.

If Sam hadn't pulled away, Wesley definitely wouldn't have stopped at kissing.

Thinking about it made heat pool in his belly. He looked down. Sure enough, he was getting hard. This wasn't morning wood that he could easily shake off either. Whatever this was, it was in his blood now, digging in roots. Could he nip into the bathroom and rub one out without waking Sam?

If I masturbate any more, I'm going to give myself a friction burn. What else can I do though? It's getting to the point where I get turned on every time I think about Sam at all. The sooner we talk, the better.

Too bad Wesley had no idea what he was going to say. He supposed he should stick to the truth and see what happened, but it didn't seem right to wing it when his closest friendship was at stake. What if Sam wanted to act like last night had never happened? Now that Wesley knew how it felt to have Sam under him—to kiss him and hold him and hear him moan—he couldn't forget about it. He wasn't going to pretend. Not with Sam. Not with his own best friend.

Resolved, Wesley hopped out of bed and tiptoed through his morning routine. Sam had started snoring cutely, a sure sign that he was dead to the world. He'd probably sleep for another hour if left to his own devices.

Once he was dressed, Wesley located his keys and slipped out the door as quietly as he could. Picking up the car was a one-man job, and it seemed Sam really needed to rest.

One twenty-minute walk later, Wesley returned from "town" with a car and two cups of coffee, courtesy of a local diner. He let himself into the room and shuffled over to Sam's bed. He set both cups on the nightstand before taking a seat next to Sam's prone form.

"Morning, Sleeping Beauty." Wesley rubbed Sam's back. "Time to face the day."

Sam groaned and peeled open the eye that wasn't buried in the pillow. "Whiskey is evil."

Wesley's heart thudded hard in his chest. "You didn't overdo it, did you?" *Please say you weren't drunk last night. Please.*

"No, I think it's all the drinking we've been doing in general. It's catching up with me." He flipped onto his back, rubbing his forehead. He'd slept in a tank top and pajama bottoms, which looked unreasonably good on him, especially when combined with the messy gold strands falling over his brow.

Wesley's gaze must've lingered for a second too long, because Sam stiffened. "Did I hear you say the car is ready?" He sat up and scooched back, supposedly to cross his legs, but Wesley knew him too well for that. He was putting distance between them.

"Yup. I picked it up a minute ago." Wesley ignored the punch of rejection Sam had delivered right to his face and forced a smile. "We can leave as soon as we're packed. But I think we should talk first."

Sam looked away. "Right now? I just woke up."

Wesley picked up the coffee and placed it directly into Sam's hand. "Drink up. Then we talk."

Sam put the coffee back down and rolled off the bed on the opposite side. "Gimme a chance to use the bathroom and shower. I need to wake myself up."

"Do you? Or do you need to avoid me?"

Sam looked back at him, eyes wide. "What?"

"I know you and all your nonconfrontational tricks, Sam. Stall all you want, but eventually, you and I are going to be in that car together, and then there's going to be nowhere for you to run. I don't want to have to trap you in a moving vehicle to get you to talk to me, so will you please sit down?" Wesley pointed to the bed opposite him.

For a moment, Sam appeared to dither. Then he sighed. "I actually do have to pee, though."

"Go ahead. Then come back."

Sam didn't argue further. He disappeared into the bathroom only to reappear five minutes later. It looked like he'd splashed some water on his face, and there was a bit of dried toothpaste at the corner of his mouth. He trudged over to the bed and climbed onto it. "I hate you."

"No, you don't."

"I do a little bit right now. This can't wait for anything, huh?" Sam's face was flushed, though it was impossible to tell if he was embarrassed or angry. "We couldn't do this when we've both had a chance to sort ourselves out? No, everything has to be upfront and uncomfortable with you."

Annoyance sparked up in Wesley. "I'd rather be uncomfortable than pretend everything is fine when it's not. I bet if it were up to you, we'd never talk about this."

His annoyance was flavored with guilt. He was no stranger to not talking about things.

"Right, because that's my whole personality in a nutshell. I'm the wimp who shuffles through life flinching away from everything unpleasant. Is that what you think? If it weren't for you forcing me to talk about this, I'd ignore something this important?"

Damn, Sam had a point. But by now, his defensiveness had set Wesley on edge. "That sounds like exactly what you did this morning. Sleeping in. Scurrying off to the bathroom. Those are classic Sam avoidance behaviors. I've lived with you, Sam. You can't lie to me."

"Oh, sorry. I forgot. You know everything about me."

Wesley started to lob a retort back, but then he realized what Sam was doing. "Why are you picking a fight with me?"

"Because I'm confused!" Sam made a frustrated sound and jumped to his feet. "I don't know what's happening, or what to do, and I *hate* this."

"Because you're overthinking it, as per usual!" Wesley was suddenly on his feet as well. "Why can't you go with it? Let things happen naturally?"

Sam scoffed. "The last time I 'went with it,' we ended up jerking off in your car together."

"Oh, so we're talking about that now?" Wesley wasn't sure when he'd taken a step forward, but Sam was suddenly right in front of him. "All I wanted to do was clear the air and try to figure some things out."

"So clear it."

Wesley had to force his mouth to form words. "Do you wish we hadn't kissed?"

Sam never raised his voice, but now he was almost shouting. "No! I don't regret anything that we did! That's what's so confusing about this. I didn't do anything I didn't want, and the only thing I regret is stopping. I can't get that night in your car out of my head!"

Wesley yelled back. "Well, I don't regret it either! In fact, it was fucking spectacular. I haven't been able to think about anything but doing that again."

"Me neither! I dreamed about kissing you last night. It's like you crawled into my brain."

"Yeah, well, same to you!" Wesley fell silent, blinking at Sam as the conversation caught up with him. When he spoke next, it was at a normal volume. "We've never argued like this before. Not once, in five years."

"No, we haven't." Sam was trembling. "Things are changing. Why is this happening now?"

"I don't know. But there's something I have to ask."

Sam's eyes were wide, but he nodded. "What?"

All the raw emotion in Wesley's blood had warped to arousal, and now he was burning up. He couldn't stop it, couldn't help but get swept up in it. With Sam standing so close, Wesley swore he could feel the heat from his body. "Are you turned on right now? Because I am."

Sam looked down, made a soft, broken sound. "Yes."

"Well, then." Wesley licked his lips. "What are we going to do about it?"

In a move that probably surprised Sam as much as anyone, Sam grabbed Wesley's face and kissed him with lip-bruising force.

After a moment of shock, Wesley kissed back with equal aggression, as if he could work off his overabundance of emotion through his mouth. No matter how much passion he spilled out, more of it bubbled up in him. He fisted a hand in Sam's shirt and hauled him closer. Sam wrapped an arm around his waist, as if he were afraid Wesley would try to get away. Wesley wasn't going anywhere.

He tilted his head to get a better angle, and Sam moved with him. His kiss was both insistent and pliant, following Wesley's lead. When Wesley nibbled on his lip, Sam sucked on Wesley's. When he brought tongues into the mix with a playful swipe, Sam was the first to sink his into Wesley's mouth. Wesley didn't realize they were moving until he was falling onto the bed.

It was the one Sam had slept in last night. Wesley could smell Sam all over it, his fresh-laundry-and-cucumber scent. It would have distracted him normally, but Wesley couldn't focus on anything but Sam as he climbed onto him. He was panting for breath as he looked down at Wesley, face unreadable.

Wesley started to say something. They could slow down if this was happening too fast. It might kill Wesley, but he'd do it. Right as he opened his mouth, Sam pounced. He kissed Wesley so hard, their teeth clicked together, but then his tongue was in Wesley's mouth, and their kissing went from desperate to filthy.

There was nothing shy about Sam as he straddled Wesley, bringing their groins flush. Wesley had changed into jeans to pick up the car, and God he regretted that as his hands found their way to Sam's cotton-clad hips. Sam's heated skin was burning through the fabric. It made Wesley's fingers itch to strip him. Especially when he felt the bulge between Sam's legs resting on top of his own, growing by the second.

There was nothing quiet about Sam either. It was like Wesley was seeing a whole new side of him. As he kissed Wesley breathless, the little pleasured noises he made pooled between Wesley's legs. He pushed at Wesley's shirt, growling when sweat made it cling to his stomach.

A second before Wesley suspected Sam was going to rip it off, he caught Sam's hands. "Sam?"

Sam stopped kissing him and pulled back far enough to look Wesley in the eye. "Yeah?"

"Are we really doing this?"

Sam licked his swollen bottom lip, and Wesley shivered. "I think we are."

"It's . . . weird how not weird this is."

"I know." Sam nosed his cheek. "I feel it too."

"Shouldn't we, I dunno, talk about it first? Sammy, this is so huge."

The smile that spread over Sam's face was slow and wicked. "You're overthinking it." His mouth found Wesley's again.

It was like Sam's words had released some sort of dam. Wesley hadn't thought he was holding back before, but now desire rushed through him, washing away everything in its path: his worries, his uncertainties, all of it. Nothing was left but the purest, simplest need. He wanted Sam naked, and he wanted it now.

Sam seemed to have the same idea. He'd abandoned Wesley's shirt in favor of groping at his pants. Having his hands in that general area felt incredible. Wesley finished pulling his shirt over his head and tossed it aside. Sam made an approving sound and trailed a hand down Wesley's chest. He stopped at one of his nipples and ran the pad of a thumb over it, but then he looked back at Wesley's still-zipped jeans. It was like he couldn't decide what new thing he wanted to experience first. It was the most relatable feeling *ever*.

Wesley took pity on him and undid his own fly, hissing when his hand brushed his erection. He thought it might rip his boxers as it strained to stick straight up. Sam stared at it, and there was a brief, surreal moment when Wesley thought, *Sam's never seen me hard before.* He moved to pull it out, but Sam went one step further.

He leaned down and wrapped his mouth around the head through his underwear.

"Oh, fuck." Wesley had to clench his hands into fists to keep from burying them in Sam's hair. "Oh God."

The heat from Sam's mouth was exquisite, and soon wetness soaked through. Sam sucked lightly and moaned, like this was somehow pleasuring him. The vibrations combined with all the other sensations, and Wesley's eyes crossed.

Sam rearranged the fabric so Wesley's cock slid through the slit in the front. He moved like he was about to take it in his mouth again, but Wesley caught him by the shoulders. "Don't. I can't take it. I'll come right now."

Sam looked at him, eyes dark, lips parted, and hovering inches from Wesley's cock. "You can come. I want you to come."

Jesus Christ, this was the most willpower Wesley had ever exerted in his life. "Not like this. Not the first time."

His words hung strangely in the air. It took Wesley a second to understand why.

There's going to be a second time, and we both know it.

Sam sat up and yanked off his shirt. His torso—which was broad with rosy nipples that Wesley knew got hard at the slightest provocation—shouldn't have been fascinating. Wesley had seen Sam naked dozens of times. This should have been like going to a movie when he already knew the ending.

But it wasn't. It was like rewatching a classic that he got something new out of every time. It was rereading a favorite passage in a book because the familiar words always struck a chord. Wesley looked at Sam's bare body and saw him in a whole new way. As Sam's eyes swept over him in turn, Wesley felt in his bones that Sam was thinking the same thing.

"We need to get a lot more naked," Sam said, breathless.

"*Fuck* yeah." Wesley was already kicking off his pants.

He shucked everything on his body and flung it away. Sam started to push his bottoms down, but Wesley grabbed his thighs and pulled him forward, like he was yanking a tablecloth out from under a pyramid of glasses.

Sam fell back against the mattress. Wesley knelt between his legs and was given the divine and utterly satisfying pleasure of stripping him. He didn't do it slowly, but he did it with reverence, kissing Sam's hip bone on one side, then the other, followed by his thighs, and then his knees.

The touch was almost innocent, but the way Sam trembled under Wesley's lips made it obscene. By the end of it, Wesley was so turned on he couldn't see straight. Sam's cock—longer than Wesley's and flushed pink just like his face—was curving toward his belly.

Wesley tossed the last of their clothing aside and crawled on top. He moved up Sam's body, kissing as he went, until they were chest to chest. Sam watched him, eyes lidded, mouth parted. Right as Wesley went to kiss him, Sam rocked his torso under him. There was so much delicious friction—so much warm skin—Wesley's heart stuttered. When their groins met, and he felt the first slide of Sam's cock against his, he pulsed with desire.

"You feel so good," Wesley murmured, skimming his mouth along Sam's collarbone. "Can't wait to fuck you."

Sam got halfway through a moan before it abruptly cut off. "Wait." He pushed Wesley back until he could look him in the eye. "Do you think you're going to top?"

Wesley blinked, hearing screeching brakes in his head. "Well, yeah. I sorta assumed."

"What, because you're the extrovert, you automatically get to top? No way."

"Are you really arguing with me while our dicks are touching?"

"Damn straight I am."

Wesley rubbed his eyes and then leaned down, bringing their mouths within a hair's breadth. "Do you actually not want to bottom, or are you making a point?"

Sam frowned, which was an answer in and of itself. "We should decide the same way we've been deciding things for years."

It took Wesley a moment to realize what he meant. "You . . . you want to play Rock, Paper, Scissors for it?"

"You got a better idea?"

Wesley laughed, shaking his head. "All right. You're on. Count of three."

Sam held up a fist. "One."

Wesley joined him. "Two."

"Three!" they said together.

Wesley kept his hand balled up while Sam threw out two fingers.

"Ha!" Wesley tapped his fist. "Rock beats scissors."

"Damn." Sam pouted. "Guess you can't win 'em all."

Wesley ground their hips together. "Bet I can make it feel like you won."

Sam moaned and grabbed his shoulders, blunt fingernails digging in. "Oh fuck. I already do."

Shuddering, Wesley was overcome by a renewed wave of lust. "What next? I didn't think to pack condoms."

"Neither did I." Sam loosened his grip on Wesley's shoulders and dragged a hand up his throat until it rested against Wesley's pulse. "Or lube, for that matter."

"That I have, for all the good it does us." Wesley turned his face to kiss the palm of Sam's hand. "We don't have to fuck. We can fool around and get supplies in the next town."

"I don't want to wait. Not after all this. I've been tested since Michael, and he was my last partner. What about you?"

"I actually get tested regularly. It's like the one adulting thing I'm serious about. Everything's fine on my end." Wesley nipped Sam's palm. "I would have mentioned way before now if it weren't. I tell you everything."

Sam scratched his nails down the back of Wesley's neck. It was probably intended as revenge for the bite, but it made Wesley shiver. "I want to do this if you do."

"Oh, Sammy." Wesley buried his face in the crook of Sam's neck and breathed deep. "I *want*."

The mood shifted from playful to serious again when Wesley slid a hand behind one of Sam's knees and eased his leg up to his chest. "Do you ever finger yourself?"

Sam's breathing started coming faster as Wesley trailed a hand down the back of his thigh, heading between his legs. "A lot, actually. I'm really sensitive."

Wesley had to bite his lip to keep himself from getting totally sidetracked by that comment. "Good. That should make this easier. One sec." He reached over the side of the bed to where he'd conveniently tossed his bag, careful not to tumble over. The lube was in a side pocket. Once in hand, he got back into position and held it up for Sam to see. "You okay with this?"

Sam nodded. "I trust you." He relaxed, pliable beneath him.

Wesley had thought the difficult part about preparing Sam was going to be having the patience to get him wet and stretched enough. As it turned out, it was not orgasming from Sam's reactions alone. Wesley barely swiped his hole with a wet thumb, and Sam moaned like he'd touched his dick.

The first finger slid in easily, earning another honeyed groan from Sam. The second took a minute and a lot more lube, but it didn't seem to make Sam uncomfortable at all. If anything, his gasps and small, pleasured noises indicated that he could have been fingered open all day. Honestly, Wesley would have done it, but he'd never wanted to fuck someone this badly before. Saying he wanted to have sex with Sam was like saying he wanted to live.

Three fingers in, Sam started to cant down in time with Wesley's rhythm, and Wesley decided he'd had enough. "You ready?" *Please say yes, holy shit.*

Sam didn't speak. His eyes had been shut ever since Wesley had first started prepping him. He nodded, and it dislodged a bead of sweat from his brow. Wesley watched it track down his cheekbone and only barely resisted the urge to kiss it from his skin.

"Say yes, Sam. I need to hear you say it." *Need it in so many ways.*

"Yes." Sam opened his eyes a sliver, tongue darting out to wet his lips. "Do it. Fuck me, Wes."

Fuck, fuck, fuck, don't come now.

Wesley bit his own lip, fighting off the threat of orgasm. And he meant *threat*. When he finally came, there was a very good chance it was going to shatter him. Break him into tiny pieces, and Sam would be left to put him back together again, as he always did.

There probably should have been a pause before the big moment—a chance for them both to soak in the gravity of what they were doing—but after all this buildup, neither of them seemed to have the patience. Wesley kneeled between Sam's legs, and as he held the base of his dick steady, Sam mouthed, *Come on.* That was all the invitation he needed. He lined himself up and sank in smoothly.

They moaned in delicious unison. Wesley had to pull back out and add more lube, but when he thrust in again, he went deeper. Sam spread his thighs wider and let his head loll back. He was gorgeous: flushed, hair dark with sweat, throat long and covered with little red marks where Wesley had sucked on him. Looking at him was almost as good as fucking him, and *holy hell*, did it feel good to fuck him. Better than Wesley had ever dreamed.

It had to be because it was Sam. The knowledge plucked something deep in Wesley.

"Sam, I'm not going to last." He shuddered, only barely holding himself still. "And I don't think I can be gentle."

"Don't be." Sam wriggled under him. "Don't you dare. I'm not fragile. You know I'm not."

That was the weirdest mixture of hot and sweet. After all the affection they'd shared over the years, this was one area where they could be rough with each other. Wesley knew he could give it to Sam fast and dirty, and Sam would take it, would ask for more.

So, Wesley did.

He set a quick, deep rhythm, one that wrung sounds out of him that would have been embarrassing in front of anyone else. Sam was every bit as vocal, garbling together swears and groans and, "Oh, Wes, God. Don't stop, don't stop."

But it was when Wesley changed angles, leaning down to bring their mouths together, open and sloppy, that Sam got *loud*. He was pliant under him, but hard in all the places Wesley wanted it: the hand that bruised the back of Wesley's neck, and the dick between their bodies. That had to be why Sam was losing it—Wesley's stomach was rubbing his cock with every thrust, slick with sweat, probably almost as good as getting to fuck someone.

The thought was obliterated before it could fully form by the bone-deep pleasure that sizzled through Wesley as he sank in and ground his hips. The sensation tightened in him, building with what felt like every breath he took.

"Gonna come," he managed to mumble. "Gonna— *Sammy*."

Sam had thrown a leg around him and was using it to pull him farther in. But that wasn't possible. Wesley was so deep in him, his balls were rubbing against Sam's ass crack. The sentiment of it, though—the profundity of that simple desire—lit Wesley's nerve endings up like a switchboard.

"I'm close." Sam words shook along with his body. "So close. Right there, Wes. Fuck."

Thank God, because Wesley was going to *die*.

He slid a hand between them, searching for Sam's dick. He didn't have the cognizance to jerk him off in any consistent way, but he had to try. The second his hand touched Sam's cock, however, Sam pulsed. He couldn't feel his come—too much sweat and heat to tell anything apart—but Sam's dick twitched with the force of it. Sam himself went rigid beneath him.

It was so raw, so visceral, Wesley orgasmed before he could prepare himself for it. He came and came and came, until he couldn't anymore. It left him shaking and so sensitive he could scream, but his throat was raw. He didn't know what he'd said during, and he didn't care. If Sam made fun of him later, Wesley would shove him off the bed.

Assuming he ever got his strength back. His arms gave out, and he very nearly crushed Sam. He managed to roll to the side with the last of his strength. He sucked in as much air as he could get, mind deliciously blank. Distantly, he realized his stomach was coated in Sam's come, and his come was in Sam, and *holy shit, he'd just had sex with Sam.*

He should say something. His mind offered up a surge of helpful feedback.

Sam beat him to it. He sounded dazed. "That . . ."

Wesley nodded, eyes on the ceiling. "Yeah."

"That was . . ."

"Yeah."

"Well." Sam blew out a breath. "I guess we're not just friends anymore."

CHAPTER NINE

They ended up extending their stay, for no reason other than they couldn't seem to leave their hotel room. Every time they started to get dressed and packed, one of them would pounce on the other, and then they'd end up in bed again. Before long, they lost track of time, forgoing silly things like sleep and food in the name of feeding the new hunger they'd discovered.

Sam had never had so much sex in his life. Sex in every way he could imagine. On every flat surface in their room, both horizontal and vertical. It was like he'd spent his whole life eating stale bread, and now someone had put a whole feast in front of him. Neither of them could seem to get enough.

The quantity alone was staggering, but the fact that it was Wesley added a whole other level. Sam had always appreciated Wesley's quick tongue, but that took on new meaning when Wesley cornered him in the shower stall, dropped to his knees, and gave him a blowjob that left him incoherent.

When Sam had collapsed onto what was now *their* bed after the fifth—sixth?—time they'd had sex, Wesley had only paused long enough to catch his breath. Then he'd wrapped a weak, sweaty Sam up in the sheets, tucking in his feet and arranging the pillows exactly the way he liked. Wesley had done it before Sam could think to ask. Sam was starting to understand why friends with benefits was such a popular arrangement. Wesley knew him inside and out, quite literally now.

The most fun, however, was when Sam took charge. Wesley was a sexy, confident top, but holy shit, as a bottom, he was insatiable. When Sam got him into the right position—on his knees, face pressed into the mattress, ass up—Wesley moaned so loud, Sam thought they were going to get noise complaints.

The little whimpering sounds he made when he was about to come were musical. They brought out something in Sam, a darker desire that had teeth. Sam spent half an hour slow-fucking him until Wesley was nearly in tears. Sam was charged by the end of it, all his nerves singing. Wesley had begged for more. He seemed content to spend all day sprawled out on the bed, Sam's hand on the back of his neck, holding him down as Sam fucked him deeply and with purpose.

When Sam finally turned serious and got them both off with fast, punishing thrusts, Wesley murmured something like, "Want you in me forever." They'd both babbled so many things in the throes, it was hard to take any of it at face value, but that one stuck with Sam.

It was easy to talk about forever when they were sequestered in their own little world, sleeping in a tangled pile and getting on a first-name basis with the pizza-delivery girl. But eventually, they were going to have to leave this room, and when that happened, the line they'd crossed—the one between friendship and something more—would have to be dealt with.

Sam had made no attempt to talk about what they were doing, mostly because he didn't know what to say. They were having sex, but they weren't lovers. He loved Wesley, but he wasn't *in love* with him. At least, he didn't think he was. That line wasn't as distinct as the others.

His brain turned into a too-small cage full of irate parrots every time he thought about what this could mean. If this was just sex, Sam could handle that. Sex wasn't scary or life-altering, like relationships were. It might make things a little awkward later, but he was confident they'd bounce back.

However, if one of them wanted a relationship—or worse, both of them—that would be when shit got complicated. Sam had thought once that no force on earth was strong enough to make him jeopardize his friendship with Wesley. Well, the joke was on him, because it seemed his sex drive had been taking steroids.

This all started because Wesley told you not to overthink it. Maybe that advice can carry you through to the end.

At one point, Sam rolled over and was blinded by sunlight streaming through the cracks around the curtains. Holy shit. What day was it?

"Wesley." Sam sat up in bed. "Wes, you awake?"

Next to him, Wesley was lying on his stomach, still mostly in the position in which Sam had last fucked him. He grunted but didn't speak. His lips were swollen from all the kissing they'd done, and there were vivid red nail marks on his shoulder blades. Sam's face heated. When had he done that?

He rooted around for his phone and found it on the floor next to the bed. He hit the home button and cursed. "We're late. We missed checkout again. If we're going to make it to New Orleans, we have to get driving. The wedding's in a little over a week."

Wesley grunted again but didn't pick his face up from the pillow. Sam's eyes lingered on the dusting of freckles across his shoulders. The urge to lean over and kiss them struck him like a gong, but he fought it off. They *had* to leave this room. What could he say to motivate Wesley to move?

Sam had no clue where the sudden burst of bravery came from, but it loosened the words that had been clinging to his tongue. "Wesley, what are we doing?"

"Sleeping." Wesley blew out a breath. "Or trying to."

"No, I mean what are we *doing*? What is this?"

Voicing the question aloud was dangerous, but it was the lesser of two evils. What he really wanted to know was if it meant anything, but he wasn't there yet. He'd have to know his own feelings in that regard before he could question Wesley.

Asking would change their friendship, but the answer could destroy it, and *that* couldn't happen. It just couldn't. Sam held his breath while he waited for Wesley to speak.

Wesley's response was anticlimactic. He didn't so much as open his eyes. "It's sex, Sammy. We took a long trip together, in extremely close quarters, with a no-hookups clause. We assembled all the ingredients; we just didn't know what we were cooking. Looking back, I dunno how I didn't see this coming, pun intended. Let's not overthink it, okay? People do weird shit when they're out of their element. When we get home, I bet we'll look back on this and laugh."

"You really think so?"

Wesley made a dismissive sound. "Dude, what are we?"

Sam answered automatically. "Friends."

"What have we *always* been?"

"Friends."

"Exactly. A little vacation sex never hurt anyone. Or a lot of vacation sex, in our case."

Wesley laughed. It rang hollow in Sam's ear, but his words offered Sam something he hadn't realized he needed: an excuse. For the past day, his heart had been a rabbit skittering from corner to corner, looking for a place to hide. Sam *needed* Wesley, needed his friendship. Especially right now. The closer they got to Montana—and the wedding, and Sam's family—the more necessary Wesley's support was.

Was Sam the most selfish person in the world for leaping at the opportunity to shelve this for now? When a solution as simple as store-bought pie came along, it took more energy than Sam had to resist it. How bad could what they were doing be if it felt this good?

A voice in his head whispered that eventually, they'd find out.

Before he could start thinking again, a knock at the door broke the spell.

Wesley finally lifted his head. His cheek had marks folded into it from the pillow. "Whossat?"

"Judging by how loud you were being before, it's the police, and they think I murdered you."

Wesley took his pillow and shoved it into Sam's face. Sam felt the mattress depress, and then he heard halting footsteps and a muttered, "Holy shit, my legs aren't working."

"Sorry," Sam said without an ounce of contrition.

Wesley, still naked, looked through the peephole. "It's housekeeping." He shouted through the door, "Do not disturb!"

A thick Southern drawl answered him. "It's checkout time, sir. You gotta pack up or pay up."

"Fuck." Wesley glanced at Sam. "Is there any way we can stay another day?"

Sam's body urged him to say yes, but in his head, a clock was counting down the few days they had left until the twenty-second. The steady *tick tick tick* prompted him to shake his head. "I'm afraid not."

"Damn." He shouted through the door again. "Give us one minute, please!" When he turned back, his eyes swept over the room, growing wide. "Do we have time to straighten up? Because honestly, housekeeping shouldn't have to deal with this."

Both beds were disasters. The sheets were tangled, a pillow had started leaking feathers at some point, and Sam didn't want to think about the various bodily fluids. None of the furniture was where it had been twenty-four hours ago, particularly the bureau that had slid across the floor a solid foot. The bathroom counter looked like something had crashed into it, which was partially true. Wesley had tackled Sam against the sink and pinned him down. Sam's smudged handprint was still on the mirror right where he'd braced himself while Wesley—

Another knock on the door.

"We'll tip them." Sam wobbled to his feet. "I'll leave a ten on the nightstand."

Wesley yanked his boxers out from under the bed and crinkled his nose. "Make it a twenty."

They packed hastily. Sam was positive they were forgetting something, but after running over a quick mental list in his head, he concluded it was their dignity. When they were dressed and ready, they opened the door and edged sheepishly past a woman with a cart of cleaning supplies. Sam might have been imagining it, but the wry look she gave them suggested she knew exactly what they'd been doing.

If she doesn't now, she will as soon as she walks in.

Sam had showered multiple times and changed clothes, yet he could still smell sex on himself. And Wesley too. When they got in the car and closed the doors, it intensified, like stepping into a hot nightclub.

"How far is the drive to New Orleans?" Sam asked, feigning nonchalance.

"Three hours." Wesley shot him a grin. "Think we'll make it?"

"We'd better. The spirit is willing, but the flesh is sore and has a hell of a kink in its neck."

Wesley chuckled and leaned over. For a second, it seemed like he was going to kiss Sam. Sam's heart thudded hard, but at the last second, Wesley seemed to realize what he was doing. He pulled back, eyes wide, and cleared his throat. "Let's get going."

It seems we've hit our first boundary. Kissing in public is something couples do. Not us.

The engine roared to life, sounding as good as ... well, not new, but as good as two days ago. They made a brief stop for food—something they both desperately needed—and then they were off.

They passed the long drive in much the same way as before. Talking. Listening to the radio. Watching the landscape change outside their windows. Trees and dirt roads melded into asphalt and gorgeous glimpses of the Gulf of Mexico. They laughed and teased each other, as always. Sam begged Wesley to stop for coffee, which led to a round of good-natured bickering about who'd had to take the most pee breaks so far.

It would have been like nothing had changed, only now when Sam laughed, his abs burned. Sitting for three hours was no picnic. When they stopped to get gas, climbing out of the car was almost too much for his aching thighs.

While Wesley pumped gas, Sam washed the windshield. Like a choreographed dance, they glanced at each other. Wesley had his sunglasses on, but Sam swore he could see a twinkle in his eye that said he was feeling it too. Could Wesley read Sam's face right now? Could he see the mark he'd left on Sam, deeper than skin? Even if they didn't kiss in public, Sam would feel the truth every time he moved.

The question bubbled up in his head again, the one he didn't dare ask.

Do you want something more?

So much for his whole don't-overthink-it plan. He should've known that'd stop being an option as soon as they couldn't distract themselves with sex.

"You need water or anything?" Wesley jerked his head toward the gas station. "I'm gonna run in and use their bathroom. I can grab you something."

"No, thanks. I'm all set."

As he watched Wesley go, Sam resolved to do something that was long overdue. He was going to call his sister.

They reached New Orleans on a gorgeous Friday afternoon. Wesley had expected that after all the buildup, the city wouldn't be able to stand up to the hype. More than a decade after Katrina had devastated it, the effects were still visible in the form of abandoned houses and crumbling steps that led to buildings that weren't there anymore.

However, once they drove over a bridge traversing a beautiful, snaking river, and it pointed them toward the sparkling heart of the city, Wesley finally understood that expression. This place had heart. He could see it in the faces of the people on the street, hear it in the muffled music drifting from the French Quarter.

"This," he said to Sam as he navigated the old cobblestone streets, "is going to be *epic*."

Their hotel was a little B&B downtown. Wesley had wanted to stay in the historic part of the city to get the "authentic experience," but according to Sam, prices there were outrageous.

They'd booked their hotel back in Charlotte—before they'd started hooking up—and though they'd pushed back their reservation date, they hadn't changed anything else. That meant it had two beds. It was silly to be disappointed, but when they walked in, and Sam threw his bag on a different bed from Wesley, emotion welled up in him. Emotion he could neither name nor justify.

Before he could think about it, he was on Sam. He kissed him, quick and eager. His lips were dry, and his jaw was sore from the sheer amount of making out they'd done in the past two days, but he ignored the dull pain and poured all his odd feelings into the kiss.

Sam responded immediately, surrendering to it. It floored Wesley every time. Sam's hands dragged up Wesley's chest to cup his face before tangling in his hair. Wesley could write sonnets about the way Sam raked his nails over Wesley's scalp with the exact right amount of pressure. And about the way he leaned into Wesley, their bodies molding together just right.

Wesley was about to break the kiss when Sam reached for his belt. Quick fingers had it open before Wesley registered what he was doing.

"Whoa, wait." Wesley grabbed his hands, chuckling. "Eager much? I know it's been four whole hours, but we have a lot of city to see. Save it for later."

His tone was light, but Sam's brow furrowed. "What?"

"I was thinking we'd hit up Bourbon Street first. Unless you want to go somewhere else?"

Sam's eyes were narrow with confusion. "You kissed me."

"Uh, yeah. So?"

Sam took a breath. "Why did you kiss me if you don't want sex?"

Oh.

The question smacked Wesley across the face. It occurred to him, far too late, that friends didn't kiss each other randomly. Even friends with benefits generally did it because they were hoping it would lead to something else.

Kissing someone for no reason is what couples do.

Shit. Wesley looked down at the carpeted floor. The closer they got physically, the more impossible it became to follow his own advice. Sam had never been the sort to wing it. Pretty soon, Sam was going to want to talk about this for real, and with Wesley doing things like kissing him for the simple pleasure of it, he couldn't blame him.

Which meant Wesley was going to have to figure out what the hell he was doing. His entire life, that was the one thing he'd never managed.

"Right." He coughed. "Sorry about that. Won't happen again."

"No, it's fine. My lips are getting a little chapped, but I don't mind."

You should mind. You should keep your distance.

Wesley clapped his hands together. "So, Bourbon Street? Beignets? There's Jackson Square too. It's still light out enough that we can go see some of the local artists."

Sam's face showed only the faintest twinge of disappointment. "Yeah, okay. Is your phone charged? Mine's dead after navigating through all that backcountry. Bad reception drains the battery apparently."

"Yeah, I'll bring it."

As they got ready to leave, Wesley's thoughts whirred. He'd made a lot of wishes over the years. Winning the lottery. Landing a job as a video game tester. Going back to kindergarten with all the knowledge he had now and convincing the world he was a prodigy. But if a genie had appeared right then and offered him one wish, Wesley would want to know what the hell he should do next.

He'd never had this before. Not just the sex—although that was a fucking cut above—but sex that gave him a deeper understanding of the person he was having it with. Wesley knew everything about Sam now. He'd joked about knowing him better than he knew himself in the past, but boy had he been wrong.

Now, he knew how Sam's skin tasted, what got him so turned on his eyes glazed over, and a hundred other nuances. It was the knowing that muddled the waters for Wesley. Because he'd loved Sam so much before, it hadn't seemed possible for that feeling to get any deeper. He'd called this *vacation sex*, something they'd laugh about later. He'd been lying through his teeth. Now that he'd had this, how could he give it up?

That scared him more than anything, because Wesley was still keeping a secret, and that meant this couldn't become more than sex. Not right now, anyway.

Sam peered at him. "Something wrong?"

It was frightening how easily the lie rolled off his tongue. "No. I'm great."

"Me too." Sam's bright smile stung Wesley's eyes.

They took the bus into town, and then a struggle presented itself: there was *so much* they wanted to do. The Museum of Death. The St. Louis Cathedral. The French Quarter. Countless little shops, art displays, and beautiful cemeteries. Hell, walking around and looking at old buildings could fill an entire day.

As they passed Café Du Monde, and the smell of sweet, fresh bread filled Wesley's nose, he nudged Sam with an elbow. "You know how you loved Atlanta?"

"Yeah?"

"This is my Atlanta."

They spent the next few hours wandering around, eating too much, and looking at absolutely everything. Wesley got his fortune told by a tarot card reader. When the woman—who was willowy as a tree and never spoke above a whisper—predicted there was someone special in his life, he winked at Sam. Sam's face turned red as the crawfish they'd had for a late lunch.

When night settled in, they googled the best bars and did a mini pub crawl. For once, Wesley didn't want to party. He tried one bayou-themed beer at each stop and then spent the evening talking to locals about the city. The scars Katrina had left were as much in the people as they were in the land, and Wesley teared up at a number of stories about people banding together: neighbors helping neighbors.

Sam, who also seemed disinterested in drinking, leaned over to Wesley at one point. "We didn't get to see a fraction of what this city has to offer today."

Hope blossomed inside Wesley. "Any chance we could stay a little longer?"

"I don't see how we have a choice." He grinned.

Wesley dragged him back to the hotel room, where they had sex that was less rigorous than before at the behest of their sore muscles, but no less enthused. After, they settled in separate beds. For all of three minutes. Then Sam crawled under the sheets with Wesley, claiming he was cold despite the fact that this was Louisiana in mid-June.

In truth, he was burning hot: chest, groin, and lips. The latter found Wesley's in the dark for a chaste kiss. Wesley rolled over to make room for him without comment. They'd been sleeping naked, and as Wesley pulled Sam to his chest, the familiar twinge of arousal was joined by something else. Something that ached and soothed at the same time. Something Wesley felt all the way through him, in his limbs, his lungs, his blood.

I am so screwed, he thought as Sam's face found its way into the crook of his neck.

They spent the whole weekend like that. They strolled along streets that'd been baked warm by the sun, drank sweet tea, and let the smell of Cajun cooking guide them. A corner deli came to know them as the "road trip guys," and they stopped correcting people who assumed they were boyfriends.

Three days was the longest they'd spent exploring any one city, but they were happy, *happy* days. Every morning, when housekeeping came in to clean the room, only one of the beds had rumpled sheets.

With every passing second that Wesley allowed this to go on, he was playing a dangerous game. But being with Sam was so . . . easy. Simple. It always had been. They were puzzle pieces that were shaped totally different, but that was what made them fit. It was only natural their chemistry had extended to the bedroom and beyond.

Wesley couldn't even begrudge the sleep he'd been losing. He was exhausted to his bones, but every time he rolled over—sweaty and sated—and Sam tangled their limbs together, Wesley would conk out like a light. He didn't usually remember his dreams, but now they were technicolor. Sensual. Heat and salt and big, brown eyes.

"I don't want to go home." Sam's whispered voice was almost lost to the shadows around them.

Wesley hummed and felt it pass from his chest to Sam's too-hot back. "To Montana or to Pennsylvania?"

"Both. I want to stay like this."

Wesley understood that sentiment well. Being on this trip was like being in a separate reality. Here, they didn't have to worry about things like rent or job interviews or what they were going to do the next time one of them got hit on. Wrapped up together in a cozy bed, it was easy to believe this would all work out.

In Wesley's head, the list of things he loved about Sam was growing daily. His hands were at the very top right now. Wesley loved how sleepy and slow they were when he woke Sam up in the morning. He loved how they turned eager when Sam remembered where he was and who he was with. He loved how Sam only called him "Wes" now when they were alone. Like an inside joke.

And Wesley hated, absolutely *loathed*, knowing that soon, he'd have to shatter Sam's image of him forever. Because if there was one thing he knew about secrets, it was that they *always* got out.

It wasn't like you didn't want to go on this trip, his brain whispered to him in his half-asleep haze. *You set yourself up for an inevitable big reveal. You're about to sleep in the bed you made.*

For some reason, the balloon metaphor he'd joked about with Sam floated into his head. He imagined Sam standing under a blue sky, holding a yellow balloon tied with red string. In this context, the metaphor suddenly took on horrifying new meaning.

Wesley really was the balloon. Fragile. Flighty. Ready to pop at the slightest provocation. He brought fun into Sam's life, sure, and Sam kept him tethered, but what if, one day, Sam couldn't anymore?

What if Wesley got caught up in something so reckless but subtle—something that was so hard to see, it'd taken his own parents years to notice—that Sam didn't realize he was being pulled off the ground? What if Sam purposefully ignored it, because he loved Wesley and wanted to think the best of him?

If he dragged Sam with him, then when he popped, they'd both plummet to the ground. That was what Wesley did after all: he made Sam forget about the gravity that'd kept him safe all this time. If Wesley went flying, Sam would follow, and then they'd both be crushed.

I can't hurt Sam. I'd end our friendship sooner. I'd die sooner. It's like I told Sam before. Until I get my shit together, I can't date anyone seriously. I never should have let this get this far.

Sam shifted in his sleep. Without waking up, he pressed back against Wesley. Their bodies were fitted together, close as nesting dolls. As if that comforted him, Sam instantly stilled. Wesley's pulse was deafening. He eased away from Sam as gently as he could and rolled onto his other side.

How much longer can I keep pretending? What will happen when my secret gets out? Sam isn't a risk-taker. He's careful and grounded. He's not going to understand why I let this happen. I've seen how Sam reacts to situations he can't control. He avoids them. What if he starts avoiding me?

The longer Wesley acted like everything was fine, the worse the lie got. But it also meant they could stay like this. Wesley could have Sam, for a little bit longer. He'd said this trip was about making memories. Maybe if he tried hard enough, he could make a lifetime of them before it all came crashing down.

CHAPTER TEN

Thanks to the extra days they'd spent in both Alabama and Louisiana, Sam was forced, for the first time since they'd left, to spend all day driving. If they were going to make it to the Pacific Ocean, *and* reach Montana before Jessica left on her honeymoon, they needed to get serious. There wasn't much between them and California—mostly desert and woods in alternating swathes—but with the help of google, they cobbled together a plan.

They rose at the crack of dawn on Monday and drove for eight hours, plus time for breaks, to Austin, Texas. They hit traffic going into Houston, and again going out, which delayed them almost as much as Wesley's constant pee breaks. For some reason, he'd been chugging water all day. Possibly because he kept sweating no matter how high he turned the air on. Sam sincerely hoped he hadn't caught some sort of bug from all the seafood they'd eaten.

Regardless, by the time they got to Austin—which someone they'd met in a bar back in Louisiana had referred to as "Texas's liberal, gay oasis"—it was too late for them to see much of the city. Wesley wanted to check it out anyway, so Sam told him to go ahead. He had something he needed to do.

He walked to a nearby park and found a bench in a secluded garden area. A nearby old-timey lamp lit up purple azalea bushes in soft yellow light. There was no one around, exactly as Sam had hoped. With five days to go until her wedding, Sam was confident Jessica would answer her phone. Though whether she'd like what Sam had to say was another matter.

True to form, Jessica answered on the first ring. "This had better be you calling to tell me there's not going to be an empty seat at my reception."

"Hello to you too." Sam tried to keep his tone light, but it came out flatter than the roadkill they'd spotted outside Audubon.

"Samuel Patrick Cooper, my wedding is on Saturday. *Saturday*. If you're calling to tell me anything that isn't good news, then I have to hang up on you."

"I'm coming to your wedding," Sam said quickly. "I'm sorry for not telling you sooner, but honestly, I wasn't sure I was going to make it."

"All right! I knew you'd come through. What made you change your mind?"

"Wesley. I'm bringing him as my date."

Jessica hissed like an agitated cat. "You didn't RSVP that you were bringing a plus-one. Actually, you didn't RSVP at all."

"He said he told you he was my plus-one."

"How was I supposed to know he was being serious? I dunno if you noticed, but Wesley's native tongue is goofball. I wasn't sure *you* were coming, let alone him."

"Shit. Can't you squeeze him in? He's the only reason I got up the courage to make the trip. He practically stuffed me into a car. He came up with this whole road trip adventure to entice me. I'm calling you from Texas right now."

"Hm." There was a pause. "Well, in that case, he can sit at the bar."

For some reason, that image bothered Sam, but he couldn't put a finger on why. He brushed it off. "Do me a favor and don't tell our parents I'm going to be there. If I know they're anticipating me, I'm going to be a ball of nerves. In fact, don't tell anyone but the caterer."

"Your secret's safe with me, little bro. I can't tell you how much this means to me. I was scared to death you weren't going to make it."

"I'm sorry. When Wesley was talking me into the trip, he told me there was no way I could miss this, and he was right. Though I'm afraid that's not the only thing I'm calling to tell you." He sucked in a breath. "Wesley and I have been hooking up."

There was dead silence. Sam checked his phone to see if the call had disconnected, but Jessica's contact picture smiled back at him. "You there, Jess?"

His question was met with five solid seconds of wordless screaming.

Sam dropped his phone. It landed on the grass with a muted *thud*. He scooped it back up. "Jessica, what the hell?"

"I'm sorry. I'm so happy, I can't contain myself." She let out another shriek. "You and Wesley? Santa read my list!"

"What's that supposed to mean?"

"Are you kidding me? I've been rooting for you guys for *years*, and now it's finally happened!"

Sam shook his head, though she couldn't see him. "You can't be serious. Wesley's my friend. I've told you before how annoyed we get when people assume we're together."

"Yeah, I've heard your spiel. You say that like you think it's your responsibility to prove to the world that you can be just friends. News flash, bro: it's not. That's not your job at all. The part of the world that isn't ignorant already knows gay men can be friends. You don't have to deny yourself happiness to prove a point."

Well, fuck. That made a lot of sense. Sam frowned. "But how can you want me to be with Wesley? He's your friend too. He had Thanksgiving at our house last year, for Christ's sake. You two ganged up on me when I mentioned I was thinking of getting highlights."

"You're welcome for that, by the way." She laughed. "And that's why it's so perfect that you two got together. All the best relationships start with friendship. Noah and I were friends first."

Sam sighed and rubbed his temple. "Wesley and I aren't *together*. We're hooking up. You're getting way ahead of us."

"You're right. Let's backtrack. Start at the beginning, and don't leave anything out."

Since Sam couldn't very well tell his sister about masturbating in Wesley's car, or the two-day sexathon, or all the hooking up that had followed, he kept it general. The road trip. Being together twenty-four seven. How he'd started looking at Wesley differently. And finally, the past few days.

"So, what's the problem?" Jessica asked. "It sounds like you two get along great, have killer chemistry, and already know each other's strengths and weaknesses. That's pretty much the ideal recipe for love."

"It's not that simple. Wesley hasn't expressed any interest in dating. In fact, the way he tells it, this is all going to stop as soon as we get home. He thinks it's some sort of vacation fling."

"What do you think?"

"I think . . . I don't want to ruin our friendship."

There was a bark of laughter that nearly startled the phone out of Sam's hand again. "Sam, you're joking, right? That's the oldest excuse in the book. That's a bad movie trope."

"No, Jessica, you don't get it." He scrubbed a hand down his face and steeled himself. "When I say I don't want to mess things up, I mean I *can't*. I need Wesley."

Jessica paused. "I don't understand."

Sam took a steadying breath. "In college, Wesley probably kept me from falling into a deep depression. I didn't make friends easily, and I was across the country from my family, so my support network was almost nonexistent. My social drive can get unhealthily low if I let it. Like, not-talk-to-another-human-for-weeks low. I'd even say I used to isolate myself. No one could reject me if I never interacted with anyone, right?"

"Right," Jessica said, sounding cautious.

"I'd go whole weekends without leaving my room under the pretense that I had to study. Wesley was the only one who could coax me out of the house. Or he'd waste a perfectly good Friday night watching movies with me when he could have been out, so I wouldn't have to be alone. Sometimes, he was the only reason I remembered to shower. I definitely wouldn't have met Michael without him, though that didn't work out so well in the end."

"Are you still like that? You need Wesley to be social?"

"It's not that extreme anymore, thank God. It got better as I got older, or maybe Wesley was a good influence. I'm not sure. The point is, I honestly don't know what I would do without him. Who would convince me to live my damn life? Who would be my best friend? What if I fell back into those old destructive habits? It's not one-way either. I keep him from doing anything *too* reckless. There's a balance, or at least, there was. Now everything's all out of whack, and it scares me."

"Wow, Sam. I knew Wesley was important to you, but I had no idea you felt this way."

"Being with him these past few days has been wonderful, but if it's between whatever this is and our friendship, I pick our friendship.

No contest. I already lost Michael and alienated people I love because I wasn't decisive. I won't lose Wesley too. I've learned my lesson. I think I should end this before it implodes."

A rare cool breeze ruffled his hair. It clung to his sweaty shirt, making him shiver. It felt weirdly ominous when paired with this heavy conversation.

Jessica was quiet for a long moment. "Well, little bro, when you put it like that, I suppose 'I don't want to ruin our friendship' isn't such a bad excuse after all. You make it sound like this is life or death."

"At times, it feels like it is." Sam sighed. "So, you think I should end it too?"

"Absolutely not."

"What?" Sam switched ears. "How can you say that?"

"Because it sounds to me like you think your options are be friends with Wesley *or* hook up with him. Did it ever occur to you that you can do both?"

"What, you mean like a friends-with-benefits thing? Those never work long-term."

"No, I mean a tell-Wesley-how-you-really-feel thing."

"That's the problem. I don't know how I feel. I have no idea what I want out of this, other than I want to keep Wesley in my life."

"I think you know perfectly well how you feel, but you're afraid to let yourself feel it. Sam, do you love him?"

"Of course I do. He's my best friend."

"Okay, let me rephrase. Are you *in* love with him?"

The question shouldn't have hit Sam as hard as it did, especially since he'd asked himself that same thing three days ago, but this time it made his chest ache. He spent a minute thinking about it before he answered. "I genuinely don't know. I only recently started thinking about him like that. I'd have to spend some time with him as a boyfriend to know for sure, but . . . I think I easily could love him."

Actually, now that the thought was in his head, Sam could imagine falling so hard and fast for Wesley, he'd be like a meteor crashing to Earth. It'd make him dizzy, same as the first time they'd kissed. He'd be light-headed and giddy with it.

Holy shit, I'm in way over my head.

Jessica tsked. "I think you're doing the thing again."

"What thing?"

"The nonconfrontational thing where you avoid risks at all costs. You tend to play it safe, Sam. Always have. Doesn't that make you wonder how many opportunities you've missed because you were too afraid to go for it?"

Sam let out a tight breath. "I think about that all the time."

"Well, this is your chance to not let it happen again. You say you've learned your lesson, but I think you learned the wrong one. You don't need to end things like you did with Michael. You need to take the plunge. I understand why you're scared, but what you stand to gain is worth the risk. You and Wesley are perfect for each other, and I think deep down you know that. I'm saying this as your big sister: this time, you need to be brave."

Her words tumbled around in the cement mixer that was Sam's brain. She was right, but fear still gripped his ribs and squeezed. "I don't know if I can be."

"You can. It's been in you this whole time, Sam. Waiting for the right motivation, and trust me, Wesley is right." She paused. "Although, there is one other thing you really need to do."

Please say fake my death and start a new life in Mexico. "What's that?"

"You need to learn to live without Wesley."

"Uh, sis, I don't know if you were listening before, but losing Wesley is exactly what I'm trying *not* to do."

"That's not how life works, little bro. Let's say you two go back to being friends, and tomorrow, he gets a job in Chicago, or wherever. What are you going to do? Move with him? Ask him to stay?"

"Um." Sam didn't have a good answer to that.

"Or what about when one of you gets married? Adopts some babies? Builds a whole other life that doesn't revolve around hanging out in bars and playing video games? Take it from someone who's about to get hitched: it changes things. Wesley won't always be available to be your social crutch. You have to function fully on your own. Otherwise, regardless of if you two are friends or lovers or whatever, your relationship won't be healthy. You can't depend on each other forever."

Sam was momentarily stunned into silence by how utterly right she was. "Jesus."

"Nope, just a know-it-all sister." There was a sound on the other end of the line like muffled talking. "Noah's home. He says there's something wrong with the centerpieces, which means I have to go have a heart attack."

"Okay. I appreciate you taking the time to talk to me."

"Anything for my precious baby brother. And honestly, the gossip perked me right up. Do you mind if I tell Noah?"

Sam's heart sputtered. "Please don't. Not until I get my head on straight."

"All right. But once I'm married, all bets are off. Apparently, married people tell each other everything."

A memory flashed before Sam's eyes. Wesley, naked on top of him, kissing his palm and smiling so sweetly it made Sam's entire body throb. *"I tell you everything."*

"You've given me a lot to think about, Jess. Thank you. I can't wait to see you at the wedding."

"You too, bro. Love you."

"Love you. Bye."

Sam hung up and let his arm go limp. It fell to the bench beside him, while his eyes drifted up to the sky. Shreds of cloud drifted over a fat moon. The biggest and brightest stars punched through the light pollution and glinted in a sea of charcoal.

His sister's words echoed in his head. *"You need to be brave."*

It was funny: when he had to buck up and get something done, he usually got moral support from Wesley. This time, he'd have to find the strength within himself. A daunting task, to say the least.

But first, he had to decide if pursuing something with Wesley was really what he wanted. Jessica's point about not owing the world a romance-free gay relationship had hit hard, but it was still an enormous paradigm shift. Thinking of Wesley as anything other than a friend after all these years was going to take some getting used to.

He also had to ask Wesley what he wanted. This whole issue was moot if Wesley had meant what he'd said. *"It's sex, Sammy. Let's not overthink it."*

This is making my head hurt. I should go back to the room and turn in early.

All the late-night activities had been adding up, in more ways than one. Sam had noticed a layer of fat working its way onto his stomach during the first week of the trip, thanks to all the greasy food. But now that Wesley and he were having sex several times a day, it was completely gone.

In fact, Sam—who had always been more of a cardio guy than a weight lifter—had glanced down once while getting dressed and had seen defined abs, even though he wasn't flexing. He supposed the moral of the story was sex did a body good. Although with Wesley, it was unlike any he'd had before. Certain aspects of Wesley's personality were more prominent in bed, while others faded. He tended to take charge, like in "real" life, but he was also a better listener. God knew he could play Sam like a damn fiddle.

Stop thinking about sex, or you're going to cause a public scene.

Sam thought about baseball for the remainder of the walk back to the room. They'd booked a cheap chain hotel, which felt a little odd after the variety of colorful places they'd stayed recently. There were no hand-knitted blankets or needlepoint pillows. Instead, the beds bore plain, white sheets, and the wall art was tastefully bland.

They'd dropped the pretense and had booked a room with one queen-sized bed. On Sam's side was his laptop. He flipped it open and checked his notifications. The comments on their pictures were more of the same. People wanted to know where they were now, what they were doing, if they'd gotten married yet. If Sam said yes, would anyone doubt it for a second?

He grabbed his phone and uploaded some of the photos they'd taken that day. They weren't exciting—they'd been driving for eight hours, after all—but there were some cute ones of them together.

Wesley had taken a selfie of him kissing Sam's cheek, complete with obnoxious smooching noises, while Sam had pretended he was focused on driving. Sam's expression was serious, except for one side of his mouth that had turned up. A second after Wesley had taken the photo, Sam had burst out laughing, unable to contain it anymore.

A thought flashed into Sam's mind as if someone had lobbed it into his skull. *If Wesley and I dated, what would change? Would we do anything that we're not already doing?*

When he thought of it like that, it didn't seem so scary.

Right on cue, the lock clicked, and in waltzed Wesley. "Sammy, I'm home!"

"Hey." Sam closed his laptop. "You're back early."

Wesley dropped onto the bed without taking his shoes off. "I was bored without you. Every time I saw something cool, I turned to tell you, and you weren't there. What were you doing?"

"Oh, I, uh . . . found a park and went for a walk. After being stuck in the car all day, I needed to stretch my legs. I finally called Jessica too. She says thank you for dragging me to the wedding."

"Your legs don't need to be stretched." Wesley inched closer. His face was red. "They're nice legs. Perfectly stretchy."

"You are drunk, my friend."

"Yes, I am!" Wesley stuck a finger up. "And you should get drunk too."

"It's a Monday night."

"I keep telling you, Sammy. We're on vacation. It's not like we've got anything else to do."

Sam was about to protest—there was plenty they could do: movies, games, or some much-needed talking—but Wesley was already rummaging in his bag, probably searching for the whiskey.

We shouldn't have a serious conversation while he's wasted anyway. It can wait until tomorrow.

"Here we are." Wesley handed the bottle over. "Drink up."

Sam eyed it. "Half-empty? I didn't think we drank that much of it."

Wesley looked down at himself and smoothed his shirt, though it wasn't wrinkled. "I had a couple of nips out of it here and there. Never when I was driving, of course. If you're not going to drink it, I certainly will."

He's really had enough. I should take the bottle.

Sam hesitated for a second longer before unscrewing the top and taking a swig. The whiskey burned his throat in the best way, and his muscles relaxed of their own volition. "You're a bad influence, you know that? In school, we called this peer pressure."

"Oooh." Wesley rolled onto his stomach and kicked his feet up. "Gonna send me to the principal's office?"

Sam laughed. "Cut it out."

Wesley pushed himself onto his hands and knees and crawled over to Sam. "Have I been a *bad boy*?"

Sam allowed Wesley to kiss him, but when Wesley tried to climb on top of him, Sam pushed him off. "Not while you're drunk."

Wesley pouted but fell back onto his haunches. "Well, there's a reason to stay sober if I ever heard one. C'mon, drink up. I'll put on a movie."

They watched part of an over-the-top action flick, but then Wesley started talking about how nothing in the genre would ever live up to the Indiana Jones films, *Crystal Skull* notwithstanding. That developed into a good-natured squabble—Sam was more of a Bruce Lee man—which turned into a pillow fight, which turned into them laughing so hard they couldn't breathe. Then they discussed the logistics of taking a helicopter down with nothing but a handgun, and the next thing Sam knew, it was three in the morning.

He swayed on the bed, more than a little drunk after hours of Wesley plying him with whiskey. "We should go to sleep."

"I don't wanna." Wesley was lying on his back, looking up at the ceiling. "Sleep is boring. I want to do something fun."

"Uh-uh." Sam shook the bottle at him. "Drunk Wesley is not allowed to leave this room. Drunk Wesley does silly things, like climbing flagpoles and swimming in fountains."

"I want to see some stars, though." He sat up. "Didn't you say you went to a park near here? Let's go there. Oh! We could watch the sunrise."

"No way. Sunrise isn't for—" Sam checked his phone "—three more hours. What are we going to do for three hours?"

"Look at the stars." Wesley's hand moved to Sam's. "Walk around. Talk." His fingers found the tender underside of Sam's wrist and stroked it lightly. "When was the last time you saw a sunrise? Sunset, sure, but a sun*rise*? My last one was with you, that night we stayed up cramming for finals. It'll be kind of romantic to watch one together, don't you think? It'll be like our thing."

The touch made Sam shiver. *Shit. Either he knows exactly how to work me, or he's the mushiest, sappiest guy I know. Possibly both. And I'm eating it up.*

Sam sighed. "Fine. But if we get arrested for being drunk in public, you realize there's no one to bail us out."

"Don't worry. If the cops show, I'll strip, and they'll be so distracted by my sexy body, you'll be able to escape. Then you can bail me out and be a character witness at my trial."

"You're ridiculous."

Wesley grinned. "You love me."

Sam choked back an affirmation that would've taken on a whole different meaning right now.

The blistering heat of the day had been subdued by a cool, windy night. The park was empty, thank God. Sam imagined murderers behind every tree. Though when Wesley dragged him over to a small pond encircled by lamps and kissed him by the sparkling water, all his worries melted away.

Between talking, laughter, and an impromptu make-out session under the bows of an old willow tree, three hours passed easily. When the sun rose, they were treated to a gorgeous view through the boughs of their tree. Bright orange and pink light filtered through the leaves.

Eventually, they trudged home. As the rest of the city was waking up, they climbed into bed and passed out. Sam slept through all of his alarms and only roused when the landline phone on the nightstand rang—or screeched, as far as his head was concerned.

He scrambled for the receiver, knocked it to the ground, and cursed as he retrieved it. "Hello?"

"This is reception, sir. Checkout was an hour ago. Would you like to stay for another day?"

"Checkout?" Sam rubbed his eyes. "Can't be. Checkout's not until two."

"It's three, sir."

Ignoring his aching head, Sam rocketed straight up in bed. "What?"

"You need to vacate the room, or we'll have to charge you for another day."

"Oh my God." Sam snatched his own phone off the nightstand and squinted blearily at it. Sure enough, the time read 3:02 p.m. Fuck.

Wesley stirred beside him, his dark hair a messy ink stain against the white pillow. "Sam? What's wrong?"

"We overslept!" Into the receiver he said, "We'll be out in two minutes. So sorry about this."

"Happens all the time, sir. Be at reception within fifteen minutes, or your card will automatically be charged." The line clicked.

"Fuck," Sam said. He looked down at himself. He was still wearing his clothes, which were now a rumpled mess. "*Fuck*."

"Stop cursing," Wesley grumbled. "You're making my head hurt."

Sam's temper swelled like a crescendo. "You know what's making my head hurt? The fucking hangover you gave me."

Wesley lifted his head, one eye open while the other remained clenched shut. "What? How is this my fault?"

An acerbic retort burned the tip of Sam's tongue, but he bit it back. Wesley was right. He hadn't forced Sam to do anything, and getting angry wasn't going to turn back time. "Hurry up. We have to get going. I can't *believe* we've done this twice now."

Wesley groaned. "Can't we stay another day and sleep it off? I'll make it worth your while." His hand slid over to Sam's thigh.

Sam pulled away. "We can't, Wes. That's what got us in this mess in the first place." He hopped out of bed and stuffed everything he could get his hands on into his bag, mind whirring. "It's Tuesday, right? The eighteenth?"

"Fuck if I know. Time stopped having meaning to me back in Alabama." Wesley rolled onto his back and groaned again. "Oh God, my head. Do we have aspirin?"

Sam didn't answer. His body had chilled as sure as if he'd walked into a meat locker. On his phone, he'd pulled up a map, and what he saw made him want to cry. "Four days. Four more days until the wedding. And we're almost as far from Montana as we were when we started."

"So?" Wesley finally sat up. "Guess we'll have to spend an extra hour or two driving every day."

"No, Wesley, you don't get it. The drive would take twenty-five hours if we didn't stop for anything. Not sleep, or food, nothing. We only have four days to get there, and the last day is the day of the wedding. Do the math. If we don't want to burst into the church in the middle of the ceremony, then . . ."

Wesley's brow furrowed. A second later, it smoothed at the same time his eyes widened. "No. Sam, don't say it."

The words were heavy on Sam's tongue. "We don't have time to drive to California. We have to head directly for Montana."

"No. No way. That was the one thing you wanted to do. We'll drive through the night. We'll stop fucking around. We're getting you to the Pacific Ocean."

Sam looked down at his bag to hide the fact that his eyes were burning. "We can't. We're both exhausted, and driving for long periods of time plays tricks on your eyes. The last thing we need is to get into an accident. We have to forget about California."

"Then we'll hit it on the way back home. After the wedding."

Sam shook his head. "It's in the opposite direction from home, and by then, we'll be going on three weeks that we've been away. I'm running low on funds as it is. After the wedding, we need to drive straight home and get back to our everyday lives."

His voice broke on the last word. In his head, he scolded himself. This wasn't life or death. He had no real reason for wanting to see the ocean. This was only upsetting because . . .

Because it's yet another thing you've missed out on.

Suddenly, two familiar, warm arms wrapped around him from behind. Wesley's nose pressed into his hair. "Sammy, I'm so sorry. This is all my fault."

The genuine contrition in Wesley's voice washed most of Sam's irritation away. He put a hand on one of Wesley's arms and leaned into his embrace. "It's not. I let this happen. I wonder if a part of me was trying to make us late so I wouldn't have to go after all. Maybe I was running away again."

"No way. Once you make up your mind, you're unstoppable. Remember what you said to me on the Ferris wheel? Nothing and no one can scare you away. You're braver than you think."

Sam sniffed. "Thank you."

They packed up, turned in their keys to reception, and hit the road. After consulting some online maps, they made a new route, one that headed almost straight for Helena. No more exploring new cities, stopping off in tourist traps, or playing around with kitten-velociraptor T-shirts.

Though it wasn't going to be totally all-work-and-no-play. They were going to drive through Denver—a city they'd both heard good things about—and toward the end of the trip, they'd pass by Yellowstone National Park. It was a small consolation for missing out on California, but it brightened the rain clouds hanging over Sam.

Today, however, the plan was to cover as many miles as they could, nurse their hangovers, and stop for the night whenever they couldn't stand to be in the car any longer.

Wesley was behind the wheel. He'd cracked the front windows, and wind ruffled his already-messy hair. His sunglasses were securely in place, and since they'd left in a hurry, he hadn't had time to shave. He should have looked unkempt, but he had a whole devil-may-care vibe going on that worked for Sam in a big way.

Wesley must've noticed him staring, because he glanced over. "What?"

"Nothing."

"Terrible liar. What's on your mind? Have you decided you're mad at me after all?"

Sam wet his lips, debated with himself briefly, and answered with the truth. "Honestly, I was thinking you look really handsome today. That scruff is sexy on you."

Back when we were just friends, I would have kept that to myself. It's nice to be able to say it out loud.

Wesley's cheeks reddened. "Thank you." He opened his mouth again only to close it. Then he reached over and tucked a loose strand of Sam's hair behind his ear before turning back to the road.

A simple compliment makes him blush, but not all the times I had him under me. Our situation is so bizarre.

Considering they were going to be stuck in the car for the indeterminable future, now might be a good time to talk. As Sam watched the pavement slip by, scenarios rolled around in his foggy head. If he didn't approach this delicately, it could end in awkward silence that neither of them could escape. Right now, he was as thin as tissue paper. Everything hurt, and his eyes twitched whenever he made them focus on something.

This was definitely his worst hangover of the trip, and he'd had plenty to choose from. There was another part of him that was sore too, the part that was still disappointed about California. They'd spent three whole days in the place of Wesley's choosing, and now they didn't have one to spare for Sam's. A fair share of the blame was his, but that didn't stop him from being bitter.

Maybe having a serious conversation right now wasn't a good idea. Sam wasn't sure what he wanted to say, exactly. He had an inkling, but so much of it depended on how Wesley felt. But then, he couldn't determine how Wesley felt until they talked about it. Sigh.

Starting fresh tomorrow seemed like the best option. They'd cover some ground, sleep off this terrible, cottony haze, and have all day tomorrow to talk when their heads were clear.

Although, one thought had been nagging at Sam ever since he'd spoken to Jessica. Was there something more holding him back? He'd meant what he'd told her about needing Wesley's friendship, but why had he been so quick to write off the opportunity to date a funny, handsome man who loved him? His brain said it was because he was happy being Wesley's friend, but as time went on, he wasn't so sure.

Am I happy being Wesley's friend the same way I was happy to marry Michael? Because it's safe? Am I choosing the path of least resistance yet again?

A bell went off in Sam's head. Damn. If that was the case, it pretty much clinched what Sam had to do. Scary as it was, Sam believed Wesley would be a part of his life no matter what. They'd make it through this. They had to.

"Seriously, what are you thinking about?" Wesley alternated between watching the road and watching him. "Your face is all scrunched like it gets when you're doing math in your head."

Sam's chest clenched. Wesley really did know him, in the most intimate, minute ways.

Tomorrow. Tomorrow I'll tell him how I feel. The words will be there when the time comes.

"It's nothing." Sam turned on the radio. "Think we can find a station that isn't country?"

The drive was long, but once Sam got some food and coffee in him, he perked up. They played games and laughed like before, and it all seemed so blissfully normal. It made it easier for Sam to tell himself that everything was going to fine.

Several hours later, they got off the highway and stopped for gas. While Wesley pumped, he tossed the keys to Sam. "You mind driving for a bit?"

Sam caught them only to fumble and let them drop. He scooped them off the dusty ground. "Not at all. I'm still hungover, though, as evidenced by my lack of coordination."

"Me too. My head's actually getting worse. I was seeing double for a minute there."

"Really? You'd think as time went on, you'd get better."

"Yeah, you'd think, but all that water I've been chugging hasn't helped, and my heart won't stop racing. I want to curl up in the back and die."

"Please don't. The car already reeks of booze and sweat."

Wesley shot him a sour look. "Uh-huh. I see where your priorities lie."

They stopped in Odessa for the night and found yet another bland, featureless motel. They were all starting to blend together in Sam's head. Once inside, Sam tossed his bag down and fell face-first onto the bed, groaning. It was a little after ten, and Sam was beyond ready for bed. He didn't even think sex could rouse him.

Although, when he felt the mattress depress next to him, and the smell of Wesley's cologne filled his nose, he was ready to have his mind changed.

A warm hand settled on his head only to drift down his nape and back. "You feeling okay?"

Sam groaned again in response.

"Here. This will help."

Sam rolled onto his side. He expected Wesley to kiss him—one of the slow, warm kisses he used to wake Sam up in the morning—but to his surprise, Wesley had the bottle of whiskey in his hand.

He proffered it to Sam. "Take a swig, and you'll feel better."

"No way." Sam crinkled his nose. "I can't hair-of-the-dog it this time. If I so much as smell alcohol, I'm gonna puke."

"Really? Damn, I was going to ask if you wanted to hit up a bar or something."

Sam laughed. When Wesley failed to join him, Sam stared at him. "Wait, are you *serious*?"

"Yeah. I mean, I'm not suggesting we pull another all-nighter, but we passed a sports bar a few blocks back. I thought a couple of beers and some hot wings would fix us right up."

Sam searched Wesley's face for any sign that this was a prank. Surely he was about to shout *Psych!* and then rib Sam for believing him. But no, Wesley's face was straight for once, absent its usual grin. In fact, he was avoiding Sam's eyes, and his mouth was set. He almost looked . . . nervous.

Sam spoke carefully. "I don't want to drink anymore. I don't think that's the solution to us being so hungover we lost half a day."

"Okay." Wesley still wasn't looking at him. "Well, do you mind if I go without you?"

Sam sat up. "Kind of? I don't want to tell you what to do, but it's already ten. A 'couple' of beers with you always means four or five. You won't be back until after midnight. We need to wake up early tomorrow."

"Hey, I can control myself." Wesley smiled and touched Sam's chin. "But you know what? You're right. We way overdid it last night. It won't kill us to spend a quiet night in the room. Besides, I have this." He unscrewed the whiskey and took a swig straight from the bottle. "I feel better already, and tomorrow will be a new day."

"Yeah." Sam's mind whirred. "Like I said before, we have four days until the wedding, and we should try to get there a day early. We have to buckle down." An idea popped into his head. "I actually don't think we should drink again until the wedding."

Anyone who knew Wesley less wouldn't have noticed the change in his expression. It was only for a second, after all. But Sam saw it. Clear as day. At the mention of being sober, Wesley's face flickered with pure, undiluted fear.

He was quick to slap on a carefree grin that to Sam looked fragile as glass.

"That's probably a good idea." Wesley stood up. "Let's sleep on it and see how we feel in the morning. I'm going to take a shower." He disappeared into the bathroom.

Sam stared at his retreating back until Wesley shut the door. In the silence of the empty room, Sam's mind was blank. Then, he started thinking back, not realizing what he was thinking about until it added up in his head.

Out of the thirteen days they'd been on this trip, Wesley had consumed at least one alcoholic beverage for seven of them. And that was just what Sam had seen.

He'd been drunk on this trip almost as much as he'd been sober. Sam hadn't paid it much mind because it was social drinking, and they were on vacation, as Wesley kept reminding him. But now that he'd noticed it, he couldn't un-notice. Like having a flaw in a piece of glass pointed out. That was a *lot* of drinking. That was the sort of drinking they used to do in college after finals week.

That . . . was way too much drinking.

Holy shit.

Sam's own words echoed in his head: *"You're not an alcoholic so long as you're in college."*

A thought snapped into Sam's head. Did Wesley drink this much all the time, or was it actually because they were on vacation? Had he made the same excuses back home? *It's a Friday*, or *It's not like we have jobs to get to*?

A floodgate opened, and memories from the past two weeks drenched Sam's mind. He heard Wesley complaining about his hangover getting worse, not better. He smelled the whiskey on Wesley's breath. He saw him chugging water and sweating, his hands shaking. He heard him complaining about his pounding heart, and wanting to go out night after night.

Sam was no doctor, but he'd been hungover enough times himself to have read up on them. Hangovers were basically miniature withdrawals. Only for Wesley, they didn't seem so miniature.

Was he . . . an addict? An alcoholic?

The door to the bathroom swung open, and out poured a cloud of steam.

"Man, I feel so much better." Wesley emerged, naked and dripping water. He was toweling off his hair, a big relaxed smile on his face. "Hey, gorgeous. Did you miss me?"

Sam's body responded to the sight of him automatically. "You were gone for five minutes."

"Is that a yes?"

Sam couldn't help but chuckle. "You know it." He looked Wesley over. All he saw was a handsome, healthy young man in his prime.

There's no way Wesley's an alcoholic. I'm his best friend. I would have noticed before now. I don't know what I was thinking.

Relief washed through him. Right up until Wesley crawled onto the bed and kissed him. His mouth tasted like whiskey, as it often had in the past two weeks.

Sam's heart sank into his stomach.

"So." Wesley's mouth moved to his jaw. "Think you can stay awake a little longer?"

"Actually, I'm really tired." Sam shifted out of Wesley's reach. "It's been a long day."

Wesley's eyes widened. "Oh. Okay, yeah. It has been. Good night, then."

"Good night." Sam yanked off his clothes but kept his boxers on for once. When he got under the covers, he faced the wall instead of Wesley's side of the bed. He heard a click behind him, and the lamp turned off. Wesley snuggled up to his back. Sam didn't push him away, but he didn't tangle their legs together like he normally did either.

Despite what he'd said about being tired, it was a long time before Sam fell asleep.

CHAPTER ELEVEN

Wesley was up at dawn the next morning. He hadn't set an alarm, so it must've been the guilt that roused him. Sam had said multiple times that it wasn't his fault they weren't going to make it to Cali, but Wesley's stomach still iced over every time he thought about it. If he hadn't wasted so much time in New Orleans . . . If he hadn't gotten so drunk . . . Sam had been distant to him the night before. Was he too polite to tell Wesley how mad he really was?

Whatever the case, Wesley was going to make it up to him. He was refreshed, hangover-free, and ready to inundate Sam with some please-forgive-me pampering.

He rolled out of bed as quietly as he could, pulled random clothes on, and snuck out of the room. Twenty minutes later, he'd procured two steaming cups of coffee and a paper bag full of blueberry muffins. It was a comfort to know that even out here in the desert, he could find an overpriced coffee shop. God bless America.

He snuck back into the room, set breakfast on the bureau, and brushed his teeth with the bathroom door shut to minimize noise. When he was minty fresh, he crawled back onto the bed. Sam was sleeping on his side, bare-chested with the sheets more off than on. Wesley paused—eyes tracking down the breadth of his shoulders to the gorgeous slope of his waist—before straddling him.

Sam stirred and made a soft, sleepy sound. Wesley made a mental note to have his phone out and recording next time. He wanted to make that his text notification. Leaning down, he kissed Sam awake, gentle and sweet.

For a moment, he expected Sam to pull away from him like he had the night before, but then Sam kissed him back with enthusiasm.

When Sam tilted his head and deepened the kiss, Wesley forgot all about food and sunk into a new hunger. Until his stomach growled.

Sam chuckled against his mouth. "Want to get some breakfast?" He blinked sleepy eyes open and smiled up at Wesley.

"Already taken care of." Wesley leaned to the side so Sam could see past him to the bureau. "Surprise!"

"Oh wow." Sam kissed him again. "Thank you."

"I figured it was the least I could do. Once we're finished eating, we'll hit the road. I bet we can make up for some lost time."

Sam's mood seemed to instantly lift. As they got ready for the day, he bounced around the room, whistling a song from the radio. Every now and then, he'd give Wesley an odd look, but Wesley chalked that up to sexual frustration. He wanted to suggest they get a quickie in before leaving, but he still had some sucking up to do. It could wait until after they'd made progress toward Montana.

"Are you getting nervous?" he asked, packing his suitcase into the trunk.

Sam hefted his bag from his shoulder to the pavement. "Off and on. Right now, it's off, but I doubt it'll stay that way."

"It's going to be okay. I know hearing that isn't any real comfort, but I swear, Sammy." Wesley squeezed his shoulder. "We'll get through this."

Sam was strangely quiet as Wesley navigated them back onto the highway, which was starting to feel like a third home, after the car and their actual homes. Wesley didn't press him. When Sam was ready to share whatever was on his mind, he would, and not a moment sooner.

Sure enough, about an hour into the drive, Sam sighed. "We need to talk."

Uh-oh. The four words of the relationship apocalypse. Does he want to talk about what we're doing again?

If so, Wesley didn't know what to say. With every passing day, it was getting harder to pretend this was all about sex, or that he believed things could go back to normal. If Sam asked him how he felt, he'd have to tell him the truth.

Wesley had been quiet for too long. He took a breath. "Oh? What about?"

"I don't really know how to say this." Sam fell silent.

Out of the corner of his eye, Wesley watched him. Sam was staring at his hands in his lap, something he did when he was fighting back embarrassment. What could Sam have to be embarrassed about?

"Whatever it is, you can tell me." Wesley let go of the steering wheel long enough to squeeze one of Sam's hands. "I promise."

Sam let out a breath and squared his shoulders. "Before I say this, I want you to know I'm not accusing you of anything. I noticed . . . Well, I was wondering about how much you've been drinking."

Wesley was so startled, he jerked the wheel. The car swerved but thankfully remained in their lane. Wesley righted them, fingers clenched so tight they were white as bone. "What?"

"Again, I'm not accusing you of anything." Sam was spitting out words now, like he couldn't get them out fast enough. "I noticed you've been drunk a lot of the nights of this trip, and I wondered if that was unusual for you, or if you drink like this all the time. I'm . . . I'm worried about you, Wes."

Wesley's heart stopped cold in his chest. It sounded even worse coming from Sam than his parents. Shame and mortification smothered him like an itchy blanket. He fought it off, thoughts darting around his brain.

Obviously, Sam wasn't buying Wesley's whole we're-on-vacation schtick. Maybe he could start hiding how much he was drinking. Sam hadn't noticed when Wesley had poured a couple of whiskeys without him. Wesley could find ways to—

Jesus, what was he thinking? Only addicts hid what they were doing from people. That wasn't him. He wasn't a fucking addict.

Sam knowing might actually be a good thing. I've been dragging my feet when I should have come clean, and now he's figured it out. Please, God, don't let him totally reject me.

"I'm sorry." Wesley swallowed. "I should have told you sooner."

Sam shifted, turning to face him. "Told me what?"

"I'm going to pull over. Is that okay?"

"Of course."

Wesley took the next exit he saw. It spat them out onto a deserted stretch of road lined with thick trees—a rare sighting after miles of sun-bleached flatland and cacti. There weren't any shops nearby, so he pulled off the road and killed the engine. For a moment, he stared forward, listening to the silence as he collected himself. Sam—wonderful Sam—waited without speaking. Wesley probably could have sat there all day, and Sam would have let him.

"You know why I wanted to take this trip?" Wesley finally looked at Sam.

"To get me to Jessica's wedding? Have a last hurrah? Get out of town for a while?"

"All of those are true, but the last one is the kicker. I was running away."

Sam's eyes searched his face. "From what?"

"My parents. Myself." Wesley sighed and rubbed his brow. "My folks want me to go to rehab."

Sam gasped. "What?"

"They've been hounding me about my drinking for a while now, but when I quit my last job, they got serious about it. They think I keep job-hopping because I can't hold anything down. I laughed and said they were being dramatic, but they wouldn't let it go. I was worried they were going to have an intervention or something. So, I left." He laughed humorlessly. "Remind me never to call you nonconfrontational again."

Sam's face was tight and neutral, as if he were fighting to keep it expressionless. "Why skip town? You must realize that's a temporary fix."

"I didn't want them to call you and tell you everything. They wanted to before, but I begged them not to. I knew eventually they'd do it against my wishes."

"You didn't want me to know?"

"I did, but I wanted to tell you myself. I didn't mean to drag it out for so long, but . . . I was scared, Sammy. I didn't know how you were going to react. I didn't want this to change how you see me."

Sam's face revealed nothing. "I take it the way you've been drinking on this trip isn't unusual?"

Fear ran cold fingers down Wesley's back. He wished Sam would react. His eyes drifted past Sam to the forest. The calm vista was incongruous with his heart hammering in his chest. This was it. The big moment. After he told Sam this, there'd be no going back.

With Sam, and with himself. Admitting it out loud made it so much more real.

"I've had at least one drink almost every day of my life since we were juniors." Forcing the words out felt like wading through waist-deep water: it fought him every step. "I knew so many people in college, I could find a party every day of the week if I wanted. Once we all started turning twenty-one, it got worse. I told myself it was okay because I was in college. Everyone was partying way too much. But then we graduated."

"We graduated," Sam said slowly, "but you kept drinking as if we hadn't."

Wesley nodded, a sickness taking root in his stomach like a choking vine. "Maybe I was trying to cling to my college days, back before I had responsibilities and bills. I told myself I'd quit once I got a job. But when I got one, I used every miniscule day-to-day stress as an excuse. 'After the day I had, I deserve a drink' or 'My boss is such an ass, I'm gonna go get beers with the guys and complain about it.' It was easy, and there was *always* someone who wanted to blow off some steam too. Not to sound cliché, but everyone was doing it."

"None of your coworkers noticed?"

"Oh no, they did. I wouldn't tell anyone when I came in hungover, but I'm sure people were aware. One time, one of the guys joked that I always smelled like a bar. After that, I had breath mints and body spray on me all the time. But there was no hiding all the times I overslept or acted irritably because I didn't feel well. A few months in, people would start asking questions, and I'd decide I didn't like that job anymore. I always left before anyone could get too close."

"I know this is a hard question to answer, but . . . why? Why do you overdrink?"

Shame suffused him, and Wesley dropped his eyes to his lap. "It's funny you should ask that, because my reason is simple. Or at least it used to be. I drink because I like it. It's fun. Takes the edge off, and I love a good party. If I'm not depressed, it's not a problem, right? That's what I used to tell myself, but the longer this has gone on, the more I've wondered. Nowadays, the best answer I can give is I'm not sure. It's become such a habit."

Sam was quiet for several of the longest seconds of Wesley's life. "Wes, do you think you have a problem?"

His first instinct was to lie—deny everything and play it all off as a joke, like he usually did—but would Sam buy that?

He knew every play in Wesley's book, and he'd seen Wesley's drinking for himself. The time for pretending was over, and Wesley didn't want to keep lying. Keeping things from his best friend had been hard enough, but now that Sam was maybe more . . . He couldn't do it anymore. Wouldn't.

His breath left him in a *whoosh*. "If you'd asked me at the beginning of this trip, I would have said no way. But now, things are different." Pain throbbed behind his eyes, and he rubbed them again. "It started when you said that thing back in Charlotte. 'You're not an alcoholic if you're in college.' That statement stuck with me, got me thinking. Then I noticed my hangovers were worse than yours, and yet I always wanted to keep drinking. Even when I knew I'd be driving."

Sam's voice seemed to reach him from a distance. Everything looked and felt surreal. "Did you ever drink and drive?"

"No, it seems I'm not quite that bad, thank God. The real clincher was when you suggested we not drink for the rest of the trip." Wesley turned in his seat to face Sam. "When you said that, I was *afraid*. I was actually scared to be sober for a week. I couldn't pinpoint why. It's totally irrational. It was like you suggested we go without food for five days, only food is necessary, and I *know* alcohol isn't. But maybe there's a part of me that thinks it is."

To Wesley's surprise, Sam looked relieved. "I'm glad to hear you say that. Not the part about you being afraid, of course, but that you're taking this seriously. That's a great sign. I have to admit, I don't really get it, though."

Wesley huffed. "Neither the fuck do I, Sammy. Honestly, I wish I could explain it better. Hell, there's a part of me that wishes I *were* drinking away some deep-seated pain, because then at least people would understand. Instead, I sound like a spoiled bastard who's being irresponsible for the hell of it."

Same shook his head. "You're explaining it great, for the record. And it's amazing that you're so self-aware about it."

Wesley chewed on his bottom lip, stomach acid burning through his lining. "You think so? You don't think I'm pathetic and weak?"

"Of course not." Sam took Wesley's hand. "Why would I think that?"

"Because *I* think I'm pathetic."

Sam shook his head. "You need help. Lots of people do, and not talking about it will make it worse. I'm glad you told me. There's nothing wrong with getting the treatment you need. If you were sick, and you went to a doctor, would that be pathetic?"

"No." Wesley nodded. "I see your point. I still wish I hadn't let it get to the point where people are worried about me. I can't seem to control myself. I should be able to turn around tomorrow and quit, but I don't want to."

"Have you ever really tried?"

Wesley shrugged. "Haven't had any reason to. Being unemployed wasn't enough of a motivator. Neither was my parents dropping the dreaded *r* word. They think rehab is some magical quick fix. Like, they'll pop me in an oven, set the dial to 'cured,' and six weeks later, out will come a brand-new me."

"What do you think will get you to quit?"

Wesley blew out a breath. "I dunno. I know I can't keep drinking every day. Cirrhosis of the liver is no joke. It'll land me in a hospital someday. But it's so hard to think about that when you're twenty-three. I can't rent a car legally. How could I be in danger of dying? But I recognize that I fucked up."

"You didn't fuck up, Wesley." Sam scooted closer, and that alone was such a comfort, it made Wesley's heart soar. "You say you were running away, but I know what that looks like. I think you were taking a step back to get some perspective, and it worked. Admitting this took guts. I'm proud of you."

"That is so sappy," Wesley teased, though his voice broke. "Thank you. I don't think I could have admitted this to anyone but you. What does this mean, though? Am I an alcoholic?"

"Honestly, I'm not sure." Sam pulled out his phone. "Google hasn't led us astray so far. Let's see what comes up." He pulled up a browser on his phone and typed something that Wesley couldn't see. "Here's a list of warning signs. You said you're not depressed, so I'll check that as a no. You haven't been injured or traumatized recently, right?"

Wesley shook his head.

"Have you been drinking alone?"

Wesley swallowed a lump in his throat that felt suspiciously like his pride. "Yes."

"For no reason?"

"What do they mean by 'reason'?"

"It says here that it means drinking for the sake of drinking and not because you're being social or celebrating."

"Then yeah. I'd say what I'm doing falls into that category."

"Have you been getting more calories from alcohol than from food?"

Wesley thought about it. "No, I eat way more than I drink." He paused. "Actually, remember that one night in the hotel when we got pizza, and I still woke up starving?"

"Yeah. You didn't drink that night. You must've been hungry because your body was missing the calories it's used to getting from booze."

"Yikes, that's scary."

"Believe it or not, that's a good sign. You're so lean. I guess this hasn't fucked with your metabolism too much."

Wesley shrugged. "I can probably thank being twenty-three for that, but I won't always be."

"True." Sam pocketed his phone. "I'm no expert, but it seems like we caught this early. It might be easier for us to get help now than if this had dragged on for years."

A smile tugged at Wesley's lips. "'We'? 'Us'?"

Sam's eyes crinkled at the corners. "Of course. We're in this together."

The heavy blanket of shame that'd been covering Wesley this whole time lifted at one corner, making room for a new emotion: joy. Hard as this conversation was, it felt good to finally say it out loud. And to tell Sam the truth.

"I have to ask, though," Sam said. "Why didn't you tell me sooner? Did you really think I was going to judge you?"

"I suppose not, but I never want to be ugly or flawed in your eyes. Also, I wanted to prolong our happy time together, so to speak. This is going to sound obvious, but once I told you, then you'd know. You know?"

Sam laughed. "Yeah, I get it. For the record, I don't think you're ugly or pathetic, and I'll let you in on a secret." He leaned in. "I already knew you're flawed."

Wesley stuck his tongue out. "What I told you . . . you're taking it awfully well. Do you really not care?"

"I care deeply, make no mistake. But God knows I'm in no place to judge. I've been drinking almost as much as you on this trip. I could stand to look at my own alcohol habits with a more critical eye. Asking for help is a sign of strength, not weakness." He paused. "I have to ask: you accept the fact that you need to get treatment, right? You have to do something about this before it gets any worse."

Wesley sighed. "I don't know. It hurts my pride to admit it. I really don't want to go to rehab."

"Maybe you don't need to. I think the first thing you need to do is commit to making a change. If you're not devoted to this, it won't work. You said before you didn't have strong enough motivation to quit. Has that changed?"

Wesley stared out the windshield. The sky had gotten overcast, and the clouds were dark and swollen. It might rain any second. It'd be fitting, atmospherically speaking.

People always say you have to change for yourself, but honestly, I want to change for Sam. I want to keep him in my life. Would it be so bad if he was my motivation?

"I think I could change." Wesley glanced back over. "I can find a powerful enough reason to quit, if I commit myself to it."

"I'm here to help you, if you want."

"Of course I do. I can't tell you how much it means to me to have your support." Wesley slid an arm behind Sam and pulled him closer. It was hard to hug in the cramped space, but Sam snaked his arms around him and squeezed him with all his wiry strength.

Eventually, Wesley's ribs started to hurt. He shifted away. "You ready to get back on the road?"

"Absolutely."

They drove for a little over six hours and stopped in Santa Fe for food and much-needed energy drinks. Then they powered through another four hours until they arrived in Denver, Colorado. Night had settled over the city, and unlike in New York, that meant people were actually sleeping. It was a shame they weren't going to be able to spend much time there, because the mountains were stunning. Literally. The first time Wesley laid eyes on them, they knocked the air from his lungs.

"We're coming back here someday," Wesley said without thinking.

Sam looked up from his phone, which he was using to find a hotel. "You think we'll ever go on another trip like this?"

"We totally should." A joke popped into his head, and he flashed a grin. "We could always get married and come here on our honeymoon."

It wasn't the best joke Wesley had ever told, but two weeks ago, it would have gotten a chuckle and a "Yeah, right" out of Sam. Now, it got dead silence.

Whoops. I read this room wrong.

Sam was staring forward a little too hard. "Um, Wesley? There's actually something else I wanted to talk to you about."

After his big confession, Wesley was both more and less prepared to have a conversation about them, if that was possible. He braced himself. "Yes?"

Sam was silent and still. Then he turned back to his phone. "Never mind. It can wait. Today was an emotional day for you. I don't want to pile too much on all at once and stress you out."

Wesley couldn't say if he was relieved or disappointed. Maybe Sam was doing him a favor. Now that he knew Wesley's secret, he might not want to hook up anymore. Sam had said he supported Wesley, but who would willing get into a relationship with a fuckup? Certainly not Sam "Play It Safe" Cooper.

Anxiety crept over Wesley again, making his heart pound. The more he thought about it, the more he realized what a precarious position his confession had put Sam in. They were going to be stuck in the car together for another two days, plus the whole trip back. If Sam was going to reject Wesley, he wouldn't do it now, when he couldn't escape. He was bringing Wesley to a wedding as his date, for Christ's sake.

What if Sam was only pretending to be supportive to get through this trip, and as soon as they got back home, he was going to tell Wesley he didn't want him anymore? What if he didn't even want to road-trip back? Helena had an airport. He might sneak out after the wedding and hop on a plane home, leaving Wesley to drive back by himself.

Stop it. Stop thinking like that. Your body is all out of whack, and it's making you paranoid. Sam would never do that. He loves you. He cares about you. You trust him implicitly.

Wesley repeated this to himself over and over, but as they pulled into the parking lot of an old, two-story motel, he felt like he was still flying down the highway at eighty miles an hour.

"This place had amazing reviews," Sam said as he lugged his bag out of the trunk.

"Good." Wesley stared off toward the mountains, mind whirring.

"They have a laundry service, so we can get our clothes cleaned."

"Uh-huh."

"And apparently you can order male strippers who will come right to your room."

"That's great." Wesley reached for his own suitcase only to drop his hand. "Wait, what?"

Sam chuckled. "I knew you weren't listening. What's up?"

Wesley looked at him for a moment. He'd failed to give Sam the benefit of the doubt before. He wouldn't make that mistake again. He was going to be upfront this time.

"Let's check in, and then I'll share with the class."

They were given a room on the second floor, which meant lugging their things up a tiny staircase. Once they were up, however, they found room 2112 to be pleasant enough, with its comfy bed, simple furniture, and gorgeous photos of snow-capped mountains on the walls.

"I'm so tired." Sam belly flopped onto the bed. "Which is funny, considering we spent most of today sitting." He rolled onto his back and patted the bed next to him. "C'mere."

Stomach churning, Wesley kicked off his shoes and sat down next to him. Sam tugged him closer. It was weird how normal touching each other had become in such a short timeframe, but it still made Wesley's heart flutter. Although right now his pulse was erratic for a different reason.

"So, tell me." Sam kissed Wesley's hair. "What were you going to say before?"

Wesley steeled himself. "I was thinking that this was way too easy."

Sam sat up. "In a good way?"

"In a way that makes me paranoid." Wesley turned to look at him. "Are you really okay with what I told you? What it means? You realize this changes everything."

"Well, I'll admit it hasn't totally hit me yet. I want to discuss some options with you and do some more googling. But I had time to process my suspicions before we talked about it, so yeah. I'm dealing. I'm more worried about you and how you're dealing, though. How are you?"

Uncomfortable truth time. Please don't let him hate me. I never realized how much power he has over me. If he wanted to, he could totally crush me.

"I guess I'm overwhelmed by it all." Wesley exhaled. "Saying it out loud made it real. I believe that you support me and that you're still my friend, but knowing this, how can you . . . Can you . . ." Wesley hadn't realized his eyes were welling up until they started to sting. He covered his face with a hand, but it was too late. "I'm sorry. I don't know what's wrong with me. I'm anxious all the time lately."

"Oh my God, Wes." Sam shushed him. "I think I get what you're trying to say. Are you upset because you think this means I'm not attracted to you anymore?"

"No." Wesley sniffed. "Maybe. You don't do messy, Sam, and I was a mess way before today. If I were you, I'd run for the hills."

"Is that so?" Sam tilted his chin up until he could look Wesley in the eye. "If our places were swapped, you'd leave me?"

That gave Wesley pause. "No. I'd never abandon you when you needed me most."

"Then what makes you think I'm going to do that to you? Is it so hard to believe I feel the exact same way? Wesley, you're not perfect, and I don't want you to be." Sam kissed him. "We can figure out what 'this' is later, when things are quieter. But for the record, I'm not going anywhere."

Wesley wiped his face and smiled. "You mean it?"

"I'll prove it."

Sam kissed Wesley with feeling, making a soft, wanting sound against his lips. Wesley hadn't realized how affection-starved he'd been until the touch unraveled something inside him: tension and pain that'd gotten knotted up. It pulled apart, and while it still hurt, it was a good hurt. A healing hurt.

He kissed Sam back with equal fervor, rolling on top of him. Sam allowed that for a whole minute, exchanging frantic, open-mouthed kisses with Wesley, but then he grabbed Wesley's shoulders and flipped him over none-too-gently.

Holy fuck, Wesley thought as his head hit a pillow, *that was hot.*

Sam's blond hair spilled in front of his eyes as he looked at Wesley from inches away. "You want to know if I still want you?" Both of his hands went to Wesley's jeans and practically ripped his fly open. "I'll show you how much, Wes."

Wesley whimpered as Sam's nimble fingers pushed his pants down and found their way into his underwear. Warm fingers curled around his cock, making him jolt from the sudden pleasure. He hadn't had enough time to get a proper erection yet, but when Sam took him out of his boxers and licked a wet stripe from root to tip, Wesley got hard in record time.

"Oh God." Wesley's head fell back. "So good. Flip your body around. I'll suck you too."

"Nuh-uh," Sam said, running the head of Wesley's swollen cock over his lips. "I've got a point to make, and I'm going to make it all over your cock."

Fuck. Hearing Sam talk dirty was a special turn-on. It reminded him of back in the car, that first furtive night when they'd still been pretending they could resist each other. That'd been the hottest sex of Wesley's life, until he'd finally gotten Sam under him. The memory made his dick harder.

Sam must've felt it because he whistled appreciatively. He suckled on him before sinking carefully down, taking him in until the head hit the back of his throat. With his eyes closed and his cheeks hollowed, he presented an image that Wesley would be masturbating to for the rest of his days.

Holy shit, his mouth was incredible. Wesley already knew that from kissing him, but feeling that wet heat and perfect suction in this way gave him new appreciation for Sam's tongue. Wesley's fingers twitched to bury themselves in Sam's hair, but if he did that, he'd end up fucking his mouth. He wanted to let Sam control this and experiment to his heart's content.

So long as he could last, at least. Not having sex for a few days after having it multiple times had taken a toll. Especially when combined with all the emotional turmoil. He was already right on the edge. How Sam could make him feel so comforted just by touching him was astounding. He was relaxed for the first time in days. He didn't think he could hold back if he tried.

"Fuck, Sammy." Wesley groaned, hands clenched into fists at his sides. "Fair warning: I could come at any second. Your mouth feels so good."

Sam hummed a response around him, and that made fireworks go off between Wesley's legs. When Sam rubbed his inner thigh and then slipped a hand down to where his balls hung heavy between them, Wesley couldn't stop the moan that poured from him.

The pièce de résistance, however, was when Sam moved his other hand to his own pants, got his cock out, and started clumsily stroking himself in time with the bobs of his head. That image shot through Wesley like lightning.

He came with a shout, finally giving in and grabbing two handfuls of Sam's hair. That seemed to turn Sam on, because he came against Wesley's calf a second later. His mouth was still full of Wesley's softening cock, but the pitiful little mewl he made as he came was world-shattering.

Sam let Wesley's spent cock slide out of his mouth, panting. He managed to haul himself up enough to collapse next to Wesley. As soon as he did, Wesley grabbed his chin and kissed him deeply, tasting salt and bitterness on his tongue.

In the postorgasm haze, a thought drifted up and broke the surface: *I love him. Fuck me, I'm so in love with him.*

"Wurff," Sam said against his mouth.

Wesley gave him a final kiss and pulled back. "Huh?"

"I was trying to say 'Wesley.'" He laughed. "I dunno about you, but I feel better."

"*Much* better."

"What do you want to do tonight? We could talk more. Or if you've had enough of that, we could cuddle for a little while." He kissed Wesley's chin. "Or wait about twenty minutes and have a lot more sex."

"Tempting, but I need to make a phone call."

Sam sat up a little. "Oh?"

"Yeah. I've been thinking about it since we talked, and I need to call my parents. They've been trying to reach me. I'm sure you've noticed."

Sam pursed his lips. "Actually, now that you mention it, yeah. You've been rejecting their calls."

"I owe them an apology. They were worried about me before, but now they must be really freaked."

"I think that's the right thing to do. What are you going to say to them?"

"I'm not sure yet." Wesley sighed. "I guess I'll do what I usually do and wing it. I really, *really* don't want to go to rehab. It sounds like prison."

"You might not need to. They were talking about rehab when you were still in denial. Now that you've come to terms with your problem, I bet there are lots of other options."

"I hope so." Wesley kissed Sam again before pulling his pants back up. "I suppose I'll do what you did with Jessica and find a park or something."

"Want me to come with you?"

"No. For this particular conversation, I'd like some privacy."

"Okay." Sam hesitated. "Wesley, I . . ."

The expression on his face, longing with a flicker of uncertainty, made Wesley's pulse double. "Yes?"

"Nothing. Good luck. I'll be here when you get back."

Wesley hid his disappointment and nodded, climbing to his feet. "Thanks."

After cleaning himself up, he exited the room, bounded down the stairs, and then paused in the parking lot, unsure of where to go. If he wanted privacy, he could always sit in the car. However, he tended to pace while on the phone. It helped him think. A park would be a good bet, if there were any nearby.

After a quick search on his phone, he headed down the street toward a little butterfly garden that should be quiet this time of night. As he walked, he passed small shops with dark windows, businesses, and restaurants. Music drifted from somewhere to the left. He paid it no mind, busy as he was rehearsing what he was going to say to his parents.

"Reed!"

That pinged distantly on Wesley's radar, but he ignored it, focused as he was on the task at hand. A second shout, however, stopped him in his tracks.

"Wesley Reed! Is that you?"

He glanced to the left. Outside of a bar, in a patio area populated by black metal tables, sat four men, one of whom looked familiar.

Wesley blinked at him. "Kurt Crocker? Holy shit!"

"I knew it!" Kurt stood up from his seat and held out his arms. He was dressed in a black shirt and jeans. A white sash across his chest read *Groom-to-Be*. "Fancy running into you here, Reed. Get your ass over here."

Wesley checked for traffic and then crossed the street. Kurt met him at the entrance to the patio area and pulled him into one of the jock-esque, back-patting hugs Wesley hadn't experienced since college.

"This is a hell of a coincidence," Wesley said. "What are you doing in Denver?"

"I live here, bro." Kurt gestured around them. His sleeves were rolled up to his elbows, showing off tattoos that barely stood out against his black skin. "Moved right after graduation. I got a job in a brewery. You know this city has a huge craft-beer scene?"

Wesley did know that. It was one of the reasons he was excited to come here. Or at least, he had been, before everything.

Guess our one-beer-per-city tradition is over. I didn't even think about that.

"Congrats on the job." Wesley pointed to Kurt's banner. "And on your future wedding. Or have you gotten into unusual accessories since college?"

"Nope, I'm getting married this weekend. Her name's Tamara, and she's amazing. These are my groomsmen." He turned to the other men. "Shawn, Timothy, and Philip. This is an old college buddy, Wesley."

The men nodded at him.

Wesley waved. "Nice to meet you."

"So, what brings you to Denver?" Kurt asked.

"A wedding, coincidentally enough. This weekend too. Though, it's in Montana. You remember my old roommate, Sam Cooper? It's his sister who's getting married. He and I are on a road trip."

Kurt tapped his chin. "I think I saw photos on Facebook. You guys have been on this trip for a long time. You finally break down and start dating?"

Wesley flushed and opened his mouth to utter the usual denials, but Kurt interrupted him with a howl of laughter.

"Oh my God, your face. I knew it! I knew you two would get together some day. It's about time."

Before Wesley could protest, a waiter walked out of the bar carrying a tray loaded with shots. "Here you are, gentlemen."

"Dude." Kurt punched his arm. "You have to stay and have a drink with us."

Two emotions hit Wesley with equal force: anxiety and eagerness. Earlier that day, he'd honestly had to ask himself if he had a drinking problem. This seemed like a prime opportunity to prove he didn't. But in truth, he would love nothing more than to have a couple of drinks with a good group of guys and catch up with Kurt. Not get drunk. Just hang out.

Don't do it. Walk away.

Wesley took a breath to steady his resolve. "I'd love to, but I really can't. I was on my way to something, and Sam's back at the hotel by himself."

"C'mon, bro. Don't give me that." Kurt grabbed his shoulder and guided him to the table, where eight shots awaited. "I'm getting married. You have to take a shot to celebrate. Do you have any idea how much bad luck it is to not toast a groom the week before his wedding?"

"He's right," one of the groomsmen piped up, a grin on his face. "Lightning will strike the church."

"The rings will get lost," another one added.

"The bride will run away with the best man," said another. "Oh wait, that's me."

They all laughed while Wesley wavered. Surely one drink couldn't hurt? It'd probably make him more prepared to call his parents. More relaxed. Less anxious. Plus, Sam had said earlier it was only bad to drink for no reason. Being social and celebrating were apparently reasons, and right now, Wesley would be doing both.

If he gave up drinking for the rest of his life, what would he do in situations like this where people were celebrating? Would he get left out? He'd have to learn what adults who didn't drink did with themselves. He'd have to remember what he used to do for fun before college.

There was a difference between having a problem and being an alcoholic, right? He couldn't imagine a life where every time someone offered him a drink, he'd have to say, *Sorry, I can't because I'm an alcoholic.* The idea made his blood curdle. That couldn't be him.

"Okay," he blurted out. "Since it's for the groom." He immediately regretted his words, but then, if he could have one drink and stop, wasn't that the surest sign that his problem wasn't that serious?

The men cheered. Kurt plucked two shots off the table and handed one to Wesley. "To my wedding."

"To your wedding!"

Wesley's shot burned going down, from both the alcohol and pure guilt. It hit his gut like acid and started chewing. At the same time, drinking again was such a relief. The familiarity of it was soothing, along with all the usual stress relief and relaxation.

Wesley set the shot glass down on the table. "Thanks for that, guys. Can I give you some money?"

"No way." Kurt waved him off. "Why don't you get the next round, though?"

"I shouldn't. I can't stay."

All the guys groaned and shouted protests.

"Come on," Kurt said. "Pull up a chair and have a beer with us. We have so much catching up to do. The guys actually know all about you. I told them about the guy I knew in college who scaled that ugly statue outside of Turlington Hall."

"That was you?" one of the guys asked. "Holy shit, dude. You're a legend."

Wesley grimaced. On one hand, hearing stories of his drunken antics highlighted the problem. On the other, it'd be nice to spend some time with other people after two weeks with Sam. Plus, after how stressful today had been, he could use a drink.

Today's ruined anyway, a voice in his head whispered. *You already had a shot. So fuck it, you might as well drink today and start fresh tomorrow. Besides, it's not like you agreed to never drink again. Sam said you would look at your options. You can do that tomorrow, and then make a decision.*

"All right, guys." Wesley flashed a grin. "The next round's on me."

CHAPTER TWELVE

S am was woken by the sound of the door slamming open. He had enough time to roll over, blink sleep from his eyes, and read 3:26 a.m. on the digital clock before something heavy landed on the bed.

"Sam!" Wesley slurred. "Sam, I have good news."

The smell of beer, stale cigarette smoke, and tequila invaded Sam's nose. "Wesley, what the—"

"I ran into Kurt Crocker. D'you remember him?" Wesley crawled on top of Sam and collapsed, crushing him. "He says hi."

Sam shoved Wesley off him and sat up. "Are you *drunk*?"

"Yeah, but it's okay. I talked to Kurt and his friends. Everything's going to be *fine*."

Sam scrubbed a hand down his face, wiping away the final remnants of sleep. "Christ, I was worried sick about you. You said you were going to be right back, and then you were gone for hours. I called you like a million times."

"Did you?" Wesley fumbled to pull his phone out of his pocket. It clattered to the carpeted floor. "Sorry, I think it's on silent."

"What the fuck, Wesley? I waited up for you. I finally had to go to sleep. I was dreaming about having to go to the police station tomorrow to report you missing."

That finally seemed to break through Wesley's drunken stupor. "Sammy, I'm so sorry. I wasn't thinking."

"No shit. What were you doing getting drunk after what we talked about earlier today?"

"That's the good news!"

Wesley tried to climb on him again, but Sam stopped him. "Jesus Christ. Stop shouting. You're going to wake our neighbors." Sam reached over and clicked on a lamp, blinking spots from his eyes.

"Sorry," Wesley whispered. "I got too excited. I have good news. I talked about my drinking problem with Kurt, and we solved it."

Sam was surprised by the pang of hurt that resonated through him. "You told a guy you haven't talked to since college about a problem you didn't feel you could come to me about?"

Wesley's smile wavered. "Well, yeah. But you know how it is. Talking to strangers is easier than talking to close friends sometimes. He had friends with 'im too. Guys I'll never see again. I thought, 'Who better?'"

"I guess." Sam sighed. "What'd they say? Nothing good, I'm guessing, since you're wasted."

"Nah, that's the thing. They were trying to get me to drink, 'n' I refused at first, which was *awesome* of me. Eventually, they were like why, and I told them what's been goin' on. I said that I was thinking of quitting, and they all said I can't. They said everyone drinks, and all I need to do is cut back. I can be, uh—" He scratched his face. "What's the word? Moderate! They said it's all about moderation, and 'm way too young to be worried about something like this."

Sam shook his head. "They were a bunch of guys in a bar. Of course they were pro-drinking. Did they get as wasted as you did?"

"Yeah."

"Did they seem at all bothered by the fact that they were drinking on a Wednesday night?"

"No." Wesley frowned.

"Is there a chance they have unhealthy relationships with alcohol as well?"

"Uh, maybe." Wesley's brow furrowed. "Come to think of it, Kurt said he got a job in a brewery for all the free beer. Maybe he's still stuck in college like I am."

"It's possible." Sam sighed and pinched his nose. "I don't think you can be moderate, Wesley. Maybe those guys can, and tonight was a fluke for them, but what you described to me earlier today was chronic overdrinking. Considering you couldn't go two days without getting drunk, I think your problem is a lot more serious than you want to believe."

"But what if—"

"But nothing!" Sam's temper finally boiled over. "You can't do this, Wesley. You can't tell me you have a problem and then turn around and keep tailspinning. For the life of me, I don't understand why, but you're clearly self-destructive, and I love you too much to watch you do this."

Wesley looked as stunned as Sam felt. "You . . . you love—"

"I need some air." Sam rolled out of bed, found his clothes, and yanked them on. "Go to sleep. In the morning, we'll talk. But for the record, you have to make a decision. You said you'd find a strong enough motivation to quit, but so much for that. It's time for you to figure out what's going on inside you that's making you be destructive, and what will give you the strength to stop."

Wesley fell silent, looking down at the bed. "What if I can't do it?"

He sounded so broken and sad, Sam wanted to reach out to him, but anger stayed his hand. "You can. I know that for certain. I said I would help you, and I meant it, but only if you commit to helping yourself. I can't watch you do this. I won't." He found his shoes and sat on the bed to tug them on, hands shaking.

"Wait, Sam, don't go." The mattress depressed behind him, and then warm arms wrapped around him. "Stay with me. Don't leave."

For a second, Sam leaned into the familiar, comforting touch. But then Wesley pulled his face to the side and tried to kiss him. The second Sam tasted alcohol, he shoved Wesley off him again.

"I'm sorry, Wesley." He climbed to his feet. "Sometimes supporting someone means storming out when they've fucked up. Don't come after me. I don't want to talk while you're like this."

Sam walked out and slammed the door behind him before Wesley could say another word. Belatedly, he checked his pockets to see if he had his room key. He'd put it in his wallet, which was mercifully in his back pocket. His phone, however, was on the nightstand. Damn.

He glanced back, debating with himself. The light filtering around the curtains disappeared, indicating that Wesley had turned off the lamp. With any luck, he was going to bed like Sam had suggested.

God, what a mess. I'm furious with him, and yet right now, all I want to do is go back inside, climb into bed, and hold him. He's probably so upset.

Sam forced himself away and headed for the stairs. He didn't know where he was going yet, but he had to get away. For once in his life, he needed to make a stand. This was a lesson Wesley had to learn, for his own good.

On the ground floor, Sam paused. To his left lay miles of dark, unfamiliar city that would probably lead to him getting lost without a phone. To his right was the parking lot, which wouldn't have offered much, except there was a light shining from a big window to the right of reception.

The hotel had a twenty-four-hour gym. Perfect. Working out seemed like the best way to sublimate all these negative emotions and clear his head. He looked down at himself. Exercising in jeans wasn't the best idea, but he wasn't about to head back into the room. It'd have to do.

The gym was empty, thanks no doubt to the late hour. There were twenty or so machines scattered around a swath of generic patterned carpet. Muted TVs mounted on the walls pictured shopping networks and late-night infomercials.

Sam started with some weight lifting. Nothing serious, since he didn't have a spot, but enough to make his triceps burn as he lifted a twenty-pound barbell slowly behind him, between his shoulder blades.

When his arm muscles threatened mutiny, he switched to cardio. He set a treadmill to a light jog, and once he fell into a rhythm, he opened his head, letting all the events of the past week spread out in front of him. Deciding to go on this impromptu trip. Seeing Wesley in a new way. Hooking up with him. Learning his "secret." And now . . . falling for him.

Sam's heart rate rose, and it had nothing to do with the jogging. He couldn't pinpoint the exact moment he'd realized it. Maybe he'd known since college and had been repressing it. It was impossible to tell. This wasn't like a movie, where music had swelled in the background, and they'd run across a beach into each other's arms.

No. Sam had fallen in love with Wesley over the course of thousands of days, hundreds of shared memories, and an immeasurable number of small but priceless moments. He'd fallen in love with the way the wind ruffled Wesley's hair, with his deep voice, and how Wesley was the only person who could get Sam to drop everything and go on a journey like this. No one else could make Sam this livid either—bursting with the kind of anger that stemmed from bone-deep fear—which was the surest sign it was love.

Naturally, Sam hadn't realized he was in love until now. Wesley was in the throes of an alcohol addiction, and Sam was about to confront his parents for the first time in over a year, in an extremely public forum, while the rest of his family looked on with judgment and disapproval.

Perfect timing.

To think, when Wesley had first admitted what was going on with him, Sam had thought they were lucky. They'd caught this in the early stages. But now, it seemed the doctors had read the charts wrong, and the disease had already sunk in its roots.

A disease was precisely what it was too. Sam believed that. He wanted to help Wesley, but there was another line he couldn't cross: the difference between being supportive and being an enabler.

Sam was going to have to learn the difference fast. In fact, if they were going to be together, Sam would have to give up drinking too. He hated to think of himself when Wesley was facing this monumental challenge, but Sam had some tough choices to make as well.

The *if* in that equation was very much a factor. If it all worked out. If they stayed together. If they dated. Sam had lost out on his chance to ask Wesley what this was in the car, and he'd done it willingly.

What was going on between them had ceased to be important the second Wesley had admitted he had a drinking problem. The question was no longer whether they had feelings for each other. The question was whether they *could* have them while Wesley was dealing with this huge, consuming thing. There were all sorts of consent and moral issues, and a million factors to consider.

It agonized Sam to admit it, but he was pretty sure the answer was no. Not right now. Not like this.

The door to the gym banged open, startling Sam so much he nearly fell off his machine.

Is someone else seriously working out this late?

Sam glanced at the clock on the wall; 5 a.m. had rolled around, which meant it wasn't late anymore. It was early. Damn.

The guy—who had so much muscle packed onto his upper body, he looked like he was going to tip over—didn't so much as glance at Sam as he trundled to the weight machines. He went straight for the bench press, loaded it with weights, and sat down.

Sam watched him with burgeoning horror. *Is he going to lift that without a spot?*

Sure enough, the guy lay down on the bench and got into position, meaty fingers flexing on the bar. He unhooked it, and it fell nearly to his neck. He caught it before it hit him and struggled to lift it up one agonizing inch at a time. His face was red within seconds, veins jutting out by his temples.

With bated breath, Sam watched the guy fight through a set of ten. Every time he lifted the bar up, Sam expected him to lose his grip and drop it, snapping his neck. By the end of the guy's first set, Sam's anxiety was through the roof.

He's going to kill himself. Of all the thoughtless, irresponsible, reckless— Does he not realize what an impact this is having on the people around him?

Avoidant as he was, Sam hadn't intended on saying anything. But then, after a short break, the guy started another set of reps. At the sight of him once more struggling, Sam's reservations shattered. He was off his treadmill and across the room in a flash.

"Hey." Sam stared down at him, arms crossed. "You need a spot?"

The guy startled, and Sam nearly had a heart attack when he briefly fumbled with the bar. He hefted it back onto the hooks and sat up, eyeing Sam. "No, thanks. I'm all right."

"No, you're not!" Sam blurted out. Rage he hadn't realized he'd been holding back flooded through him. "You're going to hurt yourself. How can you be so irresponsible? Think about how much it would hurt the people who love you if something happened to you!"

Distantly, Sam realized he was breathing hard.

The guy stared at him. "Buddy, you wanna talk about it?"

Mortification spread throughout Sam's body like poison. Blushing furiously, he mumbled an apology and scurried away. He didn't stop moving until he hit the cool morning air outside.

"Wow," he muttered to himself. "Think maybe your anger at that guy might've been a little misplaced?"

The sky was lightening with the promise of dawn. It couldn't be more than half an hour away. Sam could go back to the hotel room and catch a few hours of sleep before they had to make the final twelve-hour trek to Helena, or...

There was one other issue on Sam's mind. One he'd been thinking about off and on since his phone call with Jessica. He'd always relied on Wesley to bring fun into his life. On top of everything else, Wesley was great at getting him to socialize. That socializing in college had predominantly involved partying, and not much had changed since graduation. Had Sam contributed to Wesley's alcoholism by relying on him to be the fun one?

If—*when*—Wesley quit drinking, he was going to have to find new ways to enjoy life. He was going to need space and time to do that. It would probably be best if he wasn't around people who reminded him of the environments that triggered his drinking, like the people he'd known in college. Including Sam. That meant Sam was going to have to take his sister's advice and learn to live without Wesley. For both their sakes.

Had it been any less infuriating, Sam would have found it funny. Not a week ago, he'd explained to his sister how vital Wesley's friendship was to him. Now, it was potentially a trigger for Wesley's alcoholism. And it was keeping Sam from figuring out how to live his own life.

I need to prove something to myself. I used to think I needed Wesley to push me to live. If I can find a way to do that on my own, then that means there's hope for me. And if there's hope for me, there's hope for Wesley too.

But what could he do?

The sky—which had shifted from charcoal to gray—struck him with inspiration like a lightning bolt. Wesley's words rang in his head: *"When was the last time you saw a sunrise?"*

Well, this dawn was one Sam was going to enjoy all on his own. This would be his memory, and his alone.

And Sam knew exactly where to get the best vantage point.

He wandered over to Wesley's car, planted both hands on the trunk, and hauled himself up. He scooted back until he could rest against the slanted rear windshield. Cold dew soaked into the back of his shirt, but he paid it no mind. His head fell against the metal roof, which might as well have been ice. It smacked any trace of sleepiness from him.

He probably should have been bored, lying on a car while the sky brightened one infinitesimal degree at a time, but with his feet off the ground, and his back supported, he felt weightless. Like he might float up into the sky at any moment. It was pleasant, and admittedly a little scary, after so many years of keeping his feet firmly on the ground.

The dawn that broke over the trees was ice-white at first. It bronzed slowly, starting right at the horizon and spreading out to cover the whole dome in gold. Bits of it were blocked by buildings and billboards, but Sam could see enough. It unfurled lilac ribbons out to catch on the clouds, which blushed pink at the contact.

It was beautiful. Invigorating. Inspiring. It infused Sam with both strength and misery. He could live without Wesley, but God, he didn't want to.

The dawn reminded him of another truth: a fresh day meant new opportunities, but also new challenges. Once they got to the wedding, that wasn't the end, but rather, the beginning. They had the whole drive back, and Sam couldn't force Wesley to be sober for it. He didn't want to *force* Wesley to do anything.

The first of Sam's difficult decisions loomed over him, burning like the sun rising above the treetops. Warmth tickled his skin even as realization chilled his blood. At some point, Sam had handed his heart over to Wesley, and now it was his to protect or crush. Sam didn't expect Wesley to be perfect, or to never backslide again. But if Wesley kept hurting himself, he was going to hurt Sam too, as sure as if their hearts occupied the same space.

Sam could love Wesley with all his heart, could support him and give everything to him, and would still have to watch him self-destruct. If Wesley kept drinking, it'd kill them both.

As sunlight swept over Sam, a plan began to form in his head that would test him to the foundation of his character.

CHAPTER THIRTEEN

To say that Wesley felt like shit in the morning would besmirch the good name of shit. Physically and mentally, he might as well have been gutted and then had his insides stuffed back in his skin, sausage-style.

Sam woke him shortly after seven and asked if he'd gotten enough sleep to drive. To Wesley's complete and utter mortification, he was still a little drunk, and watching Sam's face fall as he admitted it gutted him all over again. Sam set his jaw, turned away, and walked into the bathroom. If only he'd slammed the door. Wesley would have preferred that to the too-quiet click as it shut.

What have I done?

Fifteen minutes later, Sam emerged with wet hair and his bag of toiletries. He packed them in his bag without looking at Wesley.

"Hey." Wesley sat up, wincing when the jeans he'd slept in dug into his stomach. "I can't apologize enough for last night. I fucked up, and I know it."

"We need to pick up our clothes from the laundry service." Sam unplugged his laptop and dumped that in too. "They opened a few minutes ago. Which reminds me, I want to get my formal outfit for the wedding pressed when we get to Helena. Did you think to pack something nice to wear?"

Wesley frowned, both from his pounding head and the implication. "Of course I did, Sammy. When we left, it was you who thought—"

"I don't want to hear about me or what I thought." Sam picked up his bag and tossed it onto the bed with uncharacteristic carelessness. And still, he didn't look at Wesley. "I don't want you to call me

Sammy, either. It hurts too much right now. I'm exhausted, and since you're still drunk, that means I have to drive for at least the first part of what is going to be a grueling twelve-plus hours to get to the rehearsal dinner on time. I want coffee—lots and lots of coffee—and to get going. Once we're in the car, there'll be plenty of time to talk."

Wesley swallowed, throat so dry it choked him. "Obvious question: Are you mad at me?"

Sam finally looked over. "I won't lie. I'm a lot of things, and angry is one of them. But mostly, I'm cranky as fuck because I only got a few hours' sleep. I'm sure you're not feeling like a ray of sunshine either."

Wesley shook his head.

"Let's get caffeine and food before we do anything else. I don't want to let my blood sugar do the talking and end up snapping at you."

Despite the severity of the situation, a smile slid over Wesley's face. That was so like Sam. Even when he was angry, he was still so considerate. He still watched out for Wesley.

If I lose him, I don't know what I'll do. So many people I love have been worried about me lately.

As he watched Sam, a memory drifted into Wesley's head: the conversation he'd had with his parents days before he'd talked Sam into running away on this impromptu "adventure."

"We're worried about you. Your mother and I think you should go to rehab."

Wesley jerked his head up, startled. "What?"

He'd never seen his dad's face look so sad. "You have a problem, Wesley. You need help."

"You guys are overreacting."

Mom, on the other hand, looked frightened. "You need to take this seriously. People develop liver problems all the time."

"I'm twenty-three, Mom. My liver is fine."

"If you keep drinking like this, it won't be for much longer. You could make yourself really sick."

Wesley had left the house in a huff. Days later, he'd leapt at the opportunity to get out of town with Sam. If his parents couldn't find him, they couldn't force him to check into a clinic. He'd literally run away from his problems.

Maybe this could still be fixed, though. Maybe he really didn't have a problem. Maybe— Maybe—

More excuses.

Those were the sorts of excuses he found himself making all the time lately. It was only one beer. He was on vacation. It wasn't like he had a job to go to in the morning. The easiest excuses were the ones that justified not telling Sam. If Sam looked at him with even a shadow of the disappointment that his parents had, Wesley would crumble. Shatter. Die.

I need to get my shit together, in a big way.

They gathered their things—including picking up their laundry—and headed out. Sam stopped for coffee and food, but the way he told it, he was going to haul ass to Helena. No goofing off. No stopping to check out weird shops and tourist traps. If the car caught fire, he might very well keep driving in the hopes that it'd put itself out. Once they were in Montana, he intended to sleep until the rehearsal dinner the next day.

"I booked us a place in Helena first thing this morning." Sam removed a hand from the steering wheel to stifle a yawn. "Jesus, I'm so tired. I keep picturing beds appearing out of nowhere."

Wesley didn't respond. Normally, he'd crack a joke, but for some mysterious reason, his drunkenness causing Sam to lose sleep didn't seem like a laughing matter.

Sam navigated them down a straight, tree-lined stretch of highway. It was too early for the morning rush, but not so early they had the road to themselves. Sam seemed content to let the quiet drag on as he wove them around slower-moving vehicles.

Wesley thumbed through a hundred different sentence starters only to discover he had no idea how to finish any of them. He wanted to apologize again, but words were only going to get him so far. If he was going to fix this, he needed to show Sam he wasn't going to fuck up again. That was a problem for two reasons: there was nothing he could do about it right now, and when an opportunity did present itself, there was no telling how his out-of-control ass was going to handle it.

Fifteen minutes of uncomfortable silence later, Sam beat him to the punch.

"I suppose there's no avoiding it." Sam's eyes didn't stray from the road. "We have to talk about last night."

Wesley sucked in a breath through his teeth. "Did I mention how sorry I am?"

"You could stand to say it again."

"Sam." Wesley turned in his seat as much as the belt would let him. "I'm so, so sorry."

Sam didn't respond right away. When he did, it was without so much as a glance Wesley's way. "Why'd you do it?"

Wesley put a great deal of thought into his answer before slumping down in his seat. "Because I'm an alcoholic."

Sam's head swiveled to stare at him before snapping back to the road. "Huh?"

"That probably sounds like a cop-out, but saying it out loud is . . ." He sighed. "Painful. And a relief. Like ripping off a bandage. I could lie and list other reasons. I ran into an old college friend. It put me back in that mindset. They were celebrating. I was being social. But all that is surface. Deep down, I'm a fucking alcoholic. I don't know *why*, but I am."

To his surprise, Sam perked up. "Figuring out what drives you to drink sounds like a good second step to me."

"Second step?"

Sam smiled. "You know what they say. The first step is admitting you have a problem. You just did that, for real this time. No more denial."

A spark of hope burst to life inside of Wesley. "Does this mean you forgive me?"

The smile slid off Sam's face as if it'd been oiled. In profile, his features seemed sharper than normal. "Of course I do, but I'm afraid that's not the issue. Not really, anyway. I did some thinking last night, and there are a couple of things I need to say to you."

Never in his life had Wesley wished he was sober so badly. "Okay."

A tide of terror rose up in him as a voice in his head whispered, *You brought this on yourself.*

"I'm proud of you for being up-front." Sam's eyes didn't leave the road. His hands were trembling on the steering wheel, though his voice was steady as a metronome. "I'm less proud of you for what you did last night. It's great that you're owning to it, but I'm afraid that's not enough."

Wesley's intestines tightened with misery. "Go on."

"It's important that you have support right now and that you know people love you and care about you. But I also think having a safety net could hurt you in the long run. Relapsing and backsliding are things. They've already happened to you. They might keep happening if you think your actions don't have consequences."

This is it. He's going to say he can't deal with this. Christ, and here I thought he'd at least wait until after the wedding.

Wesley hung his head. "I'm sorry about that. I'll apologize as many times as you need me to."

"I don't need apologies. I need you to understand something. At this point, you can't think that moderation is an option. If you do, then the next time you get the urge to drink, you'll go through the same old round of excuses. You'll tell yourself you're only having one, or that drinking socially is okay, or you're too young to worry about this. Tell me I'm wrong."

Wesley was dead silent.

Sam let out a strained breath. "That's why I have to do something. Something I don't want to do. But I believe in my heart it'll be better for both of us in the long run."

Here it comes. He's leaving. Oh God. Wesley braced himself.

"You have to stop drinking, completely, and promise to get help." Sam spared him a pointed look before turning back to the road. His eyes were liquid with emotion. "I'm not saying go to rehab, but you at least need counseling and to join AA, or whatever support group you choose. I'll support you through it all, but you *have* to commit to this. I hate talking about myself right now, but after last night, I need to be honest. If this is going to work, you have to show me some progress."

It took Wesley a second to process that information. "Wait, what?"

"I know it sounds like a lot right now, but we'll read up on our options. We'll find local meetings you can join and figure out what works for you. I know your parents will want to help too, and—"

"'We'?" Wesley stared at him. "As in, both of us?"

"Of course."

"You mean, you're not running for the hills?" Hope swelled up in Wesley like a balloon. "You're not leaving?"

Sam was tense as a piano string, his expression unreadable. "I'm not leaving. Yet."

The balloon burst. It seemed it'd been filled with ice cubes, because Wesley's whole body grew cold.

Sam kept talking, and each word stuck in Wesley like a knife. "I'm not going to abandon you when you're at a low point, but Wesley, you must know . . . You must have realized by now . . ."

Wesley heart stopped. "Realized what?"

Sam let out a tight breath. "How I feel about you."

Wesley's heart went from a standstill to a gallop in an instant. He tried to speak, but his lungs were on fire. He hadn't known it was possible to be so happy and so miserable at the same time.

Oblivious, Sam continued. "I would stay by your side forever, through anything, and that's precisely why I can't. I can't be selfish about this."

There was so much Wesley wanted to say. So many feelings he wanted to confess. If he could, he'd scoop Sam into his arms and hold him so tightly, all his cacophonic thoughts would transfer through their skin, and then Sam would know. He'd know how completely, uselessly in love with him Wesley was.

But Wesley couldn't say any of that. Not now. He couldn't tell Sam he loved him when Sam was talking about leaving. So instead, he said what he could.

"You're not selfish," Wesley whispered. "You're wonderful."

"I am selfish, though. If you hate me for what I'm about to say, fine. I deserve that. But at least try to understand. I've been thinking about what you said, about how hard it is to take death seriously at our age. I can't wait ten or twenty years for some health scare to make you quit. You need immediate consequences. So, here's what you stand to lose: me."

Wesley's throat tightened to the point of pain. He stayed quiet and waited for the final blow.

Sam, on the other hand, talked fast, as if the words were fighting each other to get out first. "Now that I know how serious this is, I can't watch you tailspin. I won't. Days ago, I never would have believed I was strong enough to not have you in my life, but if it'll help you, I'll do it. I'll walk right out the door. I know now that I can survive without you. This isn't an ultimatum. This is honesty. I'm telling you how far I'm willing to go."

After a breath, Wesley was able to unclench his jaw enough to say, "I understand."

If anyone else had made this declaration, Wesley might not have cared, but from Sam it was earth-shattering. It must've taken everything Sam had to work up the nerve to say it. Instantly, Wesley was terrified. What he'd told Sam in Alabama was true: once Sam made up his mind, that was it. Nothing could stop him. Including Wesley.

"There's something I need to know." Sam cleared his throat. "The other day, when you said you thought you could find a powerful enough motivator to quit, were you thinking about me?"

Wesley's voice cracked when he tried to answer, so he nodded instead.

"I was afraid of that." Sam sighed. "Not only because that never would have worked, but because of how much I wish it had, and how much I love that you thought of me. But now, you don't have that anymore. I want to support you, but I refuse to enable you. I don't care if it's cliché: you have to change for yourself."

Wesley was being drawn and quartered by his own emotions. Humiliation, uncertainty, pain, and love. Deep, frightening love like dark water. Not frightening because it was Sam, but because he might have lost it already. How could he have let himself fall so far?

"You're right," Wesley said. "You're right about everything." Suddenly, he felt dead sober. Soberer than he'd ever been in his life. "The next time we pull over for a break, let me drive."

Sam switched into the right lane to let a speeding car pass. "You mean it?"

"Yeah. I feel better now, and you should get some sleep."

"About what I said—"

"I need some time to think." Wesley blew out a breath. "Driving will be good for that. But for the record, consider me scared sober. Literally."

Sam looked pained. "I didn't mean to scare you."

"I know, Sam. Everything you said was to help me. Because you care about me. I know how much it must have hurt you to say it. Thanks for doing it anyway. Try to understand, however, how completely embarrassing this is for me. I feel about eight years old, getting scolded by a parent for pulling some stunt."

"I'm so sorry." Sam took a deep breath. "For all of this."

"No." Wesley shook his head. "I'm the one who's sorry. More sorry than I can say."

Sam got them out of mountainous Colorado and into flatter-but-less-green Wyoming before his yawning reached critical levels. Wesley took over while Sam slept in the back seat. The approximation of privacy was both a blessing and a curse. Wesley was given time to process, but unfortunately, he was given time to process.

What a mess he'd made. It was almost enough to make him wish they'd never gone on this trip in the first place. Almost. His eyes darted to the rearview window. He could see Sam's tousled blond head. His hair had fallen over his eyes. His mouth was slack, and he was snoring gently.

Gorgeous.

No, nothing could make Wesley regret this trip. He wouldn't trade the time he'd had with Sam for anything, especially now that it was running out. Wesley had never felt so motivated but also so terrified.

From where he was sitting right now, nothing in the world could make him drink again. Not if it meant losing Sam. But that meant he was still quitting for Sam and not for himself. What if it wasn't enough? What if he fucked up again? All Wesley could do was take it one step at a time and hope he found the motivation soon, or it'd be too late. For him, and for them.

It was ten at night by the time they got to Helena. Being surrounded by low mountains ever since they'd crossed the state line had made Wesley oddly claustrophobic. The small, open city was a welcome relief.

Wesley's eyes had started sliding shut of their own accord, but he powered through it. He woke Sam up to ask him the name of where they were staying and plugged it into his navigation app.

Sam sat up and propped his arms on the backrest. "Are we almost there?"

"Yeah." Wesley glanced at his phone in his lap. "It's this next right." He made the turn and pulled up to a tiny motel.

"It's only for one night." For some reason, Sam sounded nervous. "Jessica got a block of rooms in a hotel by the church. She said there's one for us, so we'll stay there tomorrow."

"It's okay. It's not like we haven't had worse. Remember New York?"

But Sam didn't relax. All through check-in—when they were given room keys and old butterscotch candy from a dusty dish on the counter—his shoulders were sharp peaks of tension.

The second Wesley got the door to their room open and flicked on the nearest light switch, he understood why.

Sam had booked them a room with two beds.

Wesley stood in the doorway, so stunned his suitcase slipped out of his grasp and hit the carpet with a soft *thud*. Behind him, Sam was silent. Stepping into the room, Wesley stared at the second bed like it'd pulled a gun on him.

"I thought this would be better," Sam said quietly. "We both need space right now. I don't think anything should happen between us until . . ."

"Until we know if I'm going relapse again," Wesley finished. *Until you know if I'm the ticking time bomb I seem to be.*

Sam's silence was the most deafening confirmation Wesley had ever received.

It would've been kinder if Sam had pulled out a knife and stabbed him right in the belly. Wesley struggled to hold in his own bleeding insides as he smiled. "That's fine. I understand."

It was true. He completely understood why Sam couldn't have sex with someone who had a habitual alcohol problem. But that didn't make him feel any less shredded, or any less like his best friend in the entire world had just rejected him both physically and emotionally.

And worst of all, it was Wesley's fault.

He threw his bag at one of the beds and, without looking to see where it landed, headed straight for the bathroom, eyes stinging.

Waking up the next morning without Sam next to him ripped his insides out all over again. Wesley stayed in bed with his eyes closed, not ready to confront the reality of his world right now.

On top of everything else, once the wedding was over, so was their trip. They'd have to go straight home, and then a new torture would begin. One where Wesley was looking for jobs and AA meetings at the same time. One where he couldn't drink to make this newfound pain go away. He'd never wanted a beer more in his life, and yet the idea that he'd let alcohol put him in this situation made him gag.

He stayed in bed until he heard rustling from the other side of the room. A soft sound drifted to his ears: bare feet on carpet. The mattress creaked beneath new weight, and warm fingers found Wesley's shoulder.

"Wesley. You awake?"

Sam's voice was both a balm and sandpaper grating against his skin. Wesley kept his eyes closed and his breathing even, beyond not ready for this.

"Wesley?" Silence. Then, the weight on the bed shifted. If Wesley knew Sam—and God, did he ever—he was moving to sit with his legs crossed. The warm fingers on Wesley's shoulder drifted up to his hair and stroked it gently.

"Yesterday killed me."

It was all Wesley could do to keep his expression from changing as the words rang in his ears.

Sam's voice was low, but Wesley could hear breaks in it, as if he were feeling cracks in a plate that had been hastily glued back together. "That was the hardest thing I've ever done in my life. I hated every second of it. I hated sleeping without you. I hated that I didn't get the chance to tell you how I—" He paused. "I've been avoiding telling you."

There was a sound like a sob. Wesley's eyelids burned to open, but he kept them closed.

"I wanted these last days together. I wanted to wait to tell you because it was going to change everything, and now I've missed my chance. I'm a coward for saying it when you can't hear me, but at least this way, no matter what happens, I'll have said it. I love you, Wesley."

Was it possible Sam couldn't hear Wesley's heart right now? Because to him, it was thunderous, making the blood in his veins roar like an angry sea.

Sam continued. "I love you so much. It's making me strong, and part of me wishes it weren't, because that's what's allowing me to distance myself from you. If I cared for you any less, I'd cover my ears and pretend this wasn't happening. I'd crawl into bed with you and kiss you and spend my life with you, for so long as we both shall live. But I can't do that. This is my fault. I should have seen it sooner. How could *I* not notice? I should have— The day I met you, I should have—" His voice broke. "I thought we had time. All the time in the world. I thought . . . I thought you were going to be my picket fence."

A choked sob. It seemed as though Sam was going to say more, but abruptly, the weight on the mattress vanished.

Sam must've turned away, or maybe he didn't notice the hot tear that escaped from under Wesley's closed eyelid and rolled down his cheek.

CHAPTER FOURTEEN

S am's finger shook as he buttoned up the dress shirt that had been taunting him from the bottom of his luggage this whole time. The bathroom mirror showed him a face that was a vague facsimile of his own, only pinched and waxen with stress.

"It's going to be fine," Wesley said from the room. He was standing at the foot of his bed, considering two outfits laid out on it.

"I didn't say anything."

"You didn't need to. I can feel you freaking out all the way over here."

Sam took a breath and ran a hand through his hair, which he'd smoothed to the point of unsmoothing it. "I don't think I've ever been this nervous."

"Don't be. You've been low-key worrying this whole trip. I'm sure you've imagined every nightmare scenario that could possibly go down. You probably lay awake one or two nights picturing your relatives pillorying you and chucking rotten tomatoes at your head."

Sam whistled. "It's not every day you hear the word 'pillorying.'"

"The point is, you're as ready as you'll ever be, and after tonight, it's over. You'll have faced your parents. The dragon will have been slain. After that, you can move on. You're free." Wesley picked up the leftmost outfit—a navy-blue cashmere sweater with white slacks and a black belt—and walked over. He stood behind Sam, slightly to the right, and held it up to himself. "What do you think?"

"Brings out your eyes." Sam wet his lips and looked at his own clothing choices: a red button-down and black trousers, paired with a white bow tie he was struggling with. They were lucky Jessica hadn't wanted a black-tie wedding, or they would have had to rent tuxes.

"Here. Let me." Wesley set his clothing aside, took Sam by the shoulders, and gently pivoted him until they were face to face. "You never could work these."

"Never needed to." Sam swallowed hard. "You're always around to do it for me."

Wesley took the lopsided bow in hand and pulled it apart, starting over. Standing this close, Sam could see the stubble scraping across his jaw, could smell his mild cologne and the soap-sweet scent of his hair. Hell, Sam could count his eyelashes and see the flecks of gray in his clear, blue eyes.

Sam's body started getting hot before he could stop it. Wesley's thumb accidentally brushed against his throat, and that light touch sizzled. Wesley finished fixing the bow tie and rested his hands on Sam's shoulders. Their eyes met. The second they did, Sam knew Wesley could feel it too. The tension between them. The magnetism.

After five years of not having sex, suddenly going a few days without it was like starving to death. Now the forbidden-fruit element was back too. Sam had forced this space between them, and he felt every inch of it like tangible distance. Heat and tongues and exploring fingers. Nothing but a memory now.

Wesley's eyes searched Sam's face, and they grew darker with every pass. He took a half step closer, and Sam's breathing hitched in his throat.

Please kiss me, Sam thought as another, smaller part of him prayed that Wesley wouldn't. If Wesley kissed him, Sam would let him, and no matter how badly he wanted it, he'd put this space between them for a reason.

Wesley's face inched closer, and Sam's heart turned into a hummingbird, fluttering frantically in his chest. At the last second, Wesley veered to the left and kissed him on the cheek. It should have been anticlimactic, but Wesley's lips seared Sam's skin.

Jesus, how had Sam ever thought he could stay away? Not just on this trip, but in general. Had there really been a point in his life when he'd believed Wesley was nothing other than a friend to him? It seemed unfathomable now.

Wesley pulled back from him slowly, eyes trained on the ground. "We should get going. Don't want to be late."

"Yeah." Sam swallowed. "Wesley?"

"Hm?"

"Stay by my side tonight. Please? I don't think I can do this without you."

Wesley's mouth curved up. "Of course."

They packed up, checked out, and drove to the venue for the rehearsal dinner. It was a restaurant Sam knew well: the View—a sprawling, ivy-covered building at the top of a large hill. As the name suggested, the outdoor seating gave spectacular vantage points of the surrounding landscape. Sam had celebrated many a life event there, from births to funerals. And now, it was possibly going to be the place he melted into the floor and died.

"Stop stressing," Wesley said as they climbed approximately forty bajillion stairs to the entrance. "It's going to be fine."

"What if it's not, though?" Sam fiddled with his tie. "Why did I tell Jessica not to let them know I'd be coming? I should have had her warn them. What if they're totally shocked? What if they're furious? What if Mom cries, and I ruin Jessica's wedding?"

"Sammy, you have to stop torturing yourself." They reached the entrance. Wesley touched Sam's hand, pulling it gently away from the bow tie he was in the process of unraveling all over again. "Whatever happens is going to happen. You're not ruining Jessica's wedding by being here. You're making her very happy. No matter what your parents think. It's not their day, it's hers."

"Right." Sam took a breath. "I should be thinking about Jessica. I'm not the important one here."

The smile on Wesley's face was beautiful. "You are to me."

Sam gave his hand a squeeze before opening the glass doors and striding inside. A hostess at a stand greeted them. "Table for two?"

"We're here for the Cooper-Velasco rehearsal." Sam could barely keep his voice steady.

"Right this way."

She led them through a sea of white tablecloths and fine china to one of the many outdoor areas. A whole veranda had been sectioned off, separating them from other diners with white trellises covered in hanging plants.

Sam followed after her with leaden feet. He recognized a handful of his cousins instantly, along with some of Jessica's friends, but there were plenty of people he didn't know seated at the four long tables.

At the far end of the patio, standing next to a man with black hair and a wide smile, was Jessica. She was talking to a table full of people and looked radiant in a purple cocktail dress and bright-blue heels. Her hair had been curled into silky ribbons. Sam's heart thumped painfully at the sight of her, in a good way.

"Is that her fiancé next to her?" Wesley whispered.

"Yeah, that's Noah. You'll like him. He's funny and a hell of a cook."

As if sensing their gazes, Jessica suddenly looked up. Upon spotting Sam, her eyes grew wide. "Sam!"

"Jess!" Sam held out his arms.

Jessica hurried over and practically threw herself at him, kicking up her heels. "I'm so glad to see you, little bro."

"It's good to see you too, sis. Congratulations."

Noah wandered over and had the good sense to wait until Jessica had finished squeezing Sam before he offered a large, square hand. "Sam! You've made my wife very happy by being here today."

Sam shook it. "I'm thrilled myself."

"I'm not your wife yet, mister," Jessica said. Her eyes fell on Wesley next. "Wesley, this is my fiancé, Noah. Noah, this is Wesley. Sam's . . . friend." Her smile was beatific.

Sam's face flashed with heat like he'd thrown it into a campfire. When Wesley reached forward to shake, his cheeks were red as well.

"I hate to interrupt our reunion," Sam said, "but where are—"

"Sam?"

He froze. He knew that voice. Slowly, he pivoted in place until he was facing the door back into the restaurant. Halfway through the door stood Sam's mother. Doe-like brown eyes stared at him, no headlight necessary. Her expression was that of total surprise, but in a moment, it would morph into something else, and that would decide the fate of the rest of the weekend.

Sam grabbed Wesley's hand instinctively. His grip had to be painful, but Wesley didn't make a peep. He held on, infusing Sam somehow with the strength to keep his knees from buckling.

Before she could react, someone came up behind her. "Dear, what are you . . ." Dad stopped short behind his wife when he spotted Sam. His face warped with nigh-identical shock. In the back of Sam's mind, a voice joked about married couples looking alike after years together.

"Mom. Dad." Sam couldn't tell if he was speaking loud enough to be heard. He scrambled for the perfect words to say to the parents he hadn't seen in over a year and ultimately came up with, "Hi."

For a moment that lasted a lifetime, everyone was still. Then, Dad slowly pushed past Mom. Every step of his shined shoes against the floor was a portent. He stopped right in front of Sam. Another second passed, and then he wrapped Sam in a tight hug.

At first, Sam was too stunned to react, but then something like a spring inside of him released, and he hugged his father back with everything he had.

Voice shaking, Dad said, "My son. We missed you so much."

A second pair of arms wound around him, and his mom's flowery perfume filled his nose. "We thought you weren't going to make it. We thought we'd chased you away. Welcome home, Sam."

Sam was not at all surprised when he burst into tears, but he was surprised when his dad joined him, his lined face turning red. Mom patted her husband on the back and kept her composure, though her eyes were brighter than normal.

When they finally let go of him, Sam realized he was still holding Wesley's hand. Miraculously, it wasn't broken. Sam released him and beckoned for him to step closer. "You guys remember, Wesley, right?"

"Of course." Mom eyed him. "I bet you had a hand in bringing Sam back."

"Not at all. It was his decision. I just provided the wheels."

"Well, thank you for whatever part you had in it." Dad gave Sam's shoulder a squeeze. "I should have known when I saw two empty seats at our table. Come sit with us. We have a lot of catching up to do."

"Of course. We'll be right there." Sam watched his parents walk away, heart pounding.

Wesley touched his shoulder. "I knew it."

"Knew what?"

Wesley grinned. "I had a feeling watching that was going to make the whole trip worth it."

Wesley spent most of the rehearsal dinner being ignored, and that was fine by him. Watching Sam with his family, particularly Jessica, was bittersweet. Sweet because Wesley was happy for them; bitter because when Wesley faced his own parents, he definitely wasn't going to get hugs and kisses out of it.

The Coopers hit Sam with questions hard and fast, wanting to know everything he'd been up to for the past year. They knew about his internship and that it had ended. What were his plans now? Where was he living? Was he seeing anyone? Sam fielded the questions with as much tact as could be expected. Wesley was exceptionally proud of him.

He was also grateful Sam was so busy, because he missed the moment when the waiter came by and asked Wesley what he wanted to drink. He hated to think of Sam staring at him, waiting to see what he'd pick.

Wesley ordered water, and immediately the person sitting next to him, who had been identified as Cousin Walter, chimed in. "Just water? At a wedding rehearsal?"

Wesley looked down at the smooth white tablecloth. "I'm not much of a drinker." *Biggest lie I've ever told, but what else can I say? "I'm a recovering alcoholic. Or at least, I hope I'm recovering. Jury's still out on that."?*

"It's a party, though." Walter took a sip from his own glass of wine, which had already been refilled several times. "You should live a little."

"Water will do fine."

"I suppose that's the responsible choice. I only drink socially, really."

"Don't listen to him." A young woman leaned over Walter and stage-whispered to Wesley. "I know how you feel. I'm vegetarian, and every time I tell people I don't eat meat, they say, 'Why not? I'd be vegetarian, except I could never give up blank.' It's the same with saying you don't drink. People are like, 'Why not? I only drink because blank.'"

That launched Walter into a diatribe about vegetarianism that sucked the girl in. Wesley was left surprisingly invigorated. He'd been dreading a lifetime of having to dodge questions about his drinking—or lack thereof—but here he'd found someone who understood in an unexpected way. Maybe this wasn't going to be so hard after all.

Although, being stuck in a room full of people he mostly didn't know, with nothing to do but eat one dinner for three hours, made him itch to do shots. But every time Sam paused in his conversation with his parents to glance at Wesley and smile, Wesley's waning determination renewed.

Don't forget what Sam said. You have to find motivation outside of him. You might as well start thinking now.

But no matter how much Wesley mulled it over, he came up blank. Health problems were too distant of a threat to motivate him. He'd successfully gotten jobs while binge drinking, so that was a no-go. He wanted to stop worrying his parents, but that was an external factor. He needed to find something that struck a chord in him on a personal level.

The dinner passed without him magically arriving at a solution. Jessica told them to follow her to the hotel where they'd be staying for the rest of the weekend.

The second they got into the car, Sam started laughing. It wasn't hysterical, exactly, but it wasn't his normal laughter either. Wesley waited it out. He started the engine and pulled onto the road behind Jessica's black sedan.

Eventually, Sam wiped his eyes. "I can't believe how well that went."

"With your parents? They weren't mad at all?"

"No, they were. That's the thing. Dad brought up the cost of the wedding-that-never-was several times, and Mom scolded me for so much as *thinking* about missing Jessica's big day, but that was nothing compared to how grateful they were to see me. I can't believe I psyched myself out so badly. Do you know they thought I was mad at *them*?"

"Really?"

"Yeah. When I stopped calling, they thought it was because they weren't more supportive when I left Michael. Convinced as they were that I didn't want to talk to them, they stopped calling too."

"So, no one was talking, and everyone thought everyone else was mad, when really everyone was not communicating." Wesley laughed. "Sounds like family all right."

Sam fell silent for a moment. "They asked about you."

Innocuous as that statement was, it made Wesley's pulse skip. "Oh?"

"They noticed us holding hands. They wanted to know if you were my date to the wedding."

What did you say? The question burned on Wesley's tongue, but he swallowed it along with the bile rising in the back of his throat. Sam's answer didn't matter. It couldn't.

In his head, he saw himself as the balloon again, dragging Sam off the stable, warm ground and into the unknown. Only now, when Wesley started to haul Sam away, Sam simply let go, allowing Wesley to drift up and up, while Sam watched him from safety. He grew smaller and smaller, until Wesley couldn't see him at all anymore.

"It looks like we're here," he said, voice tight. Following Jessica's car, he turned into a beautiful hotel with white pillars and a stone fountain in the center of the circular drive. After a brief wait in line, they pulled up to the valet, grabbed their luggage, and with great reluctance, Wesley handed his keys over to a woman in an orange vest.

"This is a beautiful car," she said, perhaps sensing Wesley's anxiety. "I'll take extra special care of it."

Wesley tipped her twenty dollars.

Jessica was waiting for them on the stairs leading up to the hotel entrance. The tightness in her shoulders made Wesley tense as they approached.

"Head to the front desk," she said without ado. "Sam, you'll have to show ID. Tell them you're with the Cooper wedding, and they'll assign you a room. They're all paid for, but there's a finite number available. I assume you two don't mind sharing?" She glanced between them.

Wesley fought back the instinct to make a joke. "We'll manage. We shared a dorm together once, after all."

"How little has changed, and yet so much," she remarked dryly before turning to face her brother. "There's something I need to tell you."

Sam gasped. "Are you pregnant?"

Jessica punched him none-too-gently on the shoulder. "Samuel Patrick! A woman says she has news, and you assume she must be pregnant? I raised you better than that. Next time, ask if I got a promotion. Hell, maybe I cured cancer. You don't know."

Wincing, Sam rubbed his shoulder. "Sorry. Also, holy shit, I'd forgotten how strong you are. What's the news?"

Jessica hesitated before reaching into the purse slung over her arm and pulling a crumpled letter out of her bag. "This arrived for you at the house."

Sam set down his bag and took it. "Why would I get mail back home? That hasn't been my address in years." His eyes swept over the envelope, and he gasped. "Michael!"

"No way." Wesley crowded next to him. "It's from your ex?"

"Yeah." Sam's hands trembled as he turned it over, as if he could glean additional information from the envelope. "Jessica, how long ago did this arrive?"

"According to Mom, about a week ago. She was going to forward it to you, but I told her I'd take it, so I'd have it here when you arrived. Honestly, I debated giving it to you. I wasn't sure what sort of place you were in. But now, I figure you're ready to hear whatever he has to say and move on." She looked directly at Wesley.

Wesley fought off a blush. "Hopefully it's not fifteen pages of curse words, front and back."

"I want to hear all about it tomorrow. Right now, I'm gonna go pass out." Jessica walked a few steps away, calling over her shoulder. "Love you both. Wish me luck. I won't see you again until the reception."

"Good luck," they both said.

"We'll look for the woman wearing white," Wesley called.

"It's more of an eggshell," she called back before slipping inside.

Sam was still staring at the envelope, seemingly mesmerized.

Wesley touched the small of his back. "Let's get to our room. We can open it there."

Their suite was a palace compared to where they'd been staying for the past two weeks. There were two queen-sized beds covered in huge pillows, plush cream carpeting, gauzy curtains hanging over bay windows, and real paintings on the walls. Not prints. Actual canvases with pigments on them. Wesley had nearly forgotten such things existed.

The place was almost nice enough to take the sting out of seeing yet another room with two beds. Although, at least these ones were queens. If by some miracle they ended up in bed together, they wouldn't have to cram two grown men into a twin like they had in the past.

Sam tossed his bag onto the ground at the foot of one of the beds and sank heavily onto it. Literally. He seemed to not notice the goose-down duvet and fancy linen that enveloped his legs.

"You read it." He glanced up at Wesley. "I can't. I'm too nervous."

"Relax, it's not a college admissions letter. There's probably some personal shit in there. Do you really want someone else reading it?"

"It's you, Wes. Come on." Sam held out the letter.

Sighing, Wesley took it. It was thin, which if it were a college admissions letter would be a bad thing. But since it was a foreboding message from a past lover, thin was good. Thin meant it probably wasn't filled with glitter that they'd still be finding on themselves twenty years from now.

Wesley tore the envelope open. Inside, he found a single sheet of notebook paper, which had writing on both sides. As he started reading, his tongue found its way between his teeth.

Dear Sam,

I didn't know where you were living these days—if you'd stayed in Williamsport or moved back home to Montana—so I sent this to your folks. I hope it finds you well. I'm sorry for not responding to your letter sooner, but I needed time to sort through my feelings and grieve for what might have been. Now, I think I'm finally in a place where I can tell you how I feel . . .

Wesley read the letter all the way through twice to himself before turning to Sam. "Do you want me to read it to you or give you the gist?"

"Just tell me if there's anything in it that's going to destroy me emotionally and leave me a husk of my former self. Because if so, it can wait until after the wedding." Sam's matter-of-fact tone made the statement comical.

"There's nothing bad in it, though it'll certainly tug at your heartstrings. I'm in it, oddly enough." Wesley handed the letter over. "Sounds to me like he's saying goodbye. I think this will give you the closure you've been looking for."

Sam took it and, in the manner of a man flinching away from the bomb he was defusing, read it. It took forever, because he seemed to reread sections of it before moving on to the next. Wesley watched him at first, but when it became clear this was going to be a long process, he kicked off his shoes at the door and undressed for bed.

Finally, Sam looked up, blowing a breath out between tight lips. "Wow. He doesn't hate me. I can hardly believe it."

"You dodged that bullet twice today. Congrats." Wesley gave him a once-over. "So? How are you feeling?"

"Honestly? It's a relief and a fresh wound. I'm glad he thinks I did the right thing, and that he's happy in his new place in Tampa. His joke about how he never could have adopted his dogs if he'd married me stings a little, but from the way he described them, we definitely wouldn't have gotten along."

"Yeah." Wesley laughed. "You plus two giant slobbering Dobermans equal a new Xanax prescription."

"The passage that really struck me was this one." Sam smoothed the letter out on the duvet and read aloud. "'When you called off our wedding, you said something to me that initially made me angry. You said you were doing this for both of us. I thought that was an excuse at the time—and not a very good one at that—but I get it now. You were trying to give both of us a chance to find who we're really supposed to be with. I haven't found that person yet, but he's out there, and as happy as I would have been with you, I want to thank you for giving me the dream of an even greater happiness.'"

Wesley nodded. "Yeah, that part got me too. I didn't know Michael was a romantic."

"That's the thing. He wasn't. He was never the type to show up unannounced with movies and takeout. Or to sing duets at karaoke night. Or whisk me off on an impromptu vacation."

Wesley snorted. "You just named three things that I've done for you in the past *month*."

Sam's face turned a lovely shade of crimson. "I suppose we should talk about your appearance in the letter."

Wesley looked down and fiddled with the drawstring on his pajama bottoms. "What's there to talk about? Your fiancé was apparently always threatened by me and resented the fact that people joked about you and me getting together even after he proposed to you. That happens all the time, right?" He looked up again and laughed, but it fell flat.

"I don't think it does, Wes." Sam chewed on his bottom lip. "Michael had a point, though. The part where he said you and I had an intimacy that he could never touch . . . That was true. I remember thinking when we were together that as much as I loved him, I didn't think I'd ever know him the way I know you."

"Maybe." Wesley shrugged. "But do me a favor. Don't torture yourself over it. There's no need to spend the rest of your life wondering if you doomed that relationship from the start, or if you never should have dated Michael at all, because deep down you knew it wasn't right."

"See? That." Sam jabbed a finger at him. "That's what I mean. How did you know exactly what I was thinking?"

Wesley raised an eyebrow. "Please. So, was the letter everything you wanted it to be?"

"Pretty much. This answered most of my questions and gave me the finality I was looking for. I can peacefully close that chapter of my life." Sam yawned. "I'm exhausted. You ready for bed?"

"Bed? I was thinking we'd go out and find a bar."

Sam froze halfway to reaching for his bag, looking stricken.

Wesley grinned. "Too soon to joke about it, huh?"

Sam picked up the nearest pillow and threw it at him with neck-wrenching force. Wesley laughed and let it hit him, a deserved punishment. They both got into their respective beds, and Sam clicked off the lamp between them. Once it was dark, Wesley settled in for another night of struggling to sleep. It wasn't the worst withdrawal symptom, but it was the most insidious. It left him with far too much time to replay every embarrassing thing he'd ever done in his life.

Tonight, however, his self-torture-fest was interrupted by rustling. He was lying on his side, facing away from the other bed. It came as a total surprise when Sam slipped under the covers with him, bringing familiar warmth.

"Sam?" Wesley asked.

Sam slid an arm around his waist and snuggled up to his back. "Is this okay? After the emotional reunion earlier, and now the letter . . . If it's all right with you, I don't want to sleep alone."

Emotions boiled over in Wesley: relief, desire, and deep, deep sadness. He exhaled sharply. "It's more than okay."

"Are you sure? I was the one who thought we needed space. I don't want you to feel used."

"No, Sammy. Please stay." *Please don't leave.*

They both grew still. Silence draped itself over them like another blanket. Wesley wasn't going to sleep anytime soon, fast as his heart was beating, but he listened for the soothing sound of Sam's steady breathing.

Instead, he heard Sam's voice, a gentle hum in the darkness. "Wesley?"

"Mm?"

"Why do you think this all happened now?"

"You mean with Michael?"

"No. With us. I've been thinking about it since Atlanta. Why now? What changed between us? Why did it wait five years?"

Wesley sucked in a breath that sounded thunderous in the quiet room. He'd been wondering the same thing off and on. With everything being so tumultuous, he hadn't planned on voicing his theory. Trust Sam to ask him when they were snuggled together, sleepy and warm. The illusion of safety gave Wesley strength.

He wet his lips and spoke in an undertone. "I don't think it waited. I think it started the moment we met. It's been growing every day since then. The catalyst was going on this trip, for sure. Being alone together. Not opening ourselves up romantically to other people. I think this ripened not one moment sooner than it was supposed to."

Sam's breathing had quickened. When he spoke, his voice was raspy. "But the timing seems awful."

"It never would have been perfect. There always would have been something. A Michael, or a job offer in another city. That's how life is. But I think we got as close to perfect as we could. We're both out of college, in a transitional period in our lives, and trying to find our place in the awkward struggle known as adulthood. It waited until we were primed, until we'd grown up enough to be ready for something like this. Then it was on us, like an avalanche. A force of nature. We couldn't have stopped it if we'd tried."

Sam snuggled closer and kissed the back of Wesley's neck. "That's beautiful."

"That's bad poetry." Wesley chuckled. "But thanks."

"You really believe that?"

Wesley's throat tightened. He whispered to hide the strain in his voice. "I do."

"Good night, Wes."

"Night, Sammy."

Wesley listened to Sam's breathing and soaked in his warmth, but they no longer brought him comfort. Now they seemed more like an omen. He'd meant what he'd said about their love being like an avalanche. The problem with that, though, was that avalanches could be deadly.

CHAPTER FIFTEEN

The wedding was a beautiful and mercifully short affair. The ceremony took place in a cottage-like church in the city, and while the vows were brief, they hit all the high notes. Wesley got the sense that the couple was eager to get to the being-married part, which was, in a way, more romantic than a long, drawn-out ritual.

The reception, however, was a special kind of torture. They'd rented the hotel's ballroom and had filled it with round white tables, candles, and black upholstered chairs. Lilies in crystal vases adorned the tables, and a huge chandelier hung from the lofty ceiling.

It was beautiful, but to Wesley, it was a giant arena where he was going to be tested for hours, expected to dodge pitfalls left and right, and at the end of it, his prize was getting to leave. He used to love weddings, but now, he wanted to skip the whole affair and head back up to the room.

Sam had warned Wesley ahead of time that Jessica had joked about seating him at the bar. Thankfully, that ended up not being the case. Instead he got seated right *next* to the bar, while Sam was up front at the bride's table.

Sam stopped by Wesley's table and squeezed his arm. "You gonna be okay?"

Wesley shrugged. "You ever come home after a long day, take your shoes off, and relax?"

"Yeah?"

"Well, in my case, my shoes are on fire, my house is on fire, and I can't relax because I've somehow wandered into hell."

Sam snorted and then looked contrite, like he hadn't meant to. "As soon as I can slip away, I will. I'll be by your side. Promise."

Wesley nodded, but the moment Sam walked away, his resolve developed hairline cracks all through it. A gentle breeze could shatter him.

It didn't help that everyone around him was drinking like the world was ending. Grandma Cooper was doing shots with the bartender, for Christ's sake. And he understood why too. This was a *wedding*. People wanted, rightly, to celebrate.

After years of drinking, his head was hardwired to make a beeline for an open bar and never look back. Now, he got to watch everyone else have fun without him. Sam had said moderation wasn't an option for him, but would having one drink really be that bad?

No, Wesley. You can do this. Now would be a good time to think about that motivation again. What would quitting do for you personally?

While he mulled it over, dinner was served. Wesley made awkward small talk with the people at his table. At least he did until the couple next to him got wasted on the freely flowing champagne and started slurring through sentences punctuated by some particularly graphic PDA.

Wesley watched out of the corner of his eye as they sloppily groped each other. They either didn't notice or didn't care about the other people at the table who were glaring at them. The woman had been talking at full volume for the past five minutes, and the guy kept mashing strawberries in the general vicinity of her mouth no matter how many times she said she didn't want them.

Jesus, the second-hand embarrassment is real. Is that what I'm like when I'm drunk?

In his experience, the answer was yes. He'd been told on a number of occasions he had no volume control as soon as he got a couple of cocktails into him. He'd always figured that was better than being angry, and since he could never remember what he said or did when he was that wasted, there was nothing to be embarrassed about. Watching these two, however, made him cringe at the idea of ever being that drunk.

At the front of the room, Mr. Cooper stood up and tapped a knife against a glass of champagne, announcing he wanted to make a toast to the newlyweds. Waiters appeared everywhere with trays of flutes. One of them placed a glass into Wesley's hand before he could stop them. The drunk couple finally broke the glue sealing their faces together and stood. The woman, in her spindly heels, held the man up all on her own.

On one hand, support goals, but on the other hand, holy shit. Are they going to remember any of this tomorrow?

A gong went off in Wesley's head, resonating through him. Of the handful of weddings he'd attended in his adult life, how many of them did he remember? He thought back and came up with a lot of ceremonies but practically no receptions. He always got smashed and then woke up in his bed the next day.

One of the main reasons he'd wanted to go on a road trip was to make memories, and he had, but he also remembered being hungover and feeling sick. All those nights they'd gone to bars faded to black halfway through. What if down the line, after years of chronic overdrinking, he barely remembered this?

Sam had confessed to him more than once that he worried about missing out. He thought Wesley was living life to the fullest, but he had it wrong. Going out and getting drunk all the time wasn't living. Neither was making friends in bars he'd never see again after that night, or forcing himself to look at sunrises that made his head throb. His "good times" were just stories that ended the same way: with him passing out.

He'd been fooling himself into thinking partying was the way to have fun, but his childhood memories said otherwise. He'd had a life before alcohol. Somewhere along the way, he'd forgotten that, and now it was time to remember.

"Holy shit, I did it," he said.

Oops.

He clapped a hand over his mouth and peeked around. Thankfully, no one seemed to have heard him. However, he did catch one person watching him from across the room.

Sam.

He was standing next to Jessica, glass of champagne in hand as Mr. Cooper finished his toast. He didn't seem to be listening, though. His eyes were fixed on Wesley's hand. Ice shot through Wesley as he realized. Sam was looking at the champagne flute. He was watching to see if Wesley was going to drink it when the speech ended.

The severity of Wesley's situation had hit him in peaks and valleys since they'd left on the trip. His parents' intervention and confessing to Sam had been peaks, but there had always been other moments—quieter ones—when he struggled to scrape up the genuine belief that he needed to make a huge lifestyle change. So long as he got to work and paid his bills, what was the harm in drinking?

Well, Wesley finally had an answer to that question.

The look on Sam's face was so sad, Wesley's stomach lurched. He didn't look afraid, however, which led Wesley to one conclusion: it wasn't that Sam thought Wesley was going to drink, it was that he hated having to watch him to make sure he didn't.

God, Wesley had made a mess of this. Cracks had found their way into the foundation of his life, and he'd done nothing to stop it. He'd given up jobs, alienated his family, and now he might lose Sam. That was everything he had. His whole world had been crumbling down around him, and he'd been too blacked out to notice.

The sick feeling in his stomach grew until he wanted to gag. How could someone ruin their life without realizing it? Slowly, he supposed. Like a cavity you couldn't see until it got big enough. Like a tumor. Like a disease.

Well, Wesley, whispered a miserable voice in his head, *it looks like you've found your motivation. Is there still time to fix this?*

The toast ended. There was applause, followed by a rustle as everyone raised their glasses. As Wesley looked around, he noticed something. There were people toasting with water, and others who had no drinks in front of them at all. Some of the guests were celebrating without alcohol. People were enjoying this big moment for what it was, and judging by the smiles on their faces, they were having plenty of fun.

I'm too young to give up on myself.

Eyes on Sam, Wesley raised his glass in salute and then set it back down on the table, untouched. The crooked smile Sam gave him dug into Wesley's skin like fingernails, leaving little crescent moons. All the faith Sam had put in him hurt as much as it healed, because Wesley knew what he had to do.

Sam had given him so many chances. Now Wesley was going to return the favor.

On Sunday, they rose early. Or at least, Sam did. Wesley couldn't wake up, considering he'd never really gone to sleep. He was still struggling to do more than doze. His body was getting used to functioning without alcohol, and he'd spent half the night agonizing about the next junction of their trip: the journey home.

They weren't taking the scenic route this time. Sam had charted a straight shot back to Pennsylvania, which was around thirty hours' worth of driving. If they pushed themselves, they could be home in three days.

Three days that were going to be simultaneously the longest and shortest of Wesley's life. Long, because he was going to be stuck in a car with nothing to do but stew on the half-cocked plan he'd made. Short, because he was trying to soak up as much Sam as he could get while he could.

Jessica met them downstairs and helped them pack the car, though they were experts at this point. Wesley figured she was doing some soaking of her own. What else could get a bride out of bed this early the night after her wedding?

"Are you sure you can't stay for the family breakfast?" she asked.

Sam lingered by the curb, his face a picture of reluctance. "I'd love to, but we have so much driving to do. You're going to dash off to your honeymoon the second breakfast is over anyway. I hope Noah and you have a blast in Scotland."

She sighed. "A month ago, I couldn't wait to waltz around a bunch of old castles. I packed a long silk dress specifically so I could drape myself dramatically over a parapet. But now, all I want is to spend more time with my *widdle brover*." She pretended to pinch Sam's cheek.

As an only child, Wesley was simultaneously jealous and horrified.

Sam laughed and pulled his sister into a hug, kissing the top of her head. "You're the little one, shorty."

"I can wear heels."

"So can I." Sam winked. "I'll let you know when we're safely back home. You can Skype me from a pub and make me jealous until you feel better."

"Deal." She turned to Wesley. "Take care of my brother, okay?"

Wesley's throat tightened. "I will."

I'll sure as hell try.

Jessica waved them off as they drove away. Wesley was behind the wheel. Sam twisted around in his seat and watched her shrinking figure until Wesley made a turn, and the hotel disappeared from view.

"Miss her already?" he asked.

"Not as much as you'd think." Sam faced forward and straightened out his seat belt. "It was great seeing everyone, and I'm glad I can call my parents now without giving myself an ulcer, but I'm so ready to go home."

"I am too. Ready to take a long shower that doesn't involve tiny shampoos."

Sam groaned. "Put on clean clothes that came out of a closet instead of a suitcase."

"Cook a meal in a real kitchen, with pots and pans and *ingredients*."

"And to sleep in my own bed."

At that, Wesley fell silent. How was his bed going to feel now that he was so used to having Sam next to him? For once, his head supplied a ready answer: empty.

Sam either sensed the awkwardness or he'd hit his talking quota for the day, because he pulled out a book and settled in. Wesley turned the radio on low and kept his eyes on the road.

In that manner, the first two days passed. They talked sometimes, but for the most part, it seemed even they'd run out of things to say. When they hit Illinois, Wesley had planned on asking if they could take a quick tour around Chicago. As it turned out, thanks to unexpected traffic and delays, they didn't get there until midnight. It was all they could do to limp to their hotel before they both passed out.

They'd reverted back to sleeping in separate beds ever since the night of the wedding, and believe it or not, Wesley was grateful. Tomorrow was the last day of their not-so-epic adventure. Tomorrow, Wesley would have to tell Sam what he'd decided. But today, he got to have a final night of peace, and Sam got to climb into bed without knowing that everything was about to change.

Their routine the next morning was appallingly familiar: wake up, clean up, get dressed, get packed, check out, and hit the road. Wesley had heard about reverse culture shock before—mainly from old classmates who'd spent a semester studying abroad and had come home with fake accents and ill-advised berets—but now he understood it. After weeks of this, *not* traveling every day was going to be an adjustment.

And I'm going to be back in the environment where I used to drink every day. Sitting alone in my apartment with nothing to do. Sam won't be around twenty-four seven to keep an eye on me.

Every time that thought popped up, it terrified him so much, he'd push it back down, like jabbing a sprout back into the dirt with his thumb. His resolve to never drink again wavered on an hourly basis. Sometimes, he felt like a gun to his head couldn't convince him to do a shot. Other times, all it took was spotting a bar on the side of the road to make him itch to pull over.

He hadn't realized how much alcohol was ingrained in his head either. A few times, he caught himself thinking things like, *Can't wait to get home and pop open a beer. No, water. A nice, ice-cold glass of water.* Or, *I should call Ben sometime and ask if he wants to get dri—dinner. Invite him to dinner.*

At this point, he and Sam had read volumes of information on alcohol addiction. According to the internet, all he could do was take it one day at a time. Focus on right now and not worry about making it to a month or a year or five years. Every day was going to be a struggle, but it was only one day.

"I'm going to miss this."

Sam's voice startled Wesley out of his thoughts. He paused to let someone merge in front of him before he briefly glanced at Sam. It'd rained that morning, and the pavement outside the window burned white-hot from the pounding sun. Sam wasn't looking at Wesley. He was gazing forward, eyes unfocused.

"Miss what?"

"This trip. I know there were ups and downs, but honestly, I had a blast, even when we were cramped in this car and sleeping in run-down motels. I don't think I ever thanked you for talking me into this." Sam turned his head toward Wesley and smiled. "So thank you."

Wesley swallowed. "You're welcome."

"Maybe we can do this again someday. I know it won't be as easy in the future, when we have jobs and mortgages, but who knows? Maybe when we're retired, we can rent an RV and do the whole West Coast."

Wesley blinked, eyes stinging. *Breaks my heart. He's still so hopeful for the future. I'm so ridiculously in love with him.*

"Sam, there's something I need to tell you."

Fuck. He hadn't meant to bring this up until they were nearly home. But then, if he waited any longer, he was going to burst like an overinflated tire.

Sam sat up straighter in his seat. "Okay. I bet I know what this is about."

"Do you?"

"Well, yeah. With everything that happened on this trip, we never got to talk about . . . us. I wanted to wait until you didn't have so much on your plate, but if you're ready, so am I."

Wesley exhaled, and the air caught in his throat. He eyed the passing green exit signs and considered pulling over. If they didn't make it back home today, however, they'd have to share a room again, and he didn't think he could handle that after the conversation they were about to have.

Eyes riveted on the road, Wesley forced himself to breathe steadily. "I do want to talk about us, but not in the way you might think."

"Oh." Sam shifted in his seat. "Is this about your plans for when we get back? Have you made any decisions?"

"Yeah. I spoke to my parents last night while you were asleep. I told them I don't think I need rehab. Not right now, anyway. I'm going to try counseling and join some support groups first. Honestly, I think getting a job will be better for me than being stuck in a care facility for however long. If I backslide again, then I'll take another look at my options, but I hope it doesn't get to that point."

Sam nodded. "That all sounds great. You've put a lot of thought into this, and I'm proud of you. Whatever I can do to help support you, let me know. I'll quit drinking when I'm around you, obviously, but I'll quit altogether if you want. To show solidarity."

Wesley's heart throbbed. "That's sweet. I appreciate the offer, but that relates to what I have to tell you. You shouldn't have to change your life too because of my mistake. I don't want this to affect you any more than it has to."

Sam's brow furrowed. "Wes, it's giving up drinking, not giving up a kidney. Yeah, it's a bit of a sacrifice, but drinking less is considered a good thing by pretty much everyone, and I was never the sort to get trashed every weekend anyway. Besides, I'm in this with you. You're a part of my life."

That might not always be the case.

"Sammy . . ." Wesley hesitated. "I heard what you said."

"What?"

"When you thought I was sleeping. The day of the rehearsal dinner. You sat on my bed, and you told me—" Wesley's voice broke. *You told me you loved me.*

Sam went rigid next to him. "You were awake? Why didn't you say something?"

"At first it was because I was tired, but then I wanted to hear what you had to say." Wesley shrugged. "I'm not a saint. I'm sorry, and I hope you'll forgive me, but honestly, I *needed* to hear it after everything." He sighed. "I have to bring up one thing in particular."

Sam looked down at his lap. "Wesley, when I said I love you, I—"

"Not that. That was . . . Sammy, it was one of the best moments of my life, but I can't think about that right now."

Sam was silent next to him.

Wesley continued. "I want to talk about the part where you said it was your fault. You're the smartest guy I know, but you couldn't have been more wrong."

Sam seemed to struggle for words. "I didn't mean it's *all* my fault, but I contributed to the problem. I still don't get how I didn't see it sooner."

"You weren't looking for flaws in me. It never occurred to you that I would have a problem like this. Because you love me." Swallowing burned Wesley's throat. "The other day, when you said you'd leave even though it'd kill you to do it, that hurt, but I thought it was so admirable. You've always been much stronger than you think. So much stronger than me. Out of the two of us, you're definitely the survivor, and I hope this trip at least taught you that. You're going to be just fine."

"Wes, you're starting to scare me. Why did that sound so much like a goodbye?"

"Because it is one." Wesley had to choke the next words out. "When we get back home, I can't see you anymore."

Sam was dead silent. Wesley blinked tears from his eyes and focused on the road. Although, if they got into an accident right now that broke every bone in his body, he wasn't certain he'd feel the difference.

"You can't . . ." Sam drew in a breath that rattled. "Is it because you can't be around people who remind you of drinking? I understand that, but you need support right now."

"It's not that. You being around makes it easier to stay sober, not harder. But I still can't see you. Not for a while, at least. You did the right thing before, when you threatened to leave. The difficult thing. Now I have to do what's difficult and right too. I don't want to be a burden on you."

"Don't say that!" Sam whipped around in his seat to face him. The belt cut into his chest. It had to hurt, but Sam didn't seem to notice. "You're *not* a burden. You're not weak, or pathetic, or any of the horrible things you've been saying. People get addicted to things. It happens. They get help, and there's zero shame in that. You're being way too hard on yourself."

"You're right. I was being harsh before, but that's not what I'm saying now, and it doesn't change the fact that we have to spend some time apart. Let me deal with this on my own. You can't fight this battle for me, and honestly, you deserve better than a lifetime of dealing with my mistakes."

"Wesley, I want a lifetime of *you*."

His words stabbed into Wesley, but Wesley held firm. "Maybe someday we'll have that. I hope we do. But for the same reason you wanted to stop sleeping together, I want us to spend some time apart. Nothing can happen until I'm sober anyway. If we got together, would you still have the strength to leave if I relapsed again? You're not my motivation anymore, but if I don't believe your threat is genuine, who's to say my resolve won't break?"

Part of Wesley prayed that Sam would argue with him, but it wouldn't change anything. One look at Sam's face told him Sam knew it too.

"Okay. I'll go quietly." Sam's expression was sharp as a knife. "But for the record, this is temporary. Bet your ass I'm going to kick your door down if you don't keep in touch. I want you to text me progress reports, and you have to swear you'll call if anything happens."

Wesley nodded, though his head was a war zone. Familiar fear tingled down his spine, similar to what he'd felt when he first thought about getting sober. Only now, he really was afraid of going without something that was necessary: Sam. He had to trust that a relationship as strong as theirs wouldn't fizzle out with time and distance. They'd be together someday, even if they went back to being friends.

One day at a time. One day at a time.

Despite what Wesley had said, the paranoia from before hadn't left him. Sam could say he wasn't a burden all day long, but that didn't make it true. All Wesley had to do was fuck up once, and Sam would have an out. He could leave, and he could convince himself that it was the right thing to do. That he was helping Wesley.

One of the many, many things Wesley loved about Sam was the quiet but firm way he had of handling big decisions. Wesley had learned that when Sam left Michael. Sam had told him later that he'd delivered that news the kindest way possible, but he'd also made it clear it wasn't up for negotiation. Same with the carney at the festival. If Sam decided to leave, that would be the end of it. Perhaps Wesley was ending things now so at least it would happen of his own volition.

No. He had to fight for this, and if fighting meant retreating, so be it. Wesley wasn't going to fuck up again. No matter what.

"Give me some space, and I'll call you when I'm ready to talk," he said, guiding the car through a gentle merge onto the highway that would take them home. "I promise."

CHAPTER SIXTEEN

S am's apartment was precisely as he'd left it. Mustier-smelling, of course, and the house plants he'd bought specifically because they were indestructible had browned around the edges, but all in all, it was home sweet home. Williamsport hadn't changed either, with its small shops, historic buildings, and sleepy serenity.

Why then did it feel like absolutely everything was different?

Over a week after they'd gotten back, Sam still hadn't unpacked. He'd taken all the electronics out of his bag, but the clothing had stayed put, despite being in desperate need of washing. Every time Sam went to pull them out, he got a whiff of Wesley, and back into the bag they went, sealed up tight.

He hadn't spoken to Wesley since that last day in the car. Not voice to voice anyway. They'd texted a couple of times. Sam had waited all of one day before asking if Wesley had looked into counseling yet. According to Google, there was an AA group in town, and plenty of qualified therapists.

Wesley had responded right away. He'd already been to a meeting and was taking to group therapy surprisingly well. He'd also met with a counselor. According to him, she was, "a straight-up emotional magician, only instead of rabbits, she Houdini-ed feelings I didn't know I had out of me."

All in all, Wesley had made it sound like he was doing well, which had done a lot to keep Sam from splitting out of his own skin. Wesley hadn't, however, asked Sam if he wanted to get together and talk. Sam took that as a sign that Wesley still needed space. Much as he was itching for more information, he had to respect that.

It was so *hard*, though. Sam had told Wesley he loved him. Wesley hadn't said it back, but his response had been enough to convince Sam the feeling was mutual. This was so huge, and they would be treating it that way, if only something even huger wasn't going on.

On some level, Sam understood that Wesley couldn't return his feelings right now. Not out loud. Wesley had said as much when he'd explained why he couldn't see him for a while. But even knowing that, the distance still stung of rejection.

He'd always thought that when he fell for the right person—found his soul mate and went head over heels—that would be it. But now, he was having to deal with the idea that even if he loved Wesley with everything he had, it might not be enough. They might still never be together.

That hurt worse than if Wesley had run him over with his car. And there was nothing Sam could do until Wesley was ready to talk.

He filled his days with job hunting and his other local friends, all two of them. Maggie and Spencer were the other interns who'd worked with him. Only, at the end of their year, they'd both been offered jobs. Listening to them complain about all the work they were doing was bittersweet, and while he enjoyed their company, neither of them were Wesley.

It didn't help that theramblingboysadventure was still getting daily notifications. It wasn't going to go viral anytime soon, but people all over the world wanted to know where they'd ended up, what they were up to now and, most frequently, if they'd ended up together.

I'd like to know that as well.

Sam tried not to look through the photos, but he couldn't seem to help himself. At times, as he scrolled from the beginning of their adventure to the end, he imagined he could see them falling in love in increments.

After the wedding, there were hardly any photos at all. There hadn't been much of a reason to take any, considering they'd been driving all day. Wesley had posted one final shot of the car—a little rougher for the wear, but still rambling—back in his dad's garage, and that was it. *Le fin.* Curtains closed. Their "adventure" must've been a good thing, because it had certainly come to an end.

"Stop moping," Sam muttered to himself as he moved around his kitchen. He was putting the finishing touches on dinner—a complicated paella recipe he never would have tried had he not discovered a newfound appreciation for his kitchen. It smelled wonderful, but the sight of the single place setting on his kitchen table depressed him.

It was a Saturday night. Normally, he'd be meeting Wesley for drinks, or Wesley would have barged into the apartment an hour ago with takeout and a bottle of wine.

Those days were over regardless of what happened. Sam wasn't going to miss the alcohol, but he missed Wesley so much it burned. Termites were gnawing at his bones, and soon he'd be so brittle he'd blow away in the wind.

Get it together, Sam. If not for yourself, then for Wesley. If space is what he needs, you have to give it to him, and you can't be a mess if—when—he finally reaches out.

Using an oven mitt, he removed a heavy cast-iron skillet from the stovetop and set it on a trivet on the table. His phone buzzed on the countertop by the sink. He ignored it. It was probably more notifications from their now-defunct Instagram.

A second later, however, a ringtone played that Sam recognized well. Only one person in his phone had a custom ring, and that was because a certain someone insisted on singing "Bohemian Rhapsody" every time they went to karaoke, despite having neither Freddie Mercury's range nor his stage presence.

"Wesley," Sam whispered.

For a second, the familiarity of the scenario sent Sam back in time, and he thought, *He must be calling to invite me out.* Then he remembered, and foreboding like ice water washed over him.

I made Wesley promise he would call if anything happened.

Sam was across the room in three strides. He snatched up his phone, almost dropping it in his eagerness. "Hello?"

"Sam." Wesley's voice was raspy and tight. "I need you to come over right now."

"I'm on my way." Sam was already running through a checklist in his head: stove off, grab keys, put on shoes if there's time. "What's wrong?"

"I'll explain when you get here."

"You sound strange. Have you been crying?"

"Sammy, please hurry. It's important." He hung up.

Sam stared at his phone, heart racing. The last time Sam had heard Wesley sound that emotional was senior year, when he'd drunk most of a twelve-pack and watched *The Notebook*. He'd ended up literally crying on Sam's shoulder and proclaiming, *"They should have eloped the night they met at the carnival!"*

Despite the fond memory, panic welled up in Sam. Had Wesley been drinking? Oh God, what if Wesley had relapsed again? What was Sam going to do?

He didn't have time to debate this right now. If Wesley had fucked up, he'd be upset about it. He might do something he'd regret. Sam had to get to him *now*.

He grabbed what he needed with trembling hands and sprinted out the door. Wesley's place was only a five-minute walk away, but Sam got in his car. Traffic laws ceased to exist. Even driving well over the speed limit, he couldn't seem to move fast enough. Everything was in slow motion.

Nightmares played out in his head, ones where he got to Wesley's place, and he was lying on the floor, surrounded by bottles. What if he'd given himself alcohol poisoning, or worse? Sam's heart shredded itself in his chest. Why had he ever let Wesley out of his sight? He should have insisted on staying with him. From the moment they met, he should have never let him go.

Please, God, let him be okay.

Wesley's apartment complex was a red-brick building with four floors. There was no gate, which was good, because Sam probably would have tried to vault it rather than wait to be let in. He raced up a flight of stairs to the second floor, found Wesley's apartment, and dropped his keys twice before he managed to let himself in.

He burst into Wesley's living room, panting for breath, and skidded to a stop.

Part of his nightmare came true before his eyes. Wesley was sitting in the center of the floor, the coffee table shoved into the couch to make room. He was surrounded by something, but it wasn't bottles.

"Construction paper?" Sam asked, blinking. The surprise in his voice rang like bells.

He had to rub his eyes before he believed he wasn't hallucinating. Wesley had scissors, glue, and piles of colorful paper spread around him, along with an open book with clear sleeves inside.

Wesley looked up at him with watery eyes, a crumpled tissue in hand, and sniffed. "Took you long enough. I've been suffering all by myself." He held up a shoebox full of photos. "Go through these and cry with me."

Sam glanced between Wesley's face and the outstretched box so many times, he rattled his brain. "What?"

"The photos. Check 'em out. They go all the way back to freshman year."

"No, I mean, what are you *doing*?"

Wesley set the box down and slid it across the wood floor to Sam's feet. "Scrapbooking. I haven't been sleeping well since I stopped drinking. My group recommended I take up a hobby to distract myself until my melanin or whatever comes back."

"Melatonin," Sam corrected on autopilot. "So . . . you're not drunk?"

Wesley, who'd been leaning over to grab a pair of scalloped scissors, jerked his head up sharply. "What? Of course not. I can't ever drink again." He frowned. "Fuck, it still hurts to say that. I'm going to bring that up to Allison when I see her Tuesday."

Sam finally uprooted himself and bent down to pick up the photos. "Jesus, Wesley, you scared the shit out of me. Who's Allison? And what are you scrapbooking?"

"She's my therapist slash sobriety coach. And I'm scrapbooking us. Our story. It was supposed to be a surprise, but then I got all emotional, and I couldn't wait. Look at these."

Sam drifted closer as he sorted through the box Wesley had passed to him. Inside were dozens of photos, all with the same subject matter: Wesley and Sam.

"Holy shit." Sam stopped at the outer ring of Wesley's supply pile. "Is this every photo we ever took together?"

"Just about." Wesley grabbed another box to his left and shook it. "I snagged the photos from our trip off Instagram too and had them printed. I thought it'd be a good event to make a scrapbook out of. But then, in a lot of the photos, I was either drunk or hungover. I didn't want to immortalize those moments, so I dug into our past—by that, I mean, our Facebooks—and found all of these from before we turned twenty-one."

"Why were you crying, though? Nostalgia doesn't seem like a strong enough emotion to justify tears."

"Not nostalgia alone. I had a revelation." Wesley flipped to a page in the scrapbook and held it up. "Remember when we went to the zoo when we were, what, nineteen?"

"Oh yeah. That was a lot of fun."

"It *was* fun. We went for the hell of it, we were sober the whole time, and we had a *blast*. I still remember when we fed lettuce to that giraffe. It licked your hand, and you shrieked."

Sam laughed. "Its tongue was black! Who the hell knew they had black tongues?"

"Pretty much everyone who graduated from kindergarten, dude. It's comforting to know there are holes in your knowledge." Wesley climbed to his feet, which brought him face to face with Sam. For some reason, the room was suddenly much warmer than it'd been a second ago.

"The point is," Wesley murmured, eyes searching Sam's face, "these photos reminded me of something I'd forgotten, and it cemented in my head that I don't need to drink. Or even want to, really. I've had enough hangovers to last me a lifetime."

"I'm glad to hear it." Sam shifted his weight from foot to foot, heat creeping into his cheeks. "You made it seem like you needed me over here urgently, though. Was that all you wanted to tell me?"

"That, and I missed you." Wesley's eyes were intense in his handsome face. "I was going to give you this book as an apology, but I couldn't wait for it to be finished. I needed to see you now."

Sam swallowed. He'd missed Wesley's company too, but standing close to him now made Sam realized he'd missed his presence as well. Not solely in a sexual way—though his body sure as fuck was happy to see him—but his closeness, and his messy hair, and the comfort that simply standing near him brought.

"You don't owe me an apology," Sam said. "You didn't do anything wrong."

Wesley brushed the back of a finger along Sam's cheek. "Oh, but I did. I didn't tell you about my drinking right away, and then I kept you at arm's length. I doubted you, more than once, when I'd trust you with my life."

"And your car," Sam joked, breathless.

Wesley smiled. "And my car. Most unforgivably, though, I didn't tell you I love you every chance I got."

A shiver played a glissando down Sam's spine. "You've told me that lots of times over the years."

"Yeah, but this time it's different." Wesley was magnetic as he stepped infinitesimally closer, pulling Sam in. "You said I scared you. Why were you scared?"

"When you called, you sounded weird. I thought maybe you'd relapsed again. I got here as fast as I could. I'm sorry for assuming you were drunk. I should have known you were too strong to quit now. But I started imagining all the things that could go wrong, and I *panicked*. If something had happened to you—" Sam's voice broke.

Wesley shushed him gently. "People relapse all the time. That's not an unfair assumption. I won't lie, every day is a struggle. This weekend in particular has been hell. I bombed a job interview, and all I wanted to do was get trashed. But I've found my motivation, and I'm sticking to it. I want to live my life and be present for every moment, without alcohol. And Sammy, I want you."

"You have me." Sam wet his lips. "You always have. You know that, right?"

"I do. But it's nice to hear it." Wesley winked and held up another photo. "Remember this?"

Sam glanced at it. It was of them, of course, though they were hardly visible. They'd turned the bunk bed in their dorm into a fort, with blankets enclosing the bottom bed and pillows lining the top. Wesley's dark head was poking out of Sam's bed on one side, while Sam peered out through the blankets at the bottom. "That was the first photo we ever took together as roommates."

"It was also the first night I ever fell asleep in your bed. And I was sober too. You got it into your head that you needed me to have fun, but I remember back when we used to go to bookstores and the aquarium and parks. I needed you to remind me how to live." Wesley leaned down until his lips were by Sam's ear. "You told me that if you could change anything, you'd get that first week back. Now, I've cost us a second one. I don't want to lose another moment that we could be spending together."

Sam nodded, breathing hard. "Me neither."

"Before, you said you love me, but a lot has happened since then. If you don't want to be with me after all, tell me now." Wesley touched Sam's chin, drawing it up. "Because otherwise, I'm going to kiss you."

"No"—Sam smiled—"you're not."

He grabbed Wesley's face and kissed him with everything he had.

Wesley's little *mmph* of surprise followed by his arms tight around Sam was the single best thing he had ever experienced in his twenty-three years on Earth. All the anxiety and weight of the past few weeks lifted off his shoulders, and he was left with the most wonderful, warm lightness.

"Wesley, I love you," Sam panted between kisses. "I love you so much."

"I love you too, Sammy." Wesley kissed him deeply, mouth open to him, teeth scraping his bottom lip and tongue slipping in. Fire spread through Sam in an instant, a frisson dancing down his spine. He pressed against Wesley, touching everything he could get. Chest to chest. Hips to hips. He spread his hands over the small of Wesley's back and squeezed, feeling muscle and hot skin through the shirt.

"Missed this," he mumbled against Wesley's lips. "Missed you."

"Never again," Wesley said. "I never want to be away from you again. Can't get enough of you."

"Have me." Sam ground their hips together. "Have all of me."

Shuddering, Wesley and grabbed him by the waist. He ran his hands up Sam's sides once before guiding him back, kissing all the skin he could find. Sam stumbled over a pack of construction paper before hitting the coffee table with the back of his calves. Wesley kicked it out of the way and pushed Sam onto the couch. Sam was already toeing off his shoes and untucking his shirt.

Wesley followed after him, and as soon as they were horizontal, the mood went from desperate to obscene. Sam was already hard and itching to feel Wesley's bare skin. How long had it been since they'd been together? Too fucking long.

Wesley nosed Sam's throat. "Love this part of you. Always have. You have the longest, most beautiful neck." He kissed Sam's shirt collar and pulled it back to expose his clavicle. "This too. Love this." He mouthed the taut skin over the bone, and then his lips found Sam's ear. "And this." He nibbled at the lobe.

Sam gasped, patience evaporating. "Clothes off. Now."

Whether spurred on by Sam's uncharacteristic command or the prospect of being naked, Wesley scrambled to obey. He sat up and yanked his shirt off before fumbling with his fly.

Sam watched him, salivating. He made quick work of his own shirt and had his pants open and cock out in record time. He'd been hard before, but as soon as he closed a hand around himself, it became clear his body had been wanting this more than he'd fathomed.

Wesley pushed his jeans down around his thighs along with his underwear. Sam expected him to undress completely, but it seemed he couldn't wait another second. As soon as his cock was free, he straddled Sam and lined them up.

"Oh, fuck yeah." Sam wanted to open his legs wider, but Wesley had him pinned. The velvety heat of his skin made Sam see stars. When Wesley rocked their hips together, Sam thought he might explode. "I love how you feel. Love you."

"Why did we wait so long to do this?" Wesley leaned down and buried his face in the crook of Sam's neck. "We could have been doing this for years."

Sam managed to nod, but ninety percent of his attention was focused on how inexplicably good it felt having Wesley on top of him, heavy and hot, their dicks sliding together just right. It was such a light sensation, lacking the finesse of fingers or the wetness of a mouth, but touching Wesley made every nerve in Sam's body light up. "Want you to fuck me, but I don't think I can wait."

"I can't," Wesley panted, grinding their hips together. "I can't. You feel— I'm so— This is plenty." His pace sped up, and Sam recognized the jerky, halting movements Wesley made when he was getting close.

The knowledge of it sent desire pulsing through Sam. Not only that Wesley was turned on, but that Sam was getting him off so fast, that Wesley felt even a fraction of the raw need Sam felt. He pushed against Sam, rubbing them both from the base of their balls all the way up, so much like sex. It wasn't enough, but somehow the intensity was far, far too much.

"Hold on," Sam said, pushing at Wesley's chest. When Wesley whined in protest, Sam shushed him. "I can make it better."

Sam spat on his palm and managed to slide it between them. Wesley seemed reluctant to move back an inch, but when Sam's hand found their cocks and slicked them up, his eager moan said he understood. The last little bit they'd been missing fell into place, and this time, when Wesley thrusted against him, desire so sharp it was almost pain sizzled through Sam.

Sam spilled over like a too-full glass, coming between them. Wesley made a surprised, pleasured sound. He probably hadn't thought there was any way Sam would beat him to it. Sam pulsed and pulsed, rigid in his orgasm. He managed to press his mouth against Wesley's and get the taste of him, which heightened his orgasm like hitting a perfect note.

Right when he thought he couldn't feel any more, Wesley moaned and came too, pressing hard against him. One final twinge of deep pleasure thrummed through Sam before he went boneless, gasping. Wesley collapsed on top of him. It made it hard for Sam to breathe, but he couldn't drum up the energy to care.

They lay together for a long, quiet moment that was pure peace and satisfaction.

Wesley was stock-still at first, but then he turned his face and kissed Sam's sweaty brow. "Seriously, we could have been doing that this whole time. We *lived* together, for Christ's sake."

Sam yawned. "It's probably better we waited until now. If we'd discovered sex with each other in college, we might never have left our room, and then we'd have flunked out."

"Yeah, but we would have been happy." Wesley rolled to the side enough so he was no longer crushing Sam, and threw an arm over him.

Sam nestled up to his chest. "I love my scrapbook. That's the most thoughtful gift anyone's ever given me."

"I'm glad, though it's not finished yet."

Sam nuzzled his cheek. "It'll never be finished. We'll keep adding pages to it until it's all filled up, and then we'll get another one."

"I like that idea." Wesley stroked the pads of his fingers down Sam's bare back. "I guess now we have to tell everyone they were right. We're not two gay guys who happen to be friends."

"Why would we lie to people?" Sam kissed his forehead. "We'll always be friends, Wes. First and foremost."

"Did you ever think we'd end up here?"

"We certainly took the long way around. But I think some part of me always knew you were boyfriend material."

"'Boyfriend'?" Wesley scrunched his mouth to the side. "I dunno. That's a big step. I'll have to think about it."

Sam bit him on the chin, and Wesley chuckled. "On second thought, being boyfriends sounds amazing. For your sake, I have to ask something, though. Aren't you worried about the future? I've only been sober for a couple of weeks now, and from what my therapist says, I'm never going to be magically cured. I'll struggle with this for the rest of my life."

"And I'll struggle with my own problems." Sam cupped Wesley's cheek in his palm. "I'll fall into unhealthy, introverted habits, and you'll help dig me out of them like always. Everyone has issues. We've both grown a lot over the years, and as much as I think we grew together, I also think we learned how to live without each other. That means when we're together, it's because we're choosing to be. I dunno about you, but that sounds pretty great to me."

"You're right." He nuzzled Sam's cheek. "What do you say to taking it one day at a time?"

"Mm-hmm." Sam closed his eyes, warm and content in Wesley's arms. "I'm looking forward to every single one of them."

EPILOGUE

Five Years Later

Wesley popped the cork on a bottle of champagne and yelped as it came gushing out. "Oh shit." He scrambled to grab a glass off the table. "Good thing this is one of the nonalcoholic bottles."

"Yeah, or we'd skin you for wasting expensive champagne," his dad called from his seat at the far end of the dining room. He held up his own glass as if in toast.

Mom elbowed him in the side. "Don't joke about skinning my baby on his special day." She smiled at him, eyes shining. "We're so proud of you, Wesley."

"Thanks, Mom." Wesley assessed the damage. Sam hadn't been happy about decorating their brand-new table with plastic confetti ("It could scratch the stain!") or glitter ("We'll never get it all off"). He definitely wasn't going to be happy about the champagne now soaking into the purple and blue paper streamers. Wesley grabbed a handful of napkins and mopped it up as best he could.

Right on cue, through a doorway to the left, Sam walked out with a tray of appetizers. "I hope you're all hungry, because I've got fifty shrimp puffs in the oven and a roast on the way."

The people at the table all perked up at the delicious smell. It was a small but significant gathering, consisting of both sets of their parents, Jessica, Noah, and some work friends who were milling around the house, admiring the décor.

Sam's mom smiled at her son. "You didn't have to go to all this trouble for us, Sam."

"Of course I did." Once Sam had placed the tray next to a glass salad bowl, he glided over to Wesley. "I wanted this dinner-slash-party-slash-housewarming to be perfect. You guys came all the way from Montana, after all. And you"—he nodded to Jessica and Noah—"had to travel even farther. Glad you could make it."

A very tan Jessica winked at him from where she was sitting. "Cali was hard to leave. You have to visit again soon."

"Definitely. I can't get enough of that ocean."

Wesley leaned toward Sam and spoke in an undertone. "I spilled the champagne. Sorry."

Sam waved him off. "Who cares? We're celebrating." He nosed Wesley's cheek. "Congratulations, my love."

Wesley closed his eyes, snaking an arm around Sam's waist. "I think this calls for a toast."

"I agree." Sam scooped his glass off the table and held it up. "To friends and family."

"To Wesley's incredible accomplishment," Jessica added.

"To getting the hell out of Montana," Noah called, eliciting laughs from everyone.

Wesley took a breath before raising his own glass. "To five years sober."

Everyone else followed suit. After a lot of hard work, Wesley was proud to say he was finally able to be around alcohol again, though Sam was drinking from the nonalcoholic bottle as well. This day marked five years of sobriety for both of them, and Wesley had never felt better. Healthier. Happier. It'd been a long road, but every step had been worth it.

"If you'll all excuse us for a moment"—Sam took Wesley by the hand—"I need to borrow the man of the hour."

"Hurry back," Sam's dad called. "I want to hear more about your trip."

Sam led Wesley through their house, which had been decorated with a mixture of tasteful antiques (Sam) and pop culture paraphernalia (Wesley). A year after they'd moved in, there were still boxes in some of the corners, but considering how busy they were with work, traveling, and everyday life, that was no surprise.

A short hallway opened into the living room. Sam made a beeline for the mantel—which boasted several framed photos of their friends and family—and plucked a present wrapped in blue paper off it.

"Where did this come from?" Wesley asked as Sam handed him the present. "This wasn't here before."

"I hid it until the party." Sam bounced on his heels. "Open it. I'm sure you already know what it is."

Wesley did, but he got his best fake-surprise face ready anyway. He ripped off the paper and revealed a beautiful hardcover photo album with a picture on the front of them kissing in front of Angel Falls.

Wesley didn't have to act surprised after all. The book was *beautiful.* "Sammy, this is amazing! Is it all the photos from our trip to South America?"

"Yup." Sam flipped it open to the first page. "I tried to do them by country, but Venezuela and Belize got a little mixed together in places." He pointed to a photo on the top right of the recto. "I couldn't remember this one at all, for obvious reasons."

It was a photo of Sam sleeping, spread out on his stomach on clean white sheets, blond hair fanned over the pillow. It wasn't moving, of course, but in Wesley's head, Sam's back was rising and falling with his gentle breaths, as it had the day he'd taken it.

He grinned. "Oh, I remember that one. That was Brazil. We spent all day on the beach, and you were so exhausted from the sun, you slept for twelve hours." He closed the book and kissed Sam. "Thank you for this. I know right where to put it."

He turned to the mantel. On it were six other photo albums. They were all bound in dark colors, like wine red and oxford blue, except for the rightmost one, which was pure white.

"Here." Wesley placed the new book on the mantel. "Next to our wedding album."

Sam reached for his hand again, but this time he took Wesley's left in his and laced their fingers together so their rings lined up. "It's almost time for another important anniversary too. Thank you for three wonderful years together."

"You mean ten." Wesley pulled him closer by the hand. "I count from the day we met."

"If we celebrated all our anniversaries, we'd never do anything else." Sam pressed their foreheads together. "The day we became roommates. Becoming friends. Becoming *best* friends."

"Our first kiss," Wesley added. "When we first started dating. Moving in together. Getting married. Buying a house. So many memories."

Sam squeezed his hand before stepping back. "You ready to make some more?"

Happiness bubbled up in Wesley, so pure and light he thought he might float off the ground after all, no balloon required. "Absolutely."

Dear Reader,

Thank you for reading Quinn Anderson's *The Long Way Around*!

We know your time is precious and you have many, many entertainment options, so it means a lot that you've chosen to spend your time reading. We really hope you enjoyed it.

We'd be honored if you'd consider posting a review—good or bad—on sites like **Amazon, Barnes & Noble, Kobo, Goodreads, Twitter, Facebook, Tumblr,** and your blog or website. We'd also be honored if you told your friends and family about this book. Word of mouth is a book's lifeblood!

For more information on upcoming releases, author interviews, blog tours, contests, giveaways, and more, please sign up for our weekly, spam-free newsletter and visit us around the web:

Newsletter: riptidepublishing.com/newsletter
Twitter: twitter.com/RiptideBooks
Facebook: facebook.com/RiptidePublishing
Goodreads: tinyurl.com/RiptideOnGoodreads
Tumblr: riptidepublishing.tumblr.com

Thank you so much for Reading the Rainbow!

RiptidePublishing.com

ALSO BY
QUINN
ANDERSON

Fourteen Summers
New Heights
On Solid Ground
All of the Above
The Other Five Percent
The Academy (Coming Soon)

The Murmur Inc. Series
Hotline
Action
Cam Boy

ABOUT THE AUTHOR

Quinn Anderson is an alumna of the University of Dublin in Ireland and has a master's degree in psychology. She wrote her dissertation on sexuality in popular literature and continues to explore evolving themes in erotica in her professional life.

A nerd extraordinaire, she was raised on an unhealthy diet of video games, anime, pop culture, and comics from infancy. Her girlfriend swears her sense of humor is just one big Buffy reference. She stays true to her nerd roots in writing and in life, and frequently draws inspiration from her many fandoms, which include Yuri on Ice, Harry Potter, Star Wars, Buffy, and more. Growing up, while most of her friends were fighting evil by moonlight, Anderson was kamehameha-ing her way through all the shounen anime she could get her hands on. You will often find her interacting with fellow fans online and offline via conventisons and Tumblr, and she is happy to talk about anything from nerd life to writing tips. She has attended conventions on three separate continents and now considers herself a career geek. She advises anyone who attends pop culture events in the UK to watch out for Weeping Angels, as they are everywhere. If you're at an event, and you see a 6'2" redhead wandering around with a vague look on her face, that's probably her.

Her favorite authors include J.K. Rowling, Gail Carson Levine, Libba Bray, and Tamora Pierce. When she's not writing, she enjoys traveling, cooking, spending too much time on the internet, playing fetch with her cat, screwing the rules, watching Markiplier play games she's too scared to play herself, and catching 'em all.

Connect with Quinn:
Facebook: facebook.com/AuthorQuinnAnderson
Twitter: @QuinnAndersonXO
Tumblr: QuinnAndersonWrites.tumblr.com
Email: quinnandersonwrites@gmail.com

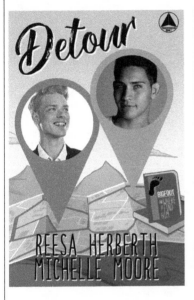
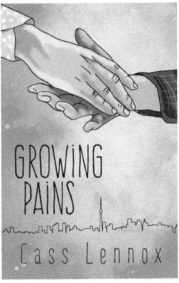

CPSIA information can be obtained
at www.ICGtesting.com
Printed in the USA
FSHW02n1108200818
51583FS